After a few moments, his eyes were drawn to the picture he'd placed beside him on the small table. The face that watched him from the photograph was smooth-skinned, framed by dark curls. He knew why he had put those signs on Cassandra's door. A part of him was furious because of the way she'd rejected him. And that part wanted to strike back, to hurt her for what she'd done.

No, he thought. That will only chase her away for good. I'll never be able to have her love.

But something else inside him was saying: *Punish her for what she's done to you. You have the chance now, the chance you never thought you'd have.*

THE ATTRACTION

B. W. Battin

FAWCETT GOLD MEDAL • NEW YORK

To Alvin and Lillian Benjamin

1

SHOULD I GO TO BED WITH HIM? CASSANDRA wondered, glancing at the man driving the car. His name was Clark Clayton. In his early thirties, he was a wiry man with thinning dark hair and blue eyes. She'd met him at a party a while back, and yesterday he'd called and asked her to go out. Since this was the weekend that Lisa spent with her father and since Cassandra had nothing planned, she'd accepted Clark's invitation. Having had dinner at a Chinese restaurant and gone to a play, they were on their way back to Cassandra's apartment in the Chicago suburbs.

Clark glanced at her, smiled, and the question hung there: *Are we going to sleep together?*

Cassandra was undoubtedly a disappointment to anyone who believed in the stereotype of the free-wheeling, liberated divorcée. Her one free weekend each month—the only time she would even consider dating—was usually devoted to things like catching up on her reading or housework. And if she did go out, she and her date normally parted at the curb.

1

But Clark had been sending out signals all evening, messages conveyed by his eyes, his movements, his frowns and smiles. Though subtle, these things, taken together, proclaimed, *I want to make love to you.* And Cassandra had found herself responding to the message.

The lights of the city were behind them now. As they drove along the freeway, they passed exits leading into the outer ring of Chicago's urban sprawl, into the world of Little League baseball, the PTA, the Neighborhood Crime Watch. It had been Cassandra's world once, before she and John had divided up the property, before they had agreed to sell the house and split the proceeds.

The marriage had failed for a variety of reasons, the big one being that John had fallen in love with another woman. Every day at the office, Janice had been there, friendly, beautiful, available. They'd had lunches together, then an affair. The affair had been going on nearly a year when he finally asked Cassandra for a divorce.

Devastated, she had cried for a week. She lost her appetite as well as fifteen pounds; then she became a nervous eater and gained them back, plus some.

Realizing that trying to force John to stay with her would be futile, she had agreed to the divorce. John moved in with Janice at once, promising to support her and Lisa until a formal arrangement could be worked out. The rest was simple. They'd seen a lawyer, agreed upon a property settlement, and determined child custody and support. The necessary papers were drawn up, signed, and filed with the court. Eventually, the final decree was signed by a judge, legally dissolving a marriage that had actually ended the second or third time John had asked Janice to lunch.

In time, the hurt, confusion, and even the extra pounds had gone away. She had her own life now, and she had her daughter; everything was fine. And yet a part of her knew that everything wasn't fine, that hidden deep inside was some hurt that time hadn't erased yet, that it might never erase. She quickly pushed this thought aside.

It was a nice spring evening, warm enough for short sleeves but still cool enough to be pleasant. The muggy summer nights were still a month or so away.

"What do you like to do besides go to restaurants and plays?" Clark asked.

"I, uh, I read, go to an occasional movie. Actually, I spend most of my time working and being the mother of a seven-year-old." She shrugged. "I guess I don't lead a very exciting life. How about you? What do you do for excitement?"

"I read, go to an occasional movie."

Cassandra laughed. "We're a real pair of swingers, huh?"

"Apparently," he said, chuckling as he reached over and touched her hand. Although the contact lasted only a fraction of a second, his flesh seemed to pulsate with the message, *I want you; I want you; I want you.* A warm tingle traveled through Cassandra's body.

Clark steered into the off ramp; a few moments later, they were driving along a tree-lined suburban street, the streetlights making occasional pools of brightness in the night. As they passed under one of the lights, she studied Clark's face. He had rugged, masculine features, and yet there was a studious look about him, as if he were a professor in some academic field who spent his spare time mountain climbing, or something like that. In reality, Clark was neither a scholar nor a mountain climber. He was a junior executive at a company that made plumbing supplies.

That was among the many things he'd told Cassandra about himself. He'd also revealed that he was thirty-

3

three and that he'd never been married. A part of her wondered whether that was a lie, whether he really had a wife he didn't want her to know about. Not wanting to consider that, Cassandra pushed the question aside.

She had enjoyed herself tonight. Her dinner—trout amandine—had been excellent, and the play, though an amateur presentation of a comedy by an unknown playwright, had been fun. Clark said he'd stumbled across the theater, located off an alley near the Loop, about a year ago and had enjoyed going there ever since.

Clark stopped at a red light, then turned left, onto a street lined with small apartment buildings. Cassandra's apartment was in the next block. It was decision time. During the eighteen months she'd been divorced, she had only slept with a man once. As scared and nervous as a teenage virgin, she'd found little pleasure in the act, and the man had never called again. But somehow she knew that Clark was different, that tonight would be different. If she allowed anything to happen tonight.

I'm afraid, she thought. I'm afraid of being so nervous that I'll bungle it. I'm afraid of doing anything that might develop into a serious relationship. Because serious relationships can lead to pain, divorce, crying all night.

Clark pulled to a stop in front of the small brick apartment building in which she lived.

An awkward moment passed during which both of them were silent. Do I send him away, Cassandra wondered, or invite him in? He looked at her and smiled.

"Would you like to come in for coffee or a nightcap?" she asked. She had merely postponed the decision. Inviting him in wasn't a commitment; she could still send him away after they'd had something to drink. And somewhere inside, two parts of Cassandra were urging her to take different actions. One part had warmed to the tingle that Clark's presence was stirring. The other part was afraid.

They walked across the lawn to the two-story brick building. Cassandra's apartment was on the ground floor, third door on the left.

"Coffee or a nightcap?" Cassandra asked as she closed the door behind him.

"Do you have any Scotch?"

She nodded. "Nothing fancy, but it's Scotch."

"On the rocks, please."

"Have a seat. I'll be right back." She hurried into the apartment's small kitchen, squatted in front of a lower cupboard, and studied her limited liquor supply. She found the Scotch, decided on white wine for herself, and set about pouring the drinks.

Returning to the living room, she found Clark standing by the bookcase, studying a framed photograph of Lisa.

"Your daughter?"

"Yes." She'd told him about the divorce and that this was the weekend for Lisa's monthly visit with her father.

He smiled. "When I see a cute little girl like this, it makes me wonder whether I made a mistake by staying single so long."

A number of questions jumped into Cassandra's head, but she remained silent, for most of them were too personal for her to ask.

He returned the picture to the bookcase, and Cassandra handed him his drink. He took a sip, nodded his satisfaction, then said, "Shall we sit down?" He seated himself on the couch.

Cassandra simply stood there, the glass of wine in her hand, staring at him. Then his eyes found hers, and they seemed to say, *It's okay. I won't bite.* Suddenly feeling silly, she sat down on the couch, leaving about two feet of cushion between herself and Clark.

As did the rest of the furniture, the expensive Early American couch looked out of place in the small living room, with its faded gold carpet. The furniture had been part of the divorce settlement. There was too much of it to fit into a little two-bedroom apartment, so a number of Cassandra's favorite pieces were in storage, awaiting—awaiting what?

Living on child-support payments and her salary, she barely had enough money left over to pay the storage fee. How was she ever going to get a place large enough to hold the things that had filled a four-bedroom house? Of course, she had received half the money from the sale of the house—$22,000. But that money was for Lisa's education, and Cassandra wouldn't even consider touching it.

She glanced at Clark, who'd been studying her silently, then quickly looked away before their eyes could meet. Calm down, she told herself. You're supposed to be one of those wicked divorcées, not a nervous wreck.

"What do you like to read?" Clark asked, his gaze shifting to the bookcase.

"Oh, uh, historical things mostly. You know, biographies and things like that. What do you like to read?"

"Well, I read an occasional spy novel." He took a drink of Scotch, then set the glass on the coffee table. "I'm afraid my interests aren't nearly as intellectual as yours."

"It's not intellectual," Cassandra said, unexplainably embarrassed at having the term applied to her. "It's just . . . well, interesting. Besides, I like spy novels, too." She named some of her favorite writers of suspense novels and quickly discovered that she and Clark had read some of the same books.

Which led to the discovery that they had enjoyed some of the same movies and that they both liked folk music.

"I'm afraid it's not very popular anymore," Clark

said as he finished his drink. "I've got records that have been out of circulation for years. I'm in the process of putting them on tape to preserve them. Someday, if you like, you can come over and listen to some of them. I've got—"

"Oh, your glass is empty," Cassandra said to change the subject. She didn't want to say anything that would commit her to visiting Clark's home. Rising, she grabbed his glass.

Standing, he gently took her arm. "No," he said, "I've had enough."

They stood there, awkwardly, both of them apparently uncertain what to do. Afraid to look into Clark's eyes, Cassandra shifted her gaze to the coffee table, spotting her empty glass and realizing that she was unable to recall having consumed the wine. Then Clark gently put his hands on her shoulders, and as if he had switched on some mechanism that controlled her muscles, her eyes rose and met his.

"Are you afraid of me?" he asked.

"I'm just afraid," she said in a shaking voice that sounded like someone else's. "I'm not afraid of you."

"Should I go?" he asked gently, his brown eyes exploring hers.

Again, she heard the strange distant voice. It said, "No. Don't go."

Slowly, gently, he took her in his arms. For a moment, he just held her; then their lips met. As the kiss became more passionate, the warm tingle that had been teasing Cassandra throughout the evening erupted into desire. As they held each other, their bodies pressing tightly together, Cassandra thought, Yes, yes. Oh, yes.

"GOOD MORNING," A MALE VOICE SAID.
Not yet fully awake, Cassandra rolled over, a part of her brain trying to determine the source of the words she'd just heard. Slowly, she realized there was a body next to hers, Clark's body. And she recalled their making love last night. This time she hadn't performed like a frightened teenage virgin. This time she'd enjoyed it, an experience she hadn't had since her divorce. No, she corrected, not since the glow wore off her marriage, which had occurred long before the marriage ended. She stretched, then slipped her arms around Clark. His body was smooth and firm.

"Good morning," she said in a sleepy voice. "Have you been awake long?"

"An hour or so, I guess," he replied, returning her hug.

"And you've just been lying there?"

"I didn't want to wake you up."

"Thanks for being so thoughtful."

Although they were in bed, their bare bodies lightly touching, somehow there didn't seem to be anything sexual about what they were doing. It was merely a cozy, comfortable way to start the morning.

"This is very nice," Clark said. "But I'm afraid I'm going to have to end it."

"Why?"

"I have to go to the bathroom."

"Oh," she said without releasing him.

"If you don't let go, I won't be responsible for what happens."

Reluctantly, she removed her arms, and Clark slipped out of the bed, his nude body disappearing into the hallway. She heard the bathroom door close. Resisting the impulse to roll over and close her eyes, Cassandra moved to the edge of the bed, pushed her feet out from under the covers, and put them on the floor. The sounds of the shower running came from the bathroom.

Pushing some dark strands of curly hair away from her face, she stared sleepily at her nakedness. Her eyes fixed on her firm breasts, then dropped to her long, slender legs, skipping quickly over her tummy, which had developed a slight outward curve. She'd first noticed it about three months ago—right after her thirtieth birthday. It was silly not to look at it, she supposed. After all, no one could expect to have an eighteen-year-old's figure forever. But at this particular moment, right after having spent the night with an extremely attractive man—well, it just wasn't the right time to stare at your once-firm tummy, which would most likely never be flat again.

If I exercise, she thought, if I eat more carefully . . . She dismissed the notion, because she knew she would never do those things, not even if—God forbid—she ever became genuinely plump. Like many people,

Cassandra had the willpower to do any number of difficult things, but not to give up the foods she liked or take up the exercise she hated. She sighed.

The sound of the bathroom door opening came from the hallway. Abruptly, Cassandra rushed to the closet and grabbed her robe. She was tying the white garment's sash when Clark, still naked, stepped into the room.

Why didn't I want him to see me nude? Cassandra wondered. I just slept with him. A few hours ago, I made love with him. Having no answer for that question, she pushed it from her thoughts.

"I think I've got some clothes around here somewhere," Clark said, his eyes exploring the room.

"On the other side of the bed. On the floor."

He grinned. "I must have been really anxious to get out of them."

Cassandra watched as he moved to the other side of the bed and began dressing. Though muscular, he was lean, built more like a long-distance runner than a weight lifter. His body had very little hair. He looked up, his eyes meeting hers, and suddenly Cassandra felt embarrassed to be staring at a naked man.

"I, uh, I'm going to take a shower now," she said, turning away from Clark. She got clean clothes from her closet and bureau, then hurried into the bathroom.

Emerging from the bathroom about fifteen minutes later, showered and dressed, Cassandra found Clark standing by the bookcase in the living room, studying Lisa's picture.

"Now I'm ready to face the day," she said. "What would you like for breakfast?"

"What are my options?"

"You're pretty much limited to eggs, pancakes, or waffles."

"Waffles," he said enthusiastically. "I haven't had them—oh, gosh, it must have been years."

"Waffles it is, then," she said, turning to leave the room.

"By the way, when am I going to meet her?"

"Meet who?" Cassandra asked, again facing Clark.

"Your daughter," He took one more look at Lisa's picture, then returned it to its spot on the bookcase.

"Well, uh, sometime, I guess," Cassandra replied, a little disconcerted.

Clark nodded, apparently satisfied with her answer. As she headed for the kitchen, Cassandra realized that if Clark planned to meet Lisa, it meant that he intended to see more of Lisa's mother. Until this moment, she hadn't given any thought to whether she would ever see Clark again.

So what were you after last night? she asked herself as she removed the electric waffle iron from one of the lower kitchen cabinets. A one-night stand? Cassandra found she had no answer for that. Last night was just a thing that happened, an unplanned thing. And, as it turned out, a good thing.

Cassandra removed a box of waffle mix and a mixing bowl from different kitchen cabinets, then got milk and eggs from the refrigerator. Apparently, Clark wanted to see her again, which meant she had to decide whether she wanted to see him.

Entering the kitchen, he sat down at the small table. "If there's anything I can do to help, just holler."

"I will," she said. And I think I'd like to see you again, she thought. I think I'd like that a lot. She put coffee and water in the coffee machine, turned it on, then shifted her attention back to waffle-making.

Half an hour later, Clark popped his last piece of syrup-drenched waffle into his mouth, washed it down with a swallow of coffee, and leaned back, looking entirely satisfied. "Damn, those were good."

"I'm afraid Aunt Jemima and General Electric get most of the credit."

Clark shook his head. "If you'd given me that waffle iron and that box of mix, I'd have produced a first-rate disaster. To make waffles as good as those I just ate takes talent."

"You're just flattering me because you want to get me into bed," she joked, a little surprised that she would say anything quite that bold.

Clark laughed. "Well, what shall we do today?"

"Do?" she said, caught off guard. It hadn't occurred to her that Clark might want to spend the day with her. It was Sunday, and this afternoon she would drive up to Milwaukee to pick up Lisa. It was the arrangement she and John had agreed upon. He picked the child up Friday evening, and Cassandra retrieved her on Sunday afternoon. In any case, she would have to explain to Clark that she had only a very limited social life.

"It's a beautiful day," he said. "How do you like this idea? Let's make some sandwiches, get some potato chips and things like that; then we can go for a drive in the country and have a picnic lunch along the way." He studied her face, eagerly awaiting her reaction.

Cassandra liked the idea—she liked it a lot—but she had to drive to Milwaukee to get Lisa, things were moving too fast. Although she liked Clark and wanted to see more of him, she hardly knew him. If they were going to have a relationship, it needed to develop slowly, over time. This was too much too soon.

You're afraid to have a relationship with any man, a part of her asserted. Your marriage didn't work, and the thought of being hurt again terrifies you. She forced that part of herself to be silent.

"Clark, I—well, I'm going to be busy today. I—"

"What do you mean?" he said, frowning.

"I mean that I have other plans, that I can't spend the day with you." And as soon as she said it, she wondered whether she was doing the right thing. She truly liked Clark. And divorced women with children didn't exactly have men beating down the door.

"What other plans?" Clark asked, his voice flat.

"I have to go to Wisconsin to pick up Lisa."

"Oh," Clark said, looking relieved. "We can have our picnic in Wisconsin and pick up your daughter afterward."

Cassandra shook her head. "She's at my ex-husband's house. I can't take you there. It would be too—too awkward."

"I can wait in the car."

"He'd see you."

"It's really none of his business, though, is it?"

"But . . ." Confused about the direction the conversation had taken and uncertain what she wanted to say, Cassandra let her words trail off.

"I mean, he's your *ex*-husband. You don't owe him any explanations."

"Clark, look, I spend most of my time working and being a mother. My daughter is the most important thing in my life. I'm only free on one weekend a month, when Lisa visits her father."

"You can always get a baby-sitter," he said. He was studying her, poker-faced, his eyes and expression completely neutral. It was a little unnerving.

"That's just not what I want to do, Clark. Look, I'm not saying we can't get together again. We just have to wait a while."

For a long moment, he stared at her, his eyes fixed

intently on hers. Finally, he said, "You're telling me to get lost."

"No, Clark, I'm not. I'm telling you that I'm only free when Lisa's visiting her father. That's the way I run my life."

Again, he stared at her, and this time his eyes were cold, cruel. "You're telling me that if I want to see you again, I should call you in a couple of weeks; is that right?"

Cassandra nodded. This conversation was making her very uneasy. She wondered whether anyone would hear her if she had to call for help, and then she forced the thought from her mind. Although Clark was behaving a little strangely at the moment, he didn't have any intention of harming her. But then she really didn't know him, did she? That thought, too, she immediately pushed from her mind.

"I'd like you to go out with me tomorrow evening," Clark said. A light film of perspiration had appeared on his forehead.

"I'm sorry," she said, trying not to betray the fears and uncertainties churning in her mind.

Suddenly, Clark's face flushed. "Why are you rejecting me?" he demanded. "Why?"

"I—I'm not. I explained—"

"You explained nothing," he said angrily. "You merely offered excuses." He raised his hand as if he were going to reach for her; then he lowered it again.

Cassandra, who'd nearly gasped when he raised his hand, forced herself to speak. "I—I think you'd better go."

Abruptly, the beligerence vanished from his face, replaced by a sad, helpless look. "I'm sorry," he said. "I didn't mean to behave like that."

Confused by his abrupt change in behavior, Cassandra

watched him warily while she tried to decide what to do. Finally, she said, "I have some errands to run before I leave for Milwaukee. I need to get started."

He nodded. "I'm sorry. I didn't mean to be pushy. Do you need any help with your errands?"

"No," she said. "But thank you for offering."

He studied her a moment, his expression something like that of a sad little boy. Suddenly, he stood up and strode from the room. Cassandra followed him into the living room. He hesitated at the door as if he were going to speak, then turned and left. As soon as he closed the door, Cassandra locked it.

For a few moments, she stood there, staring at the closed door, trying to sort out what had happened. Last night Clark had seemed warm and intelligent, an attractive man with a good sense of humor who was also a good lover. But today he'd shown her another part of his personality, a part she didn't understand. A part that made her afraid.

Returning to the kitchen, she sat down at the table and picked up her coffee cup. Last night, while she slept naked beside Clark, she'd been as vulnerable as it's possible to be. What kind of a man did I take into my bed? she wondered. The coffee cup in her hand was shaking.

It was a cool, overcast afternoon as Cassandra and Lisa drove south on Interstate 94, heading for Chicago. Ahead was the Kenosha exit. Soon they would reach the Illinois border.

"Wanna stop and get something to eat?" Cassandra asked.

"If you want," Lisa replied with no enthusiasm.

"Spend the afternoon eating ice cream and candy again?"

"A little." Which most likely meant a lot. John spoiled the child, indulging her every whim.

Inwardly, Cassandra sighed. She couldn't blame him, she supposed, not when he only got to have her one weekend each month. Were their situations reversed, she might do the same thing.

Lisa glanced knowingly at her mother, then shifted her attention to a big green bus that was passing them on the right. She was a pretty child who'd been fortunate enough to get the most desirable characteristics from each of her parents. The seven-year-old had Cassandra's curly dark hair, brown eyes, and long legs. From her father, she'd got her high cheekbones, upturned nose, and warm smile.

Glancing in the rearview mirror, Cassandra noticed the red Chevette behind her. She recalled that one had been behind her on the way to Milwaukee, too. Idly, she wondered whether it could be the same car. It seemed pretty unlikely, since hundreds, probably thousands, of people drove between Chicago and Milwaukee daily, and red Chevettes were hardly rare.

Her thoughts wandered randomly for a few moments, and then Cassandra found herself thinking about Clark Clayton. If she'd agreed to his suggestion that they have a picnic, then pick up Lisa, she and Clark would still have a relationship. Had she refused because she was incapable of having a relationship with a man? She'd had almost nothing to do with men since her divorce. Was she so afraid of being hurt again that she'd remain single forever?

Damn you, John! she thought. Damn you for doing this to me! But then it wasn't entirely John's fault, was it? Just as it took two to make a marriage work, it usually took two to make it fall apart. John had fallen in love with someone else because he *and* Cassandra had allowed their marriage to get stale and tired and uninteresting.

The divorce had been amicable—no arguments over property, John acquiescing to Cassandra's getting custody of Lisa. The only argument had come over Lisa's last name. Cassandra was taking her maiden name again, and she wanted her daughter, too, to be Jennings. John wanted her to keep his name—Browning. Cassandra had won. And the bitterness with which she fought John on the point demonstrated to both of them just how much the divorce had hurt her.

Unlike Cassandra, John hadn't had any problems with the opposite sex. As soon as the divorce was final, he married his new heartthrob. They were still married, which made it awkward for Cassandra to go to his house to pick up Lisa, even though Janice usually managed to stay out of sight whenever her husband's former wife was there.

Again, her eyes shifted to the rearview mirror. The red Chevette was still behind her, a pickup between it and Cassandra's blue Ford. She recalled how strange Clark had acted this morning, and she found herself wondering whether he might be in the red car, following her. But then that was ridiculous. For one thing, Clark's car was a large-model Oldsmobile. And it was white.

She was glad she had discovered the other side of his personality before a relationship had developed. Although he hadn't actually done anything threatening, she found his behavior very disquieting.

"Hey," she said to Lisa, "wanna play an alphabet game?"

"Sure," the girl said eagerly.

"Okay, here goes. On my vacation I went to Albany, where I ate an apple."

"Well, on *my* vacation," Lisa said, "I went to Boston and I ate a banana."

"Very good. But I'm surprised you didn't say baked beans."

"Why?" the child asked, looking puzzled.

"Haven't you ever heard of Boston baked beans?"

The girl shook her head. "You gotta do *C*, Mom. No fair talking about beans while you're trying to think of something."

Cassandra chuckled. "Okay, on my vacation, I went to Chicago, where I ate some corn bread."

"Corn bread!" Lisa said, making a face. "If it'd been me, I'd have eaten a candy bar."

"You would," Cassandra said.

The dusk had given way to complete darkness when Clark Clayton arrived at O'Hare International Airport. Following the signs that told him where to go, he parked the car, then walked to the small office, entered, and stepped up to the counter.

"Yes, sir," the young black man behind the counter said, looking up.

Without comment, Clark handed him a set of papers.

"Any problems?" the man asked, examining the papers.

"No."

"Let's see. Flat rate, paid in advance. Everything's in order as long as you didn't have any accidents or anything like that."

"No accidents," Clark said, turning to leave.

"Oh, sir," the man called.

"Yes?" Clark said, again facing the counter.

"Uh, you forgot to give me the key."

"Sorry." He handed the man the key to the red Chevette he'd rented for the day.

AFTER GETTING OFF WORK ON MONDAY, Cassandra picked up Lisa at the day-care center to which the child reported each day after school. When they got home, Cassandra collapsed on the couch.

"When are we going to eat?" Lisa asked, standing before her mother, restlessly swinging her right foot back and forth.

"As soon as I find the strength," Cassandra replied. "Go and put the silverware on the table."

"Okay," the seven-year-old said, skipping out of the room.

Unlike Lisa's father, the day-care center didn't feed the child candy, which meant she was usually hungry when she got home. The center was expensive, even though Lisa only spent the late afternoon there. Still, you couldn't allow a child Lisa's age to spend three-and-a-half hours each day unattended, so the expense was necessary.

Closing her eyes, Cassandra flexed her shoulders, trying

to get the stiffness out of them. Classified as a typist by the insurance company that employed her, she spent her days sitting at a video display terminal—usually referred to as a VDT. Customers with claims called in on the firm's 800 number, and Cassandra typed the information into the computer system. After a day of sitting in exactly the same position at her VDT, staring at the screen, she usually arrived home with a sore back, stiff shoulders, burning eyes, and a monster headache. All this for a salary that was just slightly above the minimum wage.

Oh, well, she thought as she rubbed her eyes, at least today I don't have a headache.

Opening her eyes, Cassandra again found Lisa standing before her. "Table's set," her daughter said. "You ready to make dinner?"

"Okay," Cassandra said, rising. There was some leftover macaroni casserole in the fridge. She could warm that up and steam some broccoli. Dinner in half an hour with a minimum of effort. Lisa would probably complain about the broccoli, but at the moment Cassandra was too tired to care.

She had nearly reached the kitchen when the telephone rang. Reversing direction, Cassandra headed for the phone, which was located in the hall, in one of those special little telephone alcoves people used to build. Dashing past her mother, Lisa got there first and grabbed the receiver. She'd only recently grown tall enough to reach it, so answering the phone was a new and exciting experience.

"Hello," Lisa said. "Yes, this is Lisa . . . Oh, I'm fine. How are you? . . . My mommy? Here she is." She handed the receiver to her mother.

Thoroughly puzzled, Cassandra took the phone.

"Hi," a male voice said. "It's me. I called to apologize."

"Clark?" she asked hesitantly.

"Yes. I called to say I'm sorry that I acted the way I did. I am. Honest. Will you forgive me?"

"There's nothing to forgive."

"You don't know how glad I am to hear you say that," Clark said, sounding truly relieved. "I was afraid I'd ruined everything."

Uncertain what to say, Cassandra remained silent.

"Listen, I, uh, I'd like to make it up to you. Have you had dinner yet?"

"It's cooking," Cassandra lied.

"Well, I'd really like to make it up to you. How about tomorrow night?"

"Look, Clark, I—"

"Don't worry about Lisa," he said, cutting her off. "We can take her with us. We'll just make it an early evening. We can get home by her regular bedtime. There won't be any problem with leaving her with a baby-sitter or anything."

Cassandra recalled the evening she and Clark had spent together, the warm, intelligent, attractive man she spent the night with, and a part of her wanted to say, Yes, Clark, sure I'll have dinner with you. But she also remembered the angry, frightening man who'd sat at her breakfast table the next morning, a man she did not care to meet again.

Firmly, she said, "I don't want to see you anymore, Clark."

"Don't do this to me, Cassandra," he pleaded, the desperation in his voice obvious.

"I'm sorry."

"Please give me another chance. It won't happen again. I promise."

"I've got to go now, Clark. I'm sorry, but—"

"Why?" he demanded angrily. "Why are you doing this to me?"

"I don't owe you any expl—"

"The hell you don't," he snapped. "You owe me more than—"

"Don't call me again," Cassandra said, interrupting him. Before he could respond, she hung up the phone.

For a moment, she simply stood there, trying to sort out her thoughts. Then she noticed Lisa standing beside her, looking at her questioningly.

"Who was that man?" the child asked.

"You've never met him, Lisa."

"Don't you like him, Mommy?"

Cassandra hesitated, uncertain how to respond. Finally, she said, "I don't dislike him, honey. I just want him to leave us alone."

When Cassandra and her daughter arrived home the next evening, the muffled sounds of the phone ringing were coming through the door of her apartment. Fumbling in her purse for her keys, Cassandra swore silently.

"Someone's calling you on the phone, Mommy," Lisa said.

"I know, I know," Cassandra said, still desperately trying to find her keys.

And then she had them. Quickly, she located the correct one and opened the door. The phone was still ringing. Rushing into the hallway, she grabbed the receiver.

"Hello."

Through the earpiece came the steady hum of the dial tone. She'd reached the phone a fraction of a second too late. Replacing the receiver, Cassandra headed for the kitchen, where she found Lisa standing by the stove, looking impatient.

"What are we gonna eat?" the child asked.

"What would you like?"

"Hamburgers," Lisa said hopefully.

"We don't have any buns."

"Oh."

"Is there anything else you'd like to have?"

Cassandra's daughter wrinkled her brow. "Uh . . . oh, I know. Can we have s'ghetti?"

"Spaghetti," Cassandra corrected her. "There's a *p* in it."

"Yeah," Lisa replied. "Can we have it?"

"Sure."

"Oh, boy!" As she so often did when she was pleased, Lisa grinned, pressing her palms together in front of her as if she were praying.

Such simple things can delight a child, Cassandra thought. Spaghetti for dinner, an old carton to incorporate into some imaginary play world, the wonder of a neighbor's fuzzy puppy. Why do we change so much when we grow up? she wondered. Why do we become rapists and child molesters and builders of nuclear weapons?

Suddenly, she grabbed Lisa and hugged her. "You're a pretty good kid. You know that?"

Returning the hug as best she could with her short seven-year-old's arms, Lisa said, "You're a pretty good mommy, too."

Cassandra laughed. "Come on," she said, releasing her daughter. "Let's see about that s'ghetti."

As she was reaching for the cabinet in which pasta and other dry ingredients were kept, the phone rang. Annoyed at the intrusion, she hurried to the hallway and grabbed the receiver.

"Hello."

"I've been calling and calling. I thought I'd never get you."

"Who . . ." Her voice trailed off, because she'd just realized whose voice she was hearing.

"Why don't I pick you up at seven," Clark said cheerfully.

Her thoughts churning, Cassandra tried to think of something to say.

"Cassie, you there?"

Cassie? The only one who had ever called her that had been her grandfather. It had been his private name for her, and hearing it from Clark seemed to defile it somehow.

"Listen," she said firmly, "I told you not to call me anymore. I have nothing to say to you."

"We have to talk this over, Cassie—"

"Don't call me that," she snapped.

"Look, we've got to get together and talk. I'll pick you up at seven, and—"

"No!" Cassandra shouted.

"Then when?" he demanded. "When are we going to—"

"Never!" she said, slamming down the receiver. She stared angrily at the phone, as if daring it to ring again. Don't let this jerk upset you, she told herself. He's nothing but an asshole who delights in being a persistent nuisance. But when she reached up to push some strands of hair out of her face, she realized that her hand was shaking.

After taking a moment to calm herself, Cassandra returned to the kitchen and her hungry daughter, who was sitting at the table.

"Who was it, Mommy?" Lisa asked, studying her mother's face.

"The same man who called yesterday."

"Are you mad at him?"

"I—well, let's just say I got a little annoyed with him." Before the child could respond, she added "Now, let's see about getting you some spaghetti."

She put a pot of water on to boil, then searched through the bottles and cans in an upper cabinet until she found a jar of spaghetti sauce. She was pouring it into a saucepan when the phone rang again, causing her to jump.

"I'll get it, Mommy," Lisa said, dashing from the room.

"No, wait—" But the child was already in the hallway, and Cassandra hurried after her. She found her daughter with the receiver to her ear, listening.

"I guess so," the girl said. "If it's okay with Mommy." She listened a moment, then said, "Okay." She handed the phone to Cassandra. "He wants to talk to you, Mommy."

Certain whose voice she would hear, Cassandra stared at the proffered phone, reluctant to touch it. Then, becoming aware of the worried look in her daughter's eyes, Cassandra grabbed the receiver.

"Hello," she said, the tension in her voice apparent.

"Hi," Clark said. "I—"

"I told you not to call me again. I have nothing to say to you, and I don't ever want to see you again." She hung up.

Lisa was staring at her, clearly uncertain what to make of all this.

"What did he say to you?" Cassandra asked.

"He said he wanted to meet me. He said we could have fun together."

"Did he say anything else?"

"He asked me if I'd like to have fun with him, and I said I'd have to ask you. That's all he said."

"Lisa," Cassandra said, dropping to the child's eye level, "listen to me now. I don't want you to have anything to do with this man. Do you understand?"

Lisa nodded, but then a frown came across her face. "Mommy," she said hesitantly, "I don't know what he looks like. How can I stay away from him?"

"Be careful with all strangers, Lisa. Don't ever go anywhere with a stranger. And never get into someone's car unless you know them. Okay?"

"Okay," Lisa said, looking quite serious. She cocked her head. "Mommy?"

"Yes."

"Is the man on the phone a bad man?"

"I . . ." Uncertain how to answer her daughter's question, Cassandra let her words trail off. Finally, she said, "I'm not sure, Lisa. He might be. Come on; let's get back to that spaghetti."

As they started toward the kitchen, the telephone rang again. "Lisa, don't answer it," Cassandra said quickly.

She stood there with her daughter beside her, not more than ten feet from the phone, listening to it ring but not moving. Perplexed, Lisa studied her, apparently trying to figure out why her mother wasn't answering the phone. Leave us alone, Cassandra thought. Please, just leave us alone.

Abruptly, her confusion and fear vanished, replaced by anger. Whirling around, she took three quick steps to the phone and grabbed the receiver. Unable to be absolutely certain it was Clark, she held her fury in check.

"Hello," she said flatly.

Over the line came only silence.

"Hello," she said again.

She was about to hang up when Clark said, "Why won't you talk to me, Cassandra?"

Without saying a word, she replaced the receiver,

26

then disconnected the phone's modular plug. "Come on," she said, taking Lisa's hand. "Let's have dinner."

Why won't he leave me alone? Cassandra wondered as they stepped into the kitchen. Surely he doesn't think his persistence will pay off. Doesn't he realize that the more he pesters me, the less desirable he seems?

As Cassandra made dinner, she asked herself another question: Why me? Why was he so determined to—to what? To go out with her? Have a relationship with her? To sleep with her again? She realized suddenly that she had no idea exactly what he wanted.

Why was he willing to be rejected again and again? What drove him? In a completely honest evaluation of herself, she would be forced to conclude that although she was reasonably attractive, a model or a movie star she wasn't. There was nothing in her appearance or her usually subdued personality that would warrant Clark's unrelenting persistence.

I'll leave the phone unplugged for a while, she thought. Maybe he'll get the idea and stop bothering me.

Although she tried to convince herself of that, a feeling of uneasiness settled over her. It was still with her a few hours later. When she went to bed, she tossed and turned for several hours before falling into an unsettled sleep.

Cassandra overslept the next morning. Groggy after her restless night, she shut off the alarm on the bedside table, then rolled over for a few more precious moments in bed. Half an hour later, Lisa was shaking her, urgently telling her that they were late.

Telling Lisa to get her own cereal, Cassandra rushed through her morning routine, hastily showering, doing her hair, and applying her makeup. After checking herself out in the full-length mirror on the back of her bedroom door, she decided her appearance was passable—though barely. Grabbing her purse, which hung on the doorknob, she hurried into the hallway, stopping when she noticed the disconnected phone.

I can't leave it that way forever, she thought. I'll be paying the phone bill for nothing. Grabbing the cord, she inserted the plug into its outlet, then hurried into the living room.

"Lisa, you ready?"

Lisa emerged from the kitchen, dressed in her customary costume of jeans and a T-shirt. When Cassandra had suggested once that she wear a dress to school, Lisa had been horrified, insisting that all the kids wore jeans and that to be the only one who didn't would be unthinkable. Recalling her own school days and how cruel children could be to any kid who was in any way different, Cassandra had not pushed the matter, although she would really have preferred to see Lisa in a dress.

"Come on," Cassandra said. "If I hit every green light between here and the school and the insurance company, I'm still going to be about five minutes late."

As she opened the door, the phone rang. She hesitated, uncertain what to do. It rang again, and Cassandra, deciding that she couldn't just ignore it, hurried into the hallway.

"Hello," she said impatiently.

"I'm calling to make a date with you," Clark said.

In the rush to get out of the apartment, she'd pushed Clark from her thoughts, so she was momentarily confused. "You!" she blurted.

"Yes, Cassandra, me. I—"

She cut him off by unplugging the phone.

Then she dashed into the living room, where Lisa waited, her eyes asking an unspoken question: *Was it him?* Grabbing her hand, Cassandra rushed out of the apartment. In the parking lot, she had to dig in her purse to find the keys to her blue two-door hatchback. After finding them and unlocking the door, she glanced at her watch as she climbed into the car. She was going to be late, very late.

Once more admonishing the child to be wary of strangers, Cassandra dropped Lisa off at school, then drove frantically toward the building in which she worked. She was more than a half hour late when she got there.

The insurance company occupied a modern three-story office building in the Chicago suburbs. After parking the car in the part of the lot set aside for employees, she hurried inside and took the elevator to the second floor. The room in which she worked contained five desks, each with a VDT and telephone headset. Except for hers, all the desks were occupied.

Seating herself, Cassandra slipped her purse into a desk drawer, then put on her headset and switched on her VDT. As she awaited her first call, Cassandra let her eyes take in the room. Decorated in subdued oranges and browns, it was a reasonably comfortable place in which to work. The floor was carpeted. The desks, typical of modern office furniture, were made of metal and fake wood.

Cassandra's desk was next to the wall. To her right sat Jennifer Gill, a young blond woman who had three children and was beginning to swell with the fourth. Jenny's eyes met Cassandra's, and they communicated: *Good morning. Nice to see you. I notice you're late.* Employees were not allowed to speak to each other except while on break.

Cassandra nodded her acknowledgment. She had decided that the only way to stop Clark from calling her was to get an unlisted number. Taking out the phone book, she looked up the number, then hesitated. Making personal calls was forbidden, and the phone circuits were monitored occasionally by management. Deciding that her chances of getting caught were slim, she reached for the button that would give her an outside line, but just then a call came in.

A woman in Vermont was calling to report that her big double-glazed picture window had been broken by an apparently suicidal owl. Cassandra punched up the details of the woman's homeowner's policy on her VDT, then told her to submit the bill for the window's replacement and that the company would reimburse her for anything above a hundred dollars, the deductible amount of the policy. As she ended the conversation with the woman, she typed this information on her VDT, checked to make sure she had made no errors, and sent it to the computer. Then she called the phone company.

"I've been getting threatening phone calls," she told the woman who answered. "I want to get my number changed to an unlisted one."

"You might want to consider putting a trace on your line rather than changing your number," the woman suggested. "With a tracer, we can find out where the calls are coming from. Changing a number can cause a lot of unnecessary inconvenience for you."

"No," Cassandra said. "I just want to change it." She wondered whether she should have told the truth instead of saying the calls were threatening. But then what she'd said wasn't totally untrue. Although Clark had not specifically stated his intention to harm her, there was definitely something menacing about his persistence.

"Would you like the change made right away?"

"Yes, please. Can you do it today?"

"We should be able to. Is there a number where we can reach you?"

Cassandra gave her the insurance company's number. As she broke the connection, she realized that someone was standing beside her desk. It was her boss, Nan Cosgrove.

"Personal call?" Cosgrove asked, her expression neutral. Tall and slender, with reddish-brown hair, she looked like what she was—a woman on the way up. Her hair was professionally done, her clothes conservative but quite expensive, her makeup immaculate.

"I've been getting bothersome phone calls," Cassandra explained. "I had to call the phone company. It was kind of an emergency."

Cosgrove nodded, indicating that she had noted Cassandra's explanation but giving no clues as to whether she accepted it. "Why were you late this morning?" she asked.

"Uh, my alarm clock didn't go off."

"I'd suggest you buy a new one. After all, this is your livelihood here. It's much too important to let something as inexpensive as an alarm clock interfere with it. Wouldn't you agree?"

"Yes," Cassandra said. "I'll get a new one this evening. I promise."

"Good," Cosgrove said, smiling. "I'm glad we agree. It's always better to get these little things straightened out right away."

"Yes," Cassandra said.

Giving her a curt nod, Cosgrove turned and strode from the room. Jenny, who couldn't help but witness what had transpired, rolled her eyes. Jenny had come up with a nickname for Cosgrove that had pretty much been adopted throughout the department—Nan the Nazi.

Despite having a boss who at times came on like the ruling general in some Latin American junta, Cassandra was reasonably satisfied with her work. It had taken weeks of frantic searching to find this job. Newly divorced, with a seven-year-old daughter to support, she'd been desperate enough to accept any position she could find—scrubbing toilets, cleaning sewers, anything. At least here she sat at a comfortable desk in a modern, climate-controlled office. Things could be worse.

About three-thirty that afternoon, the phone company called to let her know she had a new phone number that would not be given out. Cassandra wrote it on a slip of paper, which she put in her purse. That evening, her phone didn't ring once.

4

THE NEXT DAY, AFTER GETTING OFF WORK, Cassandra treated Lisa to one of the child's favorite meals—junk food at a burger place. Sitting at a small table, watching her daughter devour her burger, fries, and Coke, Cassandra decided that such a meal was undoubtedly a nutritionist's nightmare. It contained lots of fat and calories, a bun made from flour stripped of everything but the starch; some limp-looking lettuce was the closest thing to a green vegetable. Still, Lisa got so much pleasure from eating this sort of thing that Cassandra felt obliged to indulge her from time to time.

"We should eat here every night," Lisa said as she stuffed a french fry into her mouth.

"You'd get tired of it if we did it all the time."

The child shook her head. "We could go to McDonald's one night, then to Burger King, then to Wendy's, then to . . ." The girl's words trailed off as she tried to recall the names of other preferred eating places.

"We can eat burgers out every now and then, but not all the time."

Looking resigned to the situation, Lisa again turned her attention to her burger and fries.

Cassandra took a bite of her fish sandwich. She felt good today. She'd had no further problems with Nan the Nazi, and Clark could no longer use the telephone to pester her. She was glad now, very glad, that she hadn't allowed a relationship to develop between them. Had she done so, unaware of his almost childlike reaction to rejection . . .

She let the thought trail away uncompleted, because she had no idea what might have happened. She was just grateful that she hadn't found out. Thinking about Clark was dampening her mood, so she pushed him from her mind.

"Want to go to the ice cream place after this?" she asked.

Her mouth filled with fast food, Lisa nodded vigorously.

Forty-five minutes later, mother and daughter, having consumed a hot fudge sundae apiece, were sitting on the living-room couch, watching television.

"Can I stay up late tonight, Mommy?" Lisa asked, using her sweetest tone of voice.

"How late is late?"

"Oh, maybe ten o'clock."

"No chance."

"Nine-thirty?"

"Tomorrow's a school day."

"You always make me go to bed before I'm tired."

"Not tired, huh? You always go to sleep as soon as you hit the sheets."

"But that's because there's nothing else to do in bed."

Cassandra laughed. "You've had a hamburger and ice cream. That's enough for one night. We'll save staying up late for some other time."

Realizing the discussion was at an end, Lisa shifted

her attention back to the sitcom. Should I let her watch this junk? Cassandra asked herself. And then she decided that sitcoms, though insipid brain rot, were definitely preferable to some of the other things on TV. Like violence. Or the evening news, with its talk of an arms race that could lead to nuclear war, to the end of everything, if some lunatic pushed the wrong button.

The sitcom ended, and another began. Before it was over, Lisa was asleep. For a few moments, Cassandra studied her. She lay on the couch, her smooth child's face framed by dark curls. She looked so innocent, Cassandra thought, so uncorrupted and vulnerable. Watching this child, this piece of herself, sleep contentedly, Cassandra experienced a rush of love so overpowering that it brought tears to her eyes.

"Come on, kiddo," Cassandra said softly as she picked up her sleeping daughter.

"Nergft," Lisa muttered without opening her eyes.

After getting the child into pajamas and tucked into bed, Cassandra returned to the couch. After a moment, she switched off the TV set and picked up a magazine. It was only then that she realized that Lisa hadn't brushed her teeth. Oh, well, she thought. I'm not going to wake her up. I'll just have to make sure she doesn't get off to school in the morning without brushing.

Suddenly, the familiar double note of chimes sounded. Someone was at the door. As she headed for it, Cassandra checked her watch. It was 8:45. It was probably Grace, who lived in the apartment next door. She and Cassandra were quite friendly, often borrowing things from each other or occasionally taking each other places when one of their cars was in the shop.

Cassandra had her hand on the doorknob when she hesitated. She didn't know for sure that it was Grace out there, and she should check before opening the door.

Putting her eye to the optical peephole, she saw absolutely nothing. For a moment, she was puzzled; then she realized what was happening. The hole was covered with something. A hat, maybe, or a hand.

She backed away from the door, uncertain what to do. The chimes sounded again.

"Who's there?" she demanded.

Again, the chimes rang.

"Who's there?"

Once more, she was answered by silence. Her eyes shifted to the hallway, where the phone waited in its niche. Should she call the police?

"Cassie, it's me. Let me in. We have to talk." Though muffled by the door, it was clearly Clark's voice.

"No," she said. "Go away."

"I've been trying to call you, but you've got a new number, and the phone company won't give it to me."

"I changed it so you couldn't call me anymore. Now go away."

"I'll go away as soon as we talk. It'll only take a moment."

"No, you can't come in. Go away."

"Cassie, don't do this to me."

"I'm not doing anything to you. I just want you to leave me alone."

For a few seconds, there was only silence; then a loud boom came from the door, as if Clark had slammed it with something heavy. Then there was a resounding crash, and the door shook in its frame. My god, Cassandra thought, he's trying to break down the door.

"Stop it!" she screamed. "Stop it!"

The door shook again, and Cassandra found herself staring at it in horror, transfixed. Move! something inside her screamed. Get to the phone. Call the police.

She turned toward the phone, but then she heard another voice in the hallway.

"What the hell do you think you're doing?" a man demanded.

"This is not your concern," Clark said.

"If you're trying to break down the door of my next-door neighbor, then it's my concern, pal."

And then Cassandra recognized the other voice. It belonged to Steve Koneczny, Grace's husband. The two men were still talking to each other—mumbled words Cassandra was unable to understand. After a few seconds, the conversation stopped, and someone rapped lightly on Cassandra's door.

"Are you okay?" Grace Koneczny asked.

"That guy's gone," her husband added.

Cassandra opened the door, finding the Konecznys looking at her, a mixture of concern and curiosity on their faces. "I-I'm fine," she said.

"What was that all about?" Grace asked. She was a small woman with light brown shoulder-length hair. Her husband was a construction worker, a big muscular guy with thick sandy-colored hair. Cassandra could see why Clark had decided not to stand up to him.

"I-I went out with him once," Cassandra said. "Now he won't leave me alone. I had to change my phone number to get him to stop calling."

"He won't come back tonight," Steve said, clearly feeling pleased with himself for having run off the culprit.

Grace said, "Steve, why don't you check on Nicole? I want to talk to Cassandra for a moment."

Steve nodded. "If he comes back, just holler."

Cassandra and Grace said they would, and Steve left. The two women sat on the couch.

"You want to talk about it?" Grace asked. She was a year or two younger than Cassandra. She and Steve had one child, their ten-year-old daughter, Nicole, who some-times played with Lisa, although she apparently consid-ered a seven-year-old too young to be a serious friend.

"There's not really much to tell," Cassandra said. She gave Grace the story in more detail, including that she had spent the night with Clark, something she would have been too embarrassed to say in front of Steve.

"I think you should call the police," Grace said.

"What good would it do? There's never much they can do in cases like this."

"You could take him to court and get a judge to issue a restraining order. Then if he came around you, you could call the police and have him arrested."

"Grace, I don't want to go through all this. I just want him to leave me alone."

Grace took her hand. "I know, Cassandra, but if he won't leave you alone, you're going to have to do something."

Cassandra nodded. Grace was right. If this continued, she clearly would have to do something.

Grace looked thoughtful for a moment, then said, "Do you think there's any chance he might hurt you?"

"I don't know. Until tonight, when he tried to break down the door, he hadn't done anything physical."

"Be careful," Grace said gently but firmly. "He's shown he can be violent, and it's pretty damn apparent that there's something wrong with him."

"I know," Cassandra replied softly. She recognized the truth in Grace's words, but she didn't want to dwell on it.

"What do you think he would have done if he got in?"

Cassandra shook her head. "I don't know."

"Maybe he'll stay away now. I know I'd stay away if I were in his shoes and had just encountered the Incredible Hulk.'' It was her pet name for Steve. When she said it in his presence, he always grinned. ''You going to be okay?'' she asked as she stood up.

Cassandra nodded. ''I'll be fine.''

''You might think about putting some more locks on that door.''

''That's a good idea.''

''Well, I've got to get back to the Hulk. Holler if you need us, okay?''

''Okay.''

After Grace had gone, Cassandra slipped into Lisa's bedroom. She stood by the bed; the light from the doorway illuminated the sleeping child. Apparently, Lisa had been unaware of all the commotion. Thank goodness she's a sound sleeper, Cassandra thought. As she started to turn away, her daughter rolled over, opening her eyes.

''What was that noise, Mommy?'' she asked sleepily.

''Nothing, honey. Just someone at the door.''

''Oh,'' the girl replied, and she was sound asleep again.

Closing the bedroom door behind her, Cassandra leaned against the wall in the hallway. Suddenly, she was shaking so badly she wasn't sure she could walk. And Grace's words circled in her brain: *What do you think he would have done if he got in?*

She thought about Lisa, innocent and vulnerable in her peaceful child's sleep, and she realized that she did not want to consider what Clark might have done to them if he'd gotten in. Letting herself slide down the wall until she was sitting on the floor, Cassandra rested her head on her knees and cried.

Leave us alone, she thought. Oh, please, just leave us alone.

*   *   *

At breakfast the next morning, Cassandra poked at her scrambled eggs, then put down her fork and took a swallow of coffee. She should eat the eggs before they got cold, she knew, but she had no appetite. In her mind, she kept seeing the door shake as Clark threw his weight against it. It reminded her of a science-fiction movie she'd seen, the thing on the other side of a heavy metal door applying more and more force, the people in the room knowing that the door's collapse—and their death—was inevitable.

She pushed the image from her mind. In the movie, the trapped people had found a means of escape. Had Clark been intent on harming her and Lisa, they would most likely not have been so lucky.

She realized suddenly that the scene from the movie was appropriate in one very important respect. The thing on the other side of the door had been a monster, something to be feared, loathed. And that was what Clark had become. Something to be feared, loathed.

Across the table, Lisa was contentedly downing her customary bowl of cereal apparently unaware of her mother's somber mood. For a moment, Cassandra wished she could be a child again, with adults to protect her and shield her from all the world's nastiness. But then childhoods were allocated one to a person, and most of us wasted them by wishing we could hurry up and become grownups.

Giving up on her breakfast, Cassandra picked up her plate and took it to the counter, where she scraped the eggs into the plastic garbage container below the sink. "Time to get ready," she said to Lisa. "And don't forget to brush your teeth this morning."

"Okay," the girl said, hurrying from the room. Cassandra picked up the child's empty cereal bowl and put it in the sink.

A few minutes later, they were ready to leave. Lisa pushed ahead of her mother and started to open the door.

"No," Cassandra said. "Let me check first."

Looking at her curiously, the child asked, "Check what, Mommy?"

"We shouldn't just open the door and step into the hallway. We should—well, take a look first."

After looking through the peephole and seeing nothing but empty hallway, she unlocked the door and peeked out, again seeing nothing. She opened the door wide and peered into the hall; it was empty.

"All clear, kiddo. Let's go." Cassandra spoke calmly, hoping all this caution wouldn't upset Lisa.

They stepped into the tiled hallway, and Cassandra turned to lock her door. The corridor made a ninety-degree turn about fifteen feet to her left. The main entrance was in the other direction, about twenty-five feet from where Cassandra stood. Suddenly, she saw movement where the corridor made its turn. Clark was hurrying toward her.

Grabbing Lisa's arm, she yanked her back into the apartment.

"Wait," Clark said.

Cassandra locked the door.

"What's wrong, Mommy?" Lisa asked, somewhat bewildered.

"I don't want to hurt you," Clark said through the door. "I just want to talk."

"No," Cassandra said. "We have nothing to say to each other."

"I'm sorry about last night. I apologize. I won't do anything like that again."

"I'm going to call Steve next door."

"The big guy who was here last night?"

"Yes, him."

"I saw him come out of the building about half an hour ago, carrying his lunch box."

"Then I'll call the police."

"It's okay, Cassie. I'm going to leave. That way you'll see that I don't really mean you any harm. I'm leaving now, Cassie. If you look out your window, you'll see me drive away."

Hurrying to the window, Cassandra peered out into the hazy morning. A few moments passed, and then she saw Clark walking down the other side of the street. He stopped at a large white car, the same car in which he and Cassandra had gone into the city for a Chinese dinner and a play. Unlocking the door, Clark climbed inside, started the engine, and drove away.

"Mommy . . . ?" Lisa said, looking at her questioningly.

"That was the man who phoned us, honey. We don't want to have anything to do with him, so we're trying to avoid him."

"What does he want, Mommy?"

"I—I'm not sure, Lisa. We just want him to leave us alone."

Lisa looked at the floor and shuffled her feet. Though clearly a little uneasy, the child apparently had no more questions to ask.

"Come on," Cassandra said. "Let's go."

As she and Lisa stepped from the building, Cassandra scanned the tenants' parking area and the street. She knew that Clark hadn't necessarily left the neighborhood. He could drive around the block and wait for them to come out. Reaching her car, she slipped behind the wheel quickly and unlocked the passenger-side door for Lisa.

"Lock your door," she said as soon as the child was in the car.

Again surveying the area, Cassandra saw no sign of Clark. He meant it, she thought. He's gone. And then she allowed herself to hope that maybe, just maybe, he was gone for good.

She started the car. "Fasten your seat belt, kiddo."

Lisa complied, and Cassandra fastened her own belt, then backed out of her numbered parking space. As she drove past apartment buildings, homes, and small businesses, Lisa rode in silence, apparently trying to interpret for herself what was happening.

"Want to talk?" Cassandra asked.

Her daughter shook her head.

They continued to drive without speaking; then Lisa said, "Mommy, is that man going to go away now?"

"I hope so."

After another few moments of silence, Cassandra said, "I don't want you to worry about him, okay? Mommy will make sure he stays away from us. Uncle Steve will help, too, if we need him."

Lisa grinned. "You mean the Incred-ule Hulk?" Certain multisyllabic words, like incredible or aluminum, were just about impossible for her to pronounce.

"Yeah," Cassandra said. "The Incredible Hulk. You know what he'd do if anybody tried to bother us?"

"He'd squish 'em!" Lisa said excitedly, making squeezing gestures with her hands.

"That's right. He'd squish 'em!"

Lisa giggled. She was still in a bright mood when Cassandra left her off at school.

That evening, Cassandra and Lisa were sprawled on the living-room carpet, a checkerboard between them. Cassandra liked to play games with her daughter. Doing so not only gave them a chance to have fun together, but it cut down on TV watching, too much of which, Cassandra was convinced, was bad for children and adults alike.

"King me," Lisa said as she succeeded in moving one of her checkers all the way to Cassandra's side of the board.

Cassandra did so, saying, "I think I'm in trouble now."

Although she'd never admit it to Lisa, she carefully arranged it so the child won about half the time. This was a game Lisa was slated to win. Cassandra moved; then the girl gleefully made a triple jump, getting two of her mother's kings. The end was near.

Suddenly, a knock on the door caused Cassandra to stiffen. Although she tried to force the thought from her mind, she knew it was Clark, back to try breaking in again. Lisa was staring at her, somehow knowing that she should not go to the door.

The knock came again. "Cassandra, it's me, Grace."

Oh, thank God, she thought as relief flooded over her, washing away the fear. Quickly, she got up and opened the door.

"Hi," Grace said. "I, uh, I just went out to get the Hulk a pack of cigarettes. He's trying to quit, but all that's happened so far is that instead of keeping a supply of cigarettes around the house, we go out for a pack every time he runs out of smokes." She shrugged.

"Come in," Cassandra said. "I was just on the verge of getting trounced in a game of checkers."

"Hi, Aunt Grace," Lisa said from her position on the floor.

Grace returned the child's greeting, and Cassandra began to suspect that there was some purpose to Grace's visit besides just borrowing a little salt or some other routine matter.

Lowering her voice slightly and turning her back to Lisa, Grace said: "I, uh, I noticed something on your door as I passed by. My first inclination was to just tear it up, but then I realized that you should probably know about it." She handed a folded-up sheet of paper to Cassandra.

Unfolding it, Cassandra found herself staring at the words. Written in bold capital letters with a red felt-tip pen was the message:

KNOCK TWICE IF YOU WANT A GOOD FUCK.

"Do you think he did it?" Grace asked. "The guy who was here last night?"

Trembling, Cassandra gazed at the red letters. "Maybe not," she said. "It could have been put there by some practical joker, some kid, maybe. It doesn't mention my name or anything."

Grace studied her for a moment, then said, "Yeah, I guess it could have been some kid. Just in case, though, if you have any problems, knock on the wall. Or just plain shout. Steve will be over here real quick."

Cassandra nodded. "Thanks, Grace. I appreciate it. I really do."

Patting her purse, Grace said, "I'd better get these cigarettes to the Hulk. If he's been too long without nicotine, he gets disagreeable, and then I have to put him in his place."

Thanking her again, Cassandra let her friend out of the apartment and locked the door. Lisa, still sitting by the checkerboard, was looking at her intently. Cassandra shoved the sheet of paper that had been on her door into her pocket, then joined her daughter on the floor.

"Nothing to worry about," she said. "Just someone making signs and leaving them in the hallway."

Lisa hesitated, then asked, "Are they bad signs, Mommy?"

"Yes, honey, they're bad signs. But there's nothing to worry about. All we have to do is take them down when we see them and just not pay any attention to what they say." She smiled reassuringly. "Whose turn is it?"

The child stared at her a moment, then lowered her gaze. "Yours," she mumbled.

Cassandra kept up a stream of happy and carefree-sounding chatter, finally getting Lisa to smile, then laugh. By the time the girl went to bed, she was sleepy but in good spirits, apparently unconcerned about signs in the hall or anything else.

But for Cassandra things weren't so easy. Cheering up Lisa had distracted her, kept her from thinking about a man who had tried to force his way into her apartment, a man who might have left the unnerving notice on her door. After going to bed, she tossed and turned for several hours before finally drifting off into a shallow sleep, from which she awoke whenever she heard one of the night's noises, the little creaks and thumps that occurred when the building adjusted to the cooler night-time temperature, or when her neighbors went to the bathroom. Tonight, every sound seemed threatening, seemed to whisper, *It's me, Clark, and I'm right here in the apartment with you and your daughter*.

Once, when the noise that awakened her had been a little louder than usual, it had been all she could do to keep from screaming.

Exhausted when she got home the next evening, Cassandra decided that frozen dinners were about all the cooking she could handle. Popping two of them into the oven—roast beef for her, chicken for Lisa—she sat down on the couch to go through her mail, which she'd collected from her box in the building's foyer. It was Friday evening, and for the next two days she wanted to do nothing but rest.

Emerging from the hallway, Lisa walked over to the TV set. "Can I watch TV, Mommy?" she asked.

Realizing she was too tired tonight to entertain the child, Cassandra gave her permission. The evening news came on, and Lisa immediately began changing channels, finally settling for a game show. She sat down on the floor in front of the set.

"Not so close," Cassandra warned, and the little girl moved a foot or two farther away from the set.

Going through her mail, Cassandra found a number of ads, including one that promised her a gift with a retail value of at least fifty dollars if she would visit some land that was being developed near a rural Wisconsin lake. Lake Escape Estates, it said. Hiking trails and fishing and beautiful scenery. The perfect spot to build your summer home. The idea of her having a summer home was so ridiculous that she nearly laughed.

Cassandra's mother had been one of those traditional women who would have been delighted had her daughter married a doctor or a lawyer. You're wrong, Mom, she thought. *I* should have been a doctor or a lawyer.

She quickly pushed the thought aside. It was too late for anything like that. One failed marriage too late. One child too late.

At the bottom of her stack of ads was a hand-addressed letter with no return address. Probably more junk mail, she decided. They just want to make sure I open it. Inside the envelope was a single sheet of paper. On it, printed in ballpoint, were the words:

Cassie,

I dream about licking every inch of you, then making love to you.

Clark

Returning the letter to the envelope, Cassandra stared at the TV screen without seeing what was on it. I'm not going to let him get to me, she thought. I'm not going to have another night like the last one. I'm going to ignore him, go about my business, and eventually he'll tire of this and leave me alone.

She held that thought. After dinner, Lisa resumed her TV-watching while Cassandra wrote a letter to her sister in New Mexico.

Two years older than Cassandra, Susan had moved, with her husband, to Albuquerque about five or six years ago, and they both loved it. Susan said she didn't even like returning to the Midwest on vacations. She and Rob had two kids, and they were so happily married that death was indeed the only thing that would ever cause them to part. Ah, well, Cassandra thought, at least one of us did it right.

Her mother and father had been like that, too. When her dad died of cancer about ten years ago, her mom had been so grief-stricken that she'd simply stopped caring. Eight months later, she, too, was dead. Cassandra realized her eyes were growing moist. Despite the years that had passed, these were memories she still had trouble dealing with, and she forced them from her mind.

After putting Lisa to bed, she picked up a magazine, found she was unable to concentrate on it, and turned the TV set back on. Within moments, she was getting drowsy. She had nearly fallen sound asleep on the couch when a knock on the door awakened her.

Afraid it was Clark, she peered through the peephole,

seeing a young blond man. She vaguely recognized him as someone she'd seen around the apartment building. His name was Mike or Mark, or something like that. She opened the door.

"I decided to take you up on your offer," he said, grinning. One of his front teeth was broken. He had two pimples on his chin.

"What?" she said, confused.

"Your name's Cassandra, isn't it?"

She nodded, her uneasiness growing by the second.

He handed her a sheet of paper on which was written in red ink:

> C. JENNINGS
> SPECIALIST IN ORAL SEX
> FREE SAMPLES
> KNOCK, ASK FOR CASSANDRA

"I'm here for my free sample," he said.

"Get out of here!" she yelled, slamming the door. She leaned against it, seething, wishing she'd told Mike or Mark or whatever his name was just how much of an asshole she thought he was.

But the anger didn't last long. It died from lack of fuel. And fear took over.

Hurrying into the kitchen, she pulled the garbage container out from under the sink and retrieved the mail, which included the letter from Clark. When she located it, she compared the printing on the letter to the larger red letters on the sheet of paper that had been placed on her door. Although the larger letters were more meticulously printed, it was clear the same person had written both messages.

It'll be all right, she told herself. He'll tire of this and go away. Now go to bed and get a good night's sleep. Don't let him succeed in tormenting you.

Slowly, she got up and headed for the bedroom. After changing into her nightgown, she stepped into the bathroom, and her eyes were drawn to the mirror. A thin, pale face stared back at her. The flesh below the eyes was puffy, and in the eyes themselves she saw fear. And she knew that despite her fatigue and the strength she had urged herself to find, tonight she would not sleep well again.

Grabbing her toothbrush and a tube of toothpaste, she began brushing her teeth. When she again looked into the mirror, her vision was blurred by tears.

Sitting in the living room of his apartment, Clark Clayton studied a framed photo of the woman he so desperately desired. Leaning back in the reclining chair, he realized that although he had enjoyed having sex with her and would very much like to enjoy it again, it wasn't really the woman herself—not in the physical sense, anyway—that he craved. It was her love. More than anything else in the world he wanted Cassandra Jennings to love him.

Somewhere in a corner of his mind, he knew that the things he was doing, things like putting signs on her door, would not only never win her love but would most likely make her afraid of him, make her consider him a monster. And yet he was unable to stop doing these things, for if he did nothing, nothing would happen. He had to do something. He had to keep trying.

Putting the photo on the table beside his chair, he let his eyes wander around the room. Located in a large new complex, his apartment had thick wall-to-wall carpeting throughout. Across the room from him was a big-screen color TV and a video recorder. To his left was a costly stereo setup; to his right, equally expensive exercise equipment. His environment looked like what it was, the home of a relatively affluent and single male.

After a few moments, his eyes were drawn to the

picture he'd placed beside him on the small table. The face that watched him from the photograph was smooth-skinned, framed by dark curls. He knew why he had put those signs on Cassandra's door. A part of him was furious because of the way she'd rejected him. And that part wanted to strike back, to hurt her for what she'd done.

No, he thought. That will only chase her away for good. I'll never be able to have her love.

But something else inside him was saying. *Punish her for what she's done to you. You have the chance now, the chance you never thought you'd have.*

Violently shaking his head, he tried to push this notion from his mind. He wanted her love; he didn't want to hurt her. Besides, the idea that he finally had a chance to get even with Cassandra made absolutely no sense. He'd met her last month at a party and dated her for the first time only a few days ago.

Standing, he walked to the window and peered out. From his third-story apartment, he looked down on the subdued lights of suburbia, then shifted his gaze to the bright glow on the horizon that marked the heart of Chicago. When the clouds were low enough, the lights of the city illuminated their undersides with an eerie whitish light. It was something you never noticed when you were actually in the city, and he wondered whether the phenomenon was only visible from a distance.

Then as he turned from the window, his eyes again found the photo on the table beside his recliner. He frowned suddenly, perplexed. If he had gone out with Cassandra for the first time only a few days ago, then how did he come to have a framed photo of her?

The answer came back as a jumbled set of meaningless messages that shot into his mind with such force that he took a step backward as if he'd been punched.

For a moment, the room swirled around him, and then he found himself on the floor. Except it wasn't his floor. This one was covered with a low green carpet. It looked fairly new, and yet its style seemed years out of fashion. He sat in a corner, watching the woman use an upright vacuum.

It was Cassandra Jennings. And yet it wasn't.

She rolled the vacuum back and forth, slowly getting closer to him. He watched, oddly fascinated. "Move," she snapped, bumping him sharply with the machine, and he scrambled out of the way.

In his new position by an overstuffed chair, he watched the woman as she continued vacuuming. When he finally shifted his eyes away from her, he spotted a dead cockroach at the base of the chair. The woman, who hated cockroaches, would call an exterminator at the first sign of one. When she spotted a bug in her home, her face would twist into a look of revulsion, and she'd stare at it as if the intensity of her gaze could rid the world of all such foul creatures.

Suddenly, he knew he had the power to make her suffer. Using nothing but his mind, he called out all the roaches from their hiding places in the walls and from under the kitchen counters and from the basement. As they came, the rustle of thousands of moving legs was covered by the noise of the vacuum.

From the hallway, a reddish-brown stain spread across the carpet, as if someone had spilled an enormous chocolate shake. Clark urged them onward, toward the woman. She turned just as the roaches reached her feet. The familiar look of disgust appeared on her face, but there was no horror there. She did not scream or flail with her arms. And the roaches stopped.

The woman turned her gaze on him now, eyes that were cold and cruel, and her expression made it clear that he was even more repugnant to her than the roaches.

Suddenly, the bugs were moving again, turning away from the woman, coming toward him. He looked up at her, pleading with his eyes. No, he thought. Please don't. Please forgive me. But the woman had looked away. The spreading brown stain reached his legs, and then it was on him; roaches were climbing up his shirt, covering his arms, slipping into his clothes. He tried to stand, but the insects were holding him down. They were on his face now, trying to get into his eyes and his ears and his mouth. He screamed, a long, piercing shriek of total terror. And when that scream died from lack of breath, he started on another. And the roaches leaped into his open mouth.

And then he was on his own carpet again, spitting, wiping at his face, rolling violently from side to side, screaming. When he finally got control of himself, he lay perfectly still, listening to see whether his screams had attracted any attention. After a few moments, he decided they hadn't. His neighbor on one side liked to listen to the stereo with headphones. On the other side was a woman who worked evenings. Good, he thought. Good.

And then he began to cry, his body shaking with the sobs.

ON MONDAY, CASSANDRA WENT TO WORK
feeling much better about things. The weekend had
passed with no further contact from Clark. She'd used
her two days off to clean her apartment, do her laundry,
and catch up on her sleep.

When she stepped into the room in which she worked,
she smiled at Jenny, who whispered, "Better be careful.
Latest edict from Nan the Nazi: no smiling except on
authorized breaks."

Slipping on her headset, she flashed Jenny a big, thoroughly ridiculous grin, and the other woman chuckled.
Then both of them scanned the area to make sure the
infamous Nan wasn't watching.

It's over, Cassandra told herself. He won't bother us
again. She pushed the thought aside because a call was
coming in. Somewhere out there was a customer with a
problem. She pushed the flashing button.

That morning, Clark sat in his office, staring at a stack

of papers that had been awaiting his attention for several days. It was unlike him, ignoring his responsibilities like this. At the supervisors' meeting this morning, he'd heard almost nothing that had been said. His thoughts had been elsewhere, swirling away as they pleased, as if he had no control over them.

And do I have control? he wondered. Over anything?

He'd spent the weekend at a motel in rural Indiana, hoping that getting out of town would allow him to sort out his thoughts. It hadn't worked. His thoughts had been too confused to sort out.

He had to start paying attention to his job. He was the director of product development for one of the Midwest's largest plumbing manufacturers. He was important, and he had to act that way.

Leaning back in his chair, he rubbed his eyes. His modern, carpeted office was in a building populated by executives and secretaries and engineers. Although pipes and fixtures and things like that were being manufactured only a few hundred feet away, none of the heat or noise or grime was evident here. This was white-collar country, the territory of the powerful, who did not care to get dirt on their hands.

He did not feel powerful at the moment. He felt lost, confused, as if he were three separate selves, all of which were vying for control. One of the selves cared only about somehow gaining Cassandra's love, while another wanted only to get even with her for rejecting him. The third wanted to forget all this and start paying attention to the other things in his life, like his career.

He leaned forward again, and his eyes fixed on the telephone. For several long seconds, he stared at it, his thoughts churning. A drop of perspiration trickled down his forehead, for he knew he had reached a turning point. The two parts of him that were concerned with

Cassandra wanted him to pick up the phone and call her. He knew where she worked, because she had told him. He had already looked up the number, which was written on a pad by the phone.

The third part of him, the part that wanted to forget all this and get back to living his life as before, was pleading with him not to do it. That part of him seemed to be weakening, and if he picked up the phone, he thought it would mean the end of that portion of himself, the only portion that—that what? That was still sane? The word seemed to float across his brain. Sane, sane, sane. It was meaningless.

He reached for the phone, then hesitated as he seemed to hear one last plea from somewhere within. Again, a drop of perspiration ran down his face. He wiped it away and picked up the phone. He knew what he had to do.

Cassandra was talking to a policyholder in Kentucky when the call came in on a local line. After assuring the man that the company would pay for the damage to his car caused when a wind storm blew a large tree down on top of it, she broke the connection and punched the button for the local call.

"Telephone claims," she said. "Ms. Jennings."

"Don't hang up on me, Cassie. Please. Just listen; that's all I ask. Just give me thirty seconds and listen to what I have to say."

Cassandra stared at the button lit by the call on her headset, its innocent-looking glow proclaiming that it wasn't over, that Clark Clayton had merely taken the weekend off from tormenting her. Although she knew she should sever the connection immediately, she sat there with her finger poised above the button, uncertain why she wasn't pushing it. Her hesitation was all Clark needed.

"Good," he said, "good. You don't have to say anything. Just listen, okay? Just listen. Look, I think, uh, I think I've made a real mess of things, but it doesn't have to be like this. I'm very attracted to you, Cassandra, and I think you were attracted to me, too—at first. Then I started behaving badly and blew everything.

"It happened because, well, I was so determined to do everything right that I tried too hard. But I know better now, and if you'll give me one more chance, I'll see that it never happens again. Give us a chance, Cassie. Please. I think we could be real good together.

"That's all I've got to say, Cassie. I really wish you'd say okay, you'll give me another chance, but if you don't want to say anything, that's okay, too."

Cassandra started to press the button, then stopped herself. If Clark was truly willing to be sensible, maybe she could reason with him. "I don't want to have any kind of a relationship with you, Clark. All this—" she paused, trying to think of a word other than harassment— "this attention you've been giving me is just frightening me and my daughter. I think you should just leave us alone and we'll all be happier."

For a moment, he said nothing. Then, with an eerie calmness, he said, "I'm sorry, Cassie; I can't do that."

She broke the connection. Why won't he go away? she wondered unhappily. Why doesn't he give up? And then she imagined this continuing forever, Clark constantly pestering her, never relenting. What would she do if six months or six years from now Clark was still doing this to her? Would she capitulate just to get him off her back? Or would he drive her insane?

Insane.

She considered the term. Clark's behavior was more

than persistent. It was compulsive, the actions of someone who might be out of touch with reality. Terms she'd
learned in the psychology course she'd taken before
dropping out of college to get married. Terms that dealt
with abnormal behavior. With insanity. She shivered.

What am I going to do? she asked herself. How am I
going to protect myself? How am I going to protect
Lisa? She had no answers for these questions.

On the pad were some notes she'd made concerning
the claim phoned in by the man in Kentucky. With
shaking hands, she typed the information into the computer. As she did so, she heard Clark's voice, with its
almost offhanded calmness, saying, *I'm sorry, Cassie;
I can't do that.*

With a start, she realized she'd typed the words on
the screen of her VDT.

The next morning, Clark called her at work twice.
Both times she promptly severed the connection without
saying a word. When he called again early that afternoon, she became unnerved.

"Stop this!" she yelled. "Don't call me here again. I
hate you! Do you understand that? I'll never have anything to do with you, because I hate you!"

Breaking the connection, she sat at her desk, seething, wishing she had a real telephone instead of this
damn headset so she could get the satisfaction of slamming the receiver down. Slowly, she became aware of
the other people in the room, most of whom were staring at her. She caught Jenny's eyes, which flicked mean-
ingfully toward the front of the room, where someone
stood in the doorway, watching her.

Nan Cosgrove, a.k.a. Nan the Nazi, turned and disappeared into the hallway without a word.

*   *   *

When Cassandra came to work the following morning, she took her seat and waited for all sorts of terrible things to happen. Every time a call came in—even on the 800 number—she tensed when she answered, afraid it would be Clark.

And she had yet to explain to Nan Cosgrove about her outburst yesterday. She wasn't allowed to leave her desk, except on break, unless she was summoned by Cosgrove. On her afternoon break, she'd gone to Cosgrove's office, finding it empty. She'd tried once more after getting off work and again when she came in this morning, both times finding the office unoccupied. So the matter seemed to hang over her, something that needed to be resolved.

She'd found another letter from Clark in her mailbox when she got home last night. This one had said simply:

There are two sides of me, the side that offers you love and the other side. If you continue to reject my love, you will meet the other side.

Clark

Though not specifically threatening, the note frightened her. She wondered whether it was his "other side" that had tried to break down her door. Or was it something worse, more bizarre . . . more insane?

The word terrified her. It meant that she had a psychopath after her, someone whose mind churned along in a world all its own, seeing things through the filter of its insanity. You couldn't understand people like that; you could only avoid them, fear them.

A lunatic would pursue his goals tirelessly—a machine fueled by madness.

Her thoughts were interrupted by a call from Oregon; a policyholder's home had split in two, the separate parts creeping in opposite directions. The call provided a useful distraction. While Cassandra was dealing with the homeowner's problems, she was unable to think about her own. She explained that the company wouldn't be able to determine its liability in the matter until a claims adjuster checked out the property and reported back. When she ended the conversation, she looked up to find Clark standing beside her desk. He smiled at her. For a moment, she simply stared at him, her mouth suddenly dry. Finally, she found her voice.

"How did you get in here?" she demanded.

"I simply asked the receptionist for directions, then followed them. Anyone can walk right in."

"Get out of here," she said. "You have no right to be here."

"We have to talk," he replied.

Before Cassandra could say anything else, a call came in on the 800 number. Glancing around the room, she saw that everyone else was already on the phone, so she punched the flashing button.

"I'm calling to report that my car's been in an accident," a soft-spoken man with a southern accent said.

"I'll need your name, address, and if you've got it handy, your policy number," Cassandra said. She glared at Clark, telling him without words to go away. He smiled at her.

The caller identified himself as Jay Tiller of Shreveport, Louisiana. "Uh, let's see," he said. "I've got the policy right here in front of me. Uh, the number's 6325547-A."

Cassandra put this information into the computer, and an outline of Tiller's coverage appeared on the screen. He had liability coverage with a maximum benefit of a hundred thousand dollars and two hundred dollars' deductible collision coverage. "Can you describe the accident, please?"

"Uh, yes, I was driving along Line Avenue here in Shreveport, and another car ran a stop sign, hit me broadside."

"Was a police report taken?"

"Yes."

"All right," she said as she typed this information into the computer. "How much damage was there to the vehicles?"

"Well, on my car, the passenger-side door is pretty badly caved in, and it won't open. There are deep scratches and damaged sheet metal and missing chrome . . ." Cassandra didn't hear what else the man in Louisiana said, because hands had just taken hold of her shoulders and were gently rubbing them. It was Clark. He was standing behind her. Angrily, she knocked his hands away.

"Uh, sir, I'm sorry, but I didn't get all that. Could you—" The hands were on her shoulders again.

"Ma'am, is everything all right there?" the man in Louisiana asked.

But Cassandra only vaguely heard him. Yanking off her headset, she threw it down on her desk. "Don't you ever put your hands on me again!" she screamed.

"Now, Cassie, let's not be that way," Clark said, reaching for her.

She pushed him away. "No! Don't touch me!"

He smiled. "Stop this, Cassie," he said gently. "Just stop fighting me and everything will be all right."

He took a step toward her, and Cassandra did something she'd never done before in her life. Closing her hand into a fist, she struck him in the face. Startled, Clark took a step backward, lost his balance, and fell.

Suddenly, Jenny was standing over him, her face red with rage.

"Leave her alone, you asshole," she snapped.

And then some of the others were there, too, standing over him, daring him to do anything. All the employees in the room were women, and most of them had come to her aid. Clark looked up at them, confused.

"This—this is personal," he said.

"I think you'd better leave," Betsy Lee Adams said in her Texas drawl. A heavyset woman with curly red hair, she'd recently moved here from Austin. Betsy Lee was the sort of person who rarely took any guff from anyone.

Getting slowly to his feet, Clark rubbed his cheek, his eyes finding Cassandra's. Although they were filled with a lot of confused emotions Cassandra didn't understand, there was also loathing there, a hatred burning with such intensity that it made her feel cold inside.

"You shouldn't have done that," he said icily. And then he walked from the room.

"Thank you," Cassandra said to the women who'd come to her rescue. "Thank you so much." She flexed the fingers of her right hand, the one she'd used to strike Clark. It was a little sore, but she'd still be able to operate her VDT.

"You okay?" Jenny asked.

"Yes," Cassandra said. "Thanks to you guys."

"Hats off to you," Betsy Lee said. "Wish I'd had the nerve to deck my ex-husband like that."

"I see flashing lights all over the room," Nan Cosgrove said. "Our customers are calling, and no one's answering." Clearly annoyed, she stood just inside the room, surveying the scene.

The women returned to their desks, putting on their headsets, answering calls, avoiding Cosgrove's eyes. As

Cassandra put hers on, she said, "Hello. Sir, are you still there?"

But the man from Shreveport was no longer on the line.

Cosgrove walked purposefully to Cassandra's desk. "I want to see you in my office," she said.

Cassandra followed her boss out of the room, wondering what had happened to her life. Since the divorce, her existence had been humdrum. She went to work; she did the laundry; she watched TV or played checkers with Lisa. Every once in a while, and only on the one weekend each month Lisa spent with her father, she dated. And that was it. A routine, unexciting life.

But all that had ended the night she slept with Clark. For the past week and a half or so, she felt as though she were under siege.

Cosgrove closed the door as they stepped into her office. Taking her place behind her desk, Nan the Nazi motioned for Cassandra to take a comfortable-looking upholstered office chair.

"All right," Cosgrove said. "What's this all about?"

Cassandra told her what had been happening.

After hearing the whole story, Cosgrove frowned. "I realize that you have no control over this man's actions. Nevertheless, incidents here in this building like what happened today simply can not be tolerated. Do you understand that?"

"But it's not my fault! What can I do?"

Cosgrove sighed. "I realize that it wouldn't be fair to penalize you for this man's actions. Still, you must understand that we have a business to run here, and businesses are run on what's good for the company, not necessarily what's fair."

Cassandra got the picture. If the only way to avoid

disruptions like the one today was to get rid of her, then she was gone.

"I'm going to leave instructions with the front desk that this man is not to be admitted again under any circumstances. That may take care of the problem."

"I hope so," Cassandra said.

"Have you contacted the police?"

Cassandra shook her head. "I didn't think there was really very much they could do."

"Well, after today's incident, I think I'd contact them if I were you."

"All right," Cassandra said. "I'll do it right after work."

The police station was a modern white building with a well-cared-for lawn. This time of day, there were numerous empty parking spaces in the paved lot adjacent to the building.

She'd had to bring Lisa with her, because the day-care center was very strict about picking children up on time. But she didn't want Lisa to hear what she was going to tell the officers. She found the child a seat on a bench opposite the desk sergeant.

"You wait right here. I'll be back in just a few minutes." She gave Lisa one of the stern gazes she had learned from her own mother.

Cassandra stepped up to a counter behind which sat two uniformed officers, a man and a woman. The man had been watching her and Lisa. "Can I help you?" he asked.

"Uh, yes," she said quietly. "Uh, someone's been bothering me. He won't leave me alone. Is there anything you can do to make him stop?"

The officer shifted in his seat. He was about thirty,

blond, a little on the chubby side. "Exactly what do you mean by 'bothering' you?"

Cassandra briefly told him about Clark.

"Hmm," he said. "I'm not sure how much help we can be, but I'm going to have you talk with a detective."

He picked up the phone and held a brief conversation with someone, speaking just softly enough so that Cassandra was unable to hear what was said. When he hung up, he said, "Have a seat. Detective Hoskins will be with you in a moment."

Cassandra joined Lisa on the narrow bench against the wall. Nervously, she traced the initials and obscenities people had carved into the wood. She wondered what kind of people would deface public property in a police station, within plain view of the officers at the front desk. People who didn't care, she decided. People who'd given up on the world.

She'd been sitting there about five minutes when a tall man wearing a white shirt and tie but no jacket approached her. "I'm Detective Hoskins," he said. "Are you the one who's having a harassment problem?"

"Yes," she said.

"Why don't you come with me and we'll talk about it."

"I'll be right back," Cassandra told her daughter. "Now stay right there."

The detective led her to a small, stark room containing a wooden table and chairs. Telling her to sit down, he seated himself across the table from her.

"Okay," he said, "tell me about it."

Cassandra did so, and when she'd finished, the detective asked, "Has he threatened you or your daughter?"

"Well, there was that letter where he talked about the other side of himself. And after I hit him, he said I shouldn't have done that."

"But he hasn't ever used any words like 'hurt' or 'kill'—or phrases like 'get even,' 'make you pay,' 'teach you a lesson.' "

"No. But what about the time he tried to break down my door? Isn't that the same thing as a threat?"

Hoskins frowned. "Did he damage the door at all?"

"No."

"You'd have a tough time proving that his intention was to harm you." He sighed. "Look, I've got to tell you right out that this guy hasn't broken any laws that the criminal justice system's going to get too terribly upset about."

"Does that mean you can't do anything?"

"I didn't say that. If you'll sign a complaint against him, we can stop by and have a talk with him. Sometimes that's all it takes. The last thing a lot of these guys want is trouble with the police."

"Thank you," she said. "I appreciate this. I really do."

"I'll get a complaint form," he said.

When she and Lisa walked out of the police station a few minutes later, Cassandra thought there was an excellent chance that her troubles with Clark were over. An executive with a career to worry about, he couldn't afford to have trouble with the police.

"Can we stop and get hamburgers?" Lisa asked as her mother unlocked the car door.

"Well, if you really want to. I was kind of hoping we could stop for a pizza." It was her daughter's favorite food, and Cassandra knew what her reaction would be.

"Pizza!" the child exclaimed. "Let's have pizza. That would be even better."

"Okay," Cassandra said. "If you insist." We've got to stop eating like this, she thought. She resolved that from now on it would be balanced meals at home, with fast food a rare treat. No more frozen dinners or hastily thrown together suppers, either, she pledged.

But tonight it's okay, because tonight we're celebrating.

As she pulled away from the station, she wondered when the police would visit Clark. Tonight? Tomorrow? She pictured him turning white when Hoskins flashed his badge. She hoped the policeman would scare the hell out of him.

6

IT WAS ABOUT TEN-THIRTY THE NEXT MORN-
ing when Detective Hoskins arrived at the plumbing
manufacturing firm that employed Clark Clayton. He'd
decided to see Clayton at work, because his visit would
have maximum impact that way.

As he walked along the hallway off which Clayton's
office was located, the policeman took in his surroundings. This was clearly the domain of middle management. The floor was carpeted, but the beige-and-brown
material was a utility floor covering, not suitable for
corporate vice-presidents and the like. The offices he
passed were nice but moderate-sized, with decent but
not extremely expensive furniture.

Clayton, he discovered, had both his name and the
title DIRECTOR OF PRODUCT DEVELOPMENT on the outside
of his office door, which stood open. He also had a
secretary. Stepping up to her desk, the detective displayed his badge.

"I'm Detective Hoskins. Is Mr. Clayton in?"

"Uh, yes," she said, slightly flustered. "I'll let him know you're here." She was dark-haired, about twenty-eight, wore very little makeup, and had a wedding ring on her finger. She used the phone to let her boss know he was here, and a moment later Hoskins was in the inner office.

Again, he displayed his ID and badge. "Detective Hoskins," he said. "I take it you're Clark Clayton."

"Yes," the man behind the desk said, studying him warily. "What can I do for the police department?" Clayton was in his thirties, thin but athletic-looking, the sort of man who watched what he ate and exercised.

Pocketing his ID, the policeman sat down. "You know a woman named Cassadra Jennings?"

"Sure," Clayton replied without hesitation.

Hoskins had watched the man's face closely when he'd mentioned Cassandra Jennings. Something had registered, but the policeman was uncertain what. "She's filed a complaint against you."

Clayton looked surprised. "A complaint? For what?"

"She says you're harassing her."

"Harassing her?" He laughed. "Look, there's absolutely nothing here that should interest the police. It's more like a domestic argument than anything else. The ups and downs of lovers." He shrugged.

"You're lovers, then, you and Cassandra Jennings?"

Clayton smiled. "Sure. We've had some problems, and Cassandra overreacted a little. That's all."

"Did you try to break down her door?"

"Break down her door . . ." He shook his head. "No, no, no. She was refusing to talk to me, and I pounded on it rather angrily, but I never tried to break it down. Hell, I only weigh about 150 pounds. I'd do more damage to myself than I would to a door."

"What about yesterday?"

"Yesterday?"

"You went to the office where she works."

"I told you. We're having a—a spat. I guess that's as good a word as any. It's all very childish, really. In any case, going to the insurance company was the only way I could get to talk to her. I got directions from the receptionist. I didn't break in or anything like that."

"Wasn't there some sort of scuffle?"

Clayton grinned. "If you want to call it that. She hit me. I didn't do a thing to her."

"Did you put your hands on her?"

"I touched her shoulder."

"That could be considered assault, you know."

"You don't honestly believe you could make that stick, do you? Let's face it, if anyone was assaulted yesterday, it was me. I was the one knocked on his back."

The detective sighed. "Look, Mr. Clayton, both you and I know that what you've been doing is harassment. Now—"

"No, I don't know that at all," Clayton said, cutting him off. "I'm merely being persistent."

"The woman says she wants you to leave her alone."

Cocking his head, he smiled. "She'll change her mind. I understand that's a woman's prerogative."

"Leave her alone, Mr. Clayton."

"Is that an order, officer?"

"No, Mr. Clayton. It's advice. Good advice." Hoskins stood up. "I hope you'll pay attention to it."

As the detective turned toward the door, Clayton said, "If you decide you need to speak with me further on this matter, please let me know in advance so I can arrange to have an attorney present."

"That's your privilege, Mr. Clayton."

As he walked toward the elevator, Hoskins reviewed

his meeting with Clayton. Although he was uncertain what effect his words had on the man, he doubted very seriously that Clayton had any intention of leaving Cassandra Jennings alone. It was one of those situations in which very little could be done until something nasty happened. Until it was too late.

It was the way things worked. You couldn't arrest someone for what he was likely to do, only for what he did. It had to be that way in a free society. He understood that. But he didn't always like it.

Shaken, Clark Clayton sat at his big desk, staring at the door through which the detective had left. Although he'd known that Cassandra might go to the police, knowing something was not the same thing as experiencing it. The policeman was involved now; he could interfere, possibly even prevent Clark from doing what he had to do.

That he had to win Cassandra's love was beyond question now. The matter needed no further consideration, for it was the way things were. It was fact. His commitment was total; this was the most important thing in his life.

Punish her for this, that other part of him urged. She's betrayed you, sneered at your offer of love.

No, he thought. Not yet. I can still make her change her mind. If I can only convince her that I'm not a threat.

With a shaking hand, he got the framed photo from his top desk drawer and studied the pretty face with the dark curls. He'd started taking it with him everywhere he went. Please, Clark thought, fixing his gaze on the black-and-white eyes in the photo. Please love me. Is it so much to ask? Is it really?

Despite the interest of the detective, he had to continue, for nothing else mattered. He would have to be careful, though, not to make any overt threats, not to break any laws. As long as he was cautious, everything would be all right. There were no laws against trying to win a woman's affections, even if the technique was unorthodox.

Laying the photo on the desk, he closed his eyes. He had to find a way to make her love him. If he failed, that other part of him, the part that wanted revenge, would have its way. And it could be just as dedicated in its pursuit.

Oh, please, he thought. Please don't let that happen.

Picking up a file folder from his desk, he flipped through the typed pages and charts within. It concerned market research on a proposed new product. He was supposed to examine it and send it to his boss with a recommendation. He hadn't read it. Suddenly, he realized that he didn't even know what the product was.

For a long moment, he sat there, knowing that he should read the typed pages and study the charts. Abruptly, he closed the folder and tossed it onto his desk. It was unimportant. He got his briefcase from the closet, returned to his desk, and slipped the framed photo into the case.

Stepping into the outer office, he hesitated. Cindy, his secretary, was sitting at her desk, her back to him, unaware of his presence. Why had she told the policeman he was in? Why had she betrayed him when it would have been so easy to send the detective away? Taking two steps, he moved to within a foot of Cindy's chair. He slowly raised his hands and saw . . .

. . . his fingers closing around her throat. Struggling, she knocks some papers off the desk, then the phone, whose bell gives a single ding as it hits the floor. They are both standing now, face-to-face, and he can see the terror in her eyes. You betrayed me, he tells her, and your punishment is to die. . . .

And then the image vanished. Cindy, still unaware of his presence, sat at her desk, only inches away from him. Perspiration trickled down his back. Lowering his hands, he moved silently back to the door to his office and then stepped briskly forward as if he'd just entered the room.

"I've got a meeting," he said as he stepped past his secretary. "I'll be tied up all afternoon."

"Is there a number where I can reach you?" Cindy asked.

"No," he replied. And then he was in the hallway, walking quickly toward the elevator.

He was the only one in the car as it descended. The customary bland music played softly from an unseen speaker. Someone had to pay for that music, and he wondered what purpose it served. Why would anyone pay good money to have barely audible music playing gently in an elevator? A bell sounded, announcing the car's arrival at the ground floor, and the doors swished apart.

Clark was in the parking lot, heading for his reserved space, when a feeling of panic came over him. Suddenly, he was unable to remember having taken the picture with him. Putting the case down on the oil-stained asphalt, he popped open the catches and lifted the lid. The picture was there. Relieved, he closed the case and continued toward his car.

After he slipped behind the wheel, he opened the case again, just to make sure.

It was a few minutes before five when Nan Cosgrove entered the room and quickly walked to Cassandra's desk. "That man was here a few minutes ago," she said.

"The receptionist told him he couldn't come back here, and he left."

"Were there any problems?" Cassandra asked.

"No, he just left."

Cassandra nodded.

"Perhaps we have this thing under control now," Cosgrove said.

"I hope so."

"So do I."

Cosgrove took a moment to survey the activities of the other employees, then strode from the room. Catching Cassandra's eye, Jenny made a face. Her expression communicated, *What a bitch*.

Cassandra nodded, but the personality of her boss was of little importance to her at the moment. Clark had come back, had tried to see her again. What happened yesterday had not discouraged him. Nothing would discourage him.

Again, Jenny caught her eyes, and she apparently sensed Cassandra's mood, because she communicated, *It'll be okay*.

No, it won't, Cassandra thought.

And then she remembered that Detective Hoskins had promised to pay Clark a visit. Maybe the policeman hadn't found him yet, or maybe he hadn't had time. The thought made her feel better. Surely Clark would stop all this after a police officer paid him a visit.

As soon as she got off work, Cassandra hurried to her car without stopping to chat with her coworkers. They had all expressed concern for what was happening to her, and they all wanted to help. But at the moment she just wanted to get away as quickly as possible. She felt an overpowering need to be with her daughter, snuggly cocooned in the place they called home, with the rest of the world locked out.

When she reached her car, she scanned her surroundings. It had occured to her that Clark might wait for her outside the building, but she saw no sign of him, and none of the white cars in the lot seemed to be the same make and model as the one he drove. Slipping behind the wheel, she started the engine and pulled out of the parking area. As she drove, Cassandra regularly checked the rearview mirror. As far as she could tell, no white cars were following her.

The day was cloudy and cool. A chilly breeze was blowing in from Lake Michigan.

It took her twenty minutes to drive to the day-care center. Located in an older neighborhood, it was a two-story white frame house about two blocks from the school Lisa attended. The place was surrounded by a low chain-link fence. As she often did, Lisa was waiting for her by the gate.

"Hi," Cassandra said as her daughter climbed into the car. "Did you have a nice day?"

"Uh-huh," the child replied noncommittally, fastening her seat belt.

"What'd you do in school today?"

"Writing."

"Is that all?" Cassandra signaled her intention to pull away from the curb. Checking the side mirror, she saw that a car was coming, and she waited.

"We also did arithmetic," Lisa said.

Gloria Weinstein, the owner of the day-care facility, appeared at the gate and waved to catch Cassandra's attention. Cassandra rolled down her window as the woman came around to the driver's side of the car.

"I'm glad I caught you," Weinstein said breathlessly. She was a tall, attractive woman in her late thirties, with short dark hair.

"Is there a problem with Lisa?" Cassandra asked.

"Oh, no, nothing like that. Uh, it's your payment. It was due last week."

"Oh," Cassandra said, embarrassed. "I'm sorry. I simply forgot. I'll write you a check right now."

She dug her checkbook and a pen from her purse, wondering if she'd forgotten to pay any other bills. Since she made the mistake of saying yes to Clark's offer of dinner and a play, her life had been a mess. Although agreeing to a date with an apparently nice man had seemed such an innocent thing at the time, if there was one word she'd spoken in her life that she could take back, it would be that yes. If she'd only said she was busy or that she had a headache or just plain no, her life this past week and a half or so would have been entirely different.

She tore off the check and handed it to Weinstein. "I'm sorry. I really am. I'm usually not this forgetful."

"No problem," Weinstein said, accepting the check. "You have a good day. We'll see you tomorrow, Lisa."

"Okay, Mrs. Weinstein," the child said.

As the woman walked back into the day-care center, a familiar voice called, "Hi, Cassie. How are you today?" Cassandra's stomach tightened. Clark, who must have arrived while she was talking to Gloria Weinstein, was parked across the street in his white car.

"Listen, I tried to see you at work today, but they wouldn't let me in. Uh—"

Cassandra rolled up the window, cutting off the sound of his voice. Putting the car in gear, she quickly pulled away from the curb. From behind her came a sudden screech of tires and an irate honk. She hadn't looked to see whether anyone was coming.

"Mommy, that car almost hit us!"

"I know. I should be more careful."

Cassandra turned a corner, then another, quickly pulling to the side of the road in a neighborhood of small frame houses. She waited to see whether Clark was following her.

"Mommy, why did we stop here?"

"We're checking on something, honey. That's all."

"On what?"

Ignoring the child's question, Cassandra said, "Did you see the man in the car?"

"The man who was talking to you?"

"Yes. Would you know him if you saw him again?"

"I think so." Lisa was watching her closely, the girl's expression displaying a mixture of confusion and anxiety.

"Well, that's the man who's been calling on the telephone. Remember what he looks like, and never let him take you anywhere, all right? Stay away from him. He's a bad man."

Lisa nodded gravely.

"Also, starting tomorrow, I want you to wait for me inside with Mrs. Weinstein instead of out by the gate. Will you do that?"

"Okay, Mommy."

And what about the two blocks Lisa had to walk to get from the school to the day-care center? She was completely vulnerable when she made that walk. And then Cassandra figured out a way to deal with that.

"Lisa, honey, listen. Starting tomorrow, I'm going to have a cab start picking you up at the school and taking you to Mrs. Weinstein."

"A cab?"

"Yes, a taxi."

"I don't mind walking, Mommy. It's not far."

"No. From now on, you're going to go in a cab."

Lisa nodded. She looked bewildered.

How did Clark find the day-care center? Cassandra wondered. He hadn't followed her; she was sure of it.

But then she recalled mentioning to him that Lisa spent her afternoons at a center after getting out of school. Determining which school Lisa attended would be simple—a call to the school district's central office. A quick check of the phone book would have told him which day-care facility was closest to Lisa's school.

Satisfied that Clark wasn't following her, Cassandra put the car in gear and headed for her apartment. She was halfway there when she realized that Clark would have had absolutely no reason to follow her, because he knew where she was going. He knew where she lived.

When she reached her apartment, she drove around the block twice, making certain Clark's white Oldsmobile wasn't there. Then she quickly parked her car and hurried inside with Lisa.

"Go and put the silverware on the table, okay? I'll be there in just a moment."

As soon as the child disappeared into the kitchen, Cassandra called the police department and asked for Detective Hoskins.

"I was going to call you shortly," he said. "What I had to tell you wasn't really urgent, so I thought it might be better to wait and call you at home."

"Did you talk to him?" she asked. She hoped he hadn't, for then there would still be a chance that doing so would work.

"Yes," the police officer said, "early this afternoon. Uh, I really don't know what to say about our conversation. I warned him to stay away from you, but I'm not sure how much good it did."

"It didn't do any good at all," Cassandra said. "He showed up where I work again this afternoon, and then later he was at the day-care center where my daughter goes after school. I'm—I'm afraid for my daughter. He could try to get at me through her."

"What exactly was he doing at the day-care center?"

"He was parked across the street, watching. And he tried to talk to me, but I rolled up my window and drove away."

"Has he made any threats against the child?"

Cassandra considered lying, saying that Clark had threatened to kill Lisa, but then she dropped the idea. Distorting the truth was not the way to solve this thing. "No," she said, "not in words. But his presence seems pretty damn threatening to me."

"Do you pick your daughter up at the day-care center?"

"Yes."

"Okay, how does she get to school and from school to the center?"

"I drive her to school, and she's been walking the two blocks from there to the center. Starting tomorrow, I'm going to send a cab for her."

Hoskins whistled. "That's going to cost you a bundle."

"What else can I do?"

He was silent a moment; then he said, "As long as you can afford it, that's probably the safest thing to do. Also, I'll ask patrol division to keep an eye on things at the school. For the moment, there's not much more I can do."

"I understand," Cassandra said. "Thank you for what you've done."

"Call me if anything else happens."

Cassandra said she would, and when she hung up, she found Lisa standing a few feet away, staring up at her.

"Table's set, Mommy," she said. She hesitated, as if she had something else to say, but then she turned and headed back toward the kitchen.

How am I going to protect her? Cassandra wondered.

How can I keep this lunatic from hurting her? And how can I shield her from the ugliness of all this?

It occurred to her suddenly that there was a way; that she would even consider it showed how desperate she was becoming. She could send Lisa to stay with her father. Though aware that her ex-husband lived in Wisconsin, Clark didn't know John's name. He could never find Lisa there.

No, she thought. Not that. Lisa was everything to her, and to send her to John's would be one thing; to get her back again, another.

Besides, John and Janice might not even want to have the child thrust into their lives. They might refuse. But Cassandra knew that just wasn't so. John would not only take Lisa; he'd be delighted. Perhaps he could use what was happening to his ex-wife to get the custody matter reopened. *The child's not safe with her, your honor. Lisa needs the stable sort of environment Janice and I can give her.*

Am I being selfish? Cassandra asked herself. Am I putting my own needs before the safety of my child? Uncertain whether she could answer that question honestly—even to herself—Cassandra pushed it from her thoughts unanswered. Things weren't bad enough yet for her to be faced with that hard decision. There had been no direct threats against Lisa.

Things weren't bad enough *yet*. Cassandra wished she hadn't let that word slip into her thoughts. She wished she had some magic saying she could utter that would make the word go away.

Yet.

As she stepped into the kitchen, she tried to empty her mind, to purge her brain of everything pertaining to Clark. She was only partially successful.

7

WILLIAM RICHWELL, VICE-PRESIDENT IN charge of research and development, walked along the carpeted hallway, heading for the office of Clark Clayton. His mind on the disturbing situation he had to deal with, he barely noticed the young man in a blue suit who smiled and wished him a good morning as they passed each other.

A tall man with dark hair and blue eyes, Richwell had a long stride that moved him rapidly, purposefully, along the corridor. He'd heard it said that he always walked as if he were in a hurry, which he supposed was not a bad image to have in a company that expected hustle from its executives.

What was troubling him this morning was the behavior of Clayton, the director of product development. Richwell was Clayton's boss, and Clayton had not been himself lately. A handsome, intelligent young man who was ordinarily a hard worker, he'd abruptly started letting his job slide. He'd missed appointments. He'd disappeared for hours without letting anyone know where he was going.

Clayton was a bright young man with a good future, which he was on the verge of destroying. There was still time to save his career, but something had to be done quickly, and that was why Richwell was on the way to Clayton's office.

"Good morning, Mr. Richwell," Cindy Waller, Clayton's secretary, said as the vice-president stepped up to her desk.

"Is he in?" Richwell asked, inclining his head toward the closed door to the inner office.

"He's out right now," Cindy Waller replied. Absently, she reached up and touched her dark hair.

"Where can he be reached?"

"I, uh, I don't have a number for him." She was watching him, clearly uncertain how to handle this. Apparently she knew something was wrong with her boss, but she was unsure whether her allegiance was to Clayton or to the company.

"Has he been in this morning?"

"No, sir."

"Have you heard from him at all?"

Cindy Waller shook her head, then shifted her eyes to the surface of her desk.

"Would you tell him to see me when he gets in, please?"

"Yes, sir." The secretary pulled over a pad and made a note.

As he left Clayton's office, Richfield decided that he approved of Cindy Waller's reluctance to betray her boss. If it turned out that Clark Clayton's career was unsalvageable, he would make it a point to find another spot for her in the company.

Richfield truly hoped it wouldn't come to that. He

genuinely liked Clayton, and he wanted to see him succeed. The young man had always been bright, friendly, one of the few junior executives who weren't constantly jockeying for position, back-stabbing, brownnosing. An honest, hard worker. At least he had been until about two weeks ago, when something happened.

As he stepped into the elevator and pressed the button for the next floor, Richfield wondered what had happened to make Clayton change so abruptly. Richfield had checked Clayton's personnel file, discovering that he had never been married and that both his parents were deceased. Which ruled out all sorts of possibilities. Clayton was coping neither with marital problems nor with the expense of medical treatment for an elderly mother or father. What did that leave? Burnout? Breakdown? Gambling? Trouble with his love life?

The vice-president shook his head. He didn't know. He only knew that something had to be done, and quickly.

Cassandra sat at her desk, waiting for the next call to come in from a policyholder with a claim. Only two of the room's five telephone claims operators were on the line at that moment. There were lulls like this every now and then; at other times, everyone would have two or three callers on hold, listening to music and occasionally being reminded by a tape-recorded voice that someone would be with them shortly.

If too many calls came in at one time, the callers would get a busy signal, which was why there were five employees here. The company thought it was bad public relations to have policyholders get a busy signal when they called about a claim.

She looked up as a man with shaggy red hair stepped into the room. He paused at the entrance, then walked directly toward Cassandra, his eyes meeting hers. He was about three paces from her desk when he pulled off the wig. It was Clark.

"I walked right by the receptionist," he said, smiling. "She never even recognized me."

"Get out of here," Cassandra said firmly but softly. She didn't want to make another scene, for she knew doing so could cost her her job.

"I want you to go out with me," he said. "I want you to find out that I'm not what you think I am."

"I've already been out with you," she said. "Now, if you don't leave, I'm going to call building security and have you thrown out." She reached for the button that would connect her headset to an in-house line, hoping she wouldn't have to make the call, because it would ultimately bring Nan the Nazi as well as a guard.

Clark put his hand in front of the button. "No," he said. "You're going to listen to me." Cassandra thought his hand was shaking slightly.

Glancing around the room, she saw that the lull had ended and everyone else was now on the phone, although their eyes shifted between their VDTs and Clark. She would have help if she needed it. Another call came in, and she reached for the button to take it, but again Clark blocked her hand with his.

"I have to take this call," she said.

"No. Let it ring. I have to talk to you."

"I have nothing to say to you except that I want you to leave me alone."

"If you'll see me one more time, give me one more chance, then I'll go away afterward if you want me to."

There had been desperation in his voice as he said that, and she was tempted. If she agreed, maybe he'd keep his word and leave her alone afterward. Maybe this was her only chance to get rid of him.

"Would you promise—give me your absolute word—that you'd go away and never bother me again?"

"Yes. Just give me this one chance. Please."

And then she recalled what had happened the last time she'd agreed to go out with Clark. It had been the start of all this. "I'm sorry, Clark, but as I said before, I've already been out with you once. And once was enough."

For a moment, he simply stared at her miserably. Then his expression changed, and he was looking at her with cruel, hate-filled eyes. "You didn't just go out with me," he said loudly. "You took me home and bedded me, you slut—you whore. Do all these people here know about you? Do they know you're a whore?"

Suddenly afraid he might try to attack her, Cassandra said nothing. Although she tried to appear calm, beneath her desk her legs were shaking.

"Is that any way to treat a child?" he demanded. "Answer me, you slut. Is that any way to treat a child—to whore around with men instead of loving her, cherishing her?" He stared at her, his eyes burning into hers. He was waiting for her to say something, demanding that she say something.

"I don't know what you're talking about," she said softly.

"What? Speak up."

"I said I don't know what you're talking about," she snapped, anger suddenly overriding her fear. "I love my daughter, and you've got no right saying I don't. You're sick; do you understand that? You're mentally sick. Now—" She abruptly stopped, because Clayton's face had reddened. He looked ready to attack her.

"I'm not the one who's sick," he said, his voice wavering. "No, I'm not the one at all. I'll tell you what sick is. Sick is—"

Two brown-uniformed security guards hurried into the room, one quickly moving to either side of Clayton. One of her coworkers must have called them, Cassandra realized.

"You'll have to leave the building, sir," the guard on Clark's right said.

Clark glared at Cassandra, and for a moment she thought that he was going to lunge at her. But then the rage in his eyes faded.

"I was just leaving, anyway," he said, and the two guards escorted him from the room.

Cassandra spent the rest of the day waiting for Nan Cosgrove to show up. Early in the afternoon, she had a taxi pick up Lisa, then called the day-care center to make sure the child arrived safely. There were no problems. When four o'clock came and went with still no sign of her boss, Cassandra decided that everything must be all right. Clark's actions are beyond my control, she thought. I'm the victim in all this, not the bad guy. Even Nan the Nazi wouldn't penalize me for that.

It was Friday afternoon. Cassandra planned to spend the weekend with Lisa, doing nothing in particular. Maybe we should go on a picnic, she thought. The weather's been nice, and the countryside's starting to turn green and beautiful. And Lisa loves outings of any sort.

She had just decided that going on a picnic was definitely what she wanted to do this weekend when Nan Cosgrove entered the room, walking directly to Cassandra's desk.

"Can you come with me for just a moment?" Cosgrove said.

As she followed her boss from the room, Cassandra wondered why people phrased orders as questions. *Can you come with me for just a moment?* She wondered what Cosgrove's reaction would have been if she'd said no.

As Cassandra stepped into the hallway, she noticed a clock on the wall that indicated the time was 4:45. Fifteen minutes before quitting time on Friday. It should be a happy time. But happiness was not among the emotions churning within Cassandra's mind.

Cosgrove's office was across the hall and a door or two down from the room in which Cassandra worked. As she seated herself, she looked across the desk at Nan the Nazi, and she knew what was about to happen. Cosgrove got right to the point.

"I'm letting you go," she said. "Your presence has become a disruptive force in the department, and the situation can not be allowed to continue."

Cassandra said nothing. Even though she'd known what was coming, she was stunned. She'd just been fired, and the cold, hard reality was just now settling over her.

Looking at Cosgrove, she decided that Nan the Nazi was an apt name. What did this woman care that she had a seven-year-old daughter to support? What did she care that none of this was her fault? Cosgrove's sole concern was her own advancement up the corporate ladder. The Cosgrove rule for success: Allow no disruptive influences in the domain for which you will be held accountable.

"I've got your check here," Nan the Nazi said, producing an envelope. "It pays you through five o'clock today."

Accepting the envelope, Cassandra rose.

"I'm sorry it worked out this way," Cosgrove said. "But you seemed unable to control the situation, and it simply could not be allowed to go on. If you're ever in a position like mine, you'll most likely have to make a similar decision. And you'll have to do what I did. You'll have to consider the interests of the company first." She gave Cassandra her most efficient, business-like smile.

As Cassandra walked from Cosgrove's office, clutching her final paycheck from the company, she resolved that if she ever did become a supervisor, she would never be anything like Nan the Nazi. Getting her purse from her desk, she avoided the questioning look from Jenny. She quickly strode from the office.

It was only five minutes until five, and she wanted to be gone before her coworkers were able to question her, offer their sympathies, say good-bye. She knew she'd be unable to handle that right now. She simply wanted to get away.

Cassandra was only a few blocks from the day-care center when the full emotional impact of what had just happened caught up with her. Her vision blurring with tears, she pulled her car to the curb in front of an old three-story house, rested her head on the steering wheel, and cried.

When the tears stopped, she found herself staring at the traffic on a through street at the end of the next block. People on the way home from work on a Friday afternoon, their cares set aside for the next two days—TGIF and all that. Cassandra recalled how she'd been planning a picnic with Lisa. Now the notion seemed inappropriate, absurd. A tear trickled down her cheek, and she wiped it away.

Come on, she told herself. Pull yourself together. On Monday, you can start looking for another job, and in the meantime, don't let your unhappiness rub off on Lisa.

It took months to find that job, she thought. How am I going to find another?

Although she'd known that she could lose her job because of Clark, she hadn't really considered what to do in the event Cosgrove actually sacked her. A large part of her simply hadn't believed it could happen, she supposed. Well, it's happened, she thought, and now I've got to deal with it.

There was nothing she could do at the moment. On Monday, she'd go to a couple of employment agencies and see what happened. Before, when she'd been job hunting, she'd had an incomplete college education and no skills. At least now she could do something. Her previous employer had trained her to use a VDT. The experience had to be worth something.

Using the rearview mirror to see what she was doing, she wiped away her tear-streaked eye makeup. Then she started the car and headed for the day-care center. Although she had no idea what would happen to her and Lisa, at least she had a pretty good idea of what she had to do.

And what about the person who was causing her all this grief? What would he do now? Clark Clayton, she was sure, was not through with her. I hate you, Cassandra thought angrily. I hate you. And she realized suddenly that this was the first time she'd ever truly despised someone, detested a person enough to wish him harm.

Nor had she ever feared anyone as much as she feared Clark Clayton. She shivered. Cassandra decided to phone Detective Hoskins when she got home.

"The only thing we could arrest him for would be a misdemeanor trespass charge or something like that," Hoskins said. "He'd be out in an hour. I'm sorry."

Cassandra sighed. "The man cost me my only source of income other than child support, and there's nothing I can do about it."

"You could file a civil action against him, ask for damages and a restraining order."

"Could I win?" she asked. While she stood in the hallway, talking on the phone, she'd been twisting the curly cord into a tangled mess.

"I don't know. A guy like Clayton will get himself a good lawyer, and the lawyer will keep you tied up in legal maneuvering as long as possible, hoping you'll give up and drop the matter. So even if you do win eventually, nothing's going to happen very quickly."

"You mean that—that I just have to take this?"

Hoskins hesitated, then said, "He's getting pretty bold. Pretty soon he'll make a mistake, do something we can arrest him for, something that'll give us some leverage."

"What do you mean, leverage?"

"I mean we'll have something we can hold over him. Either he leaves you alone or we prosecute—his choice."

"And just what is this thing he has to do? Break my legs, burn down my apartment, kid—" She stopped in mid-word, because she didn't want to speak the unthinkable. She didn't even want to suggest that Clark might abduct Lisa. She glanced toward the living room. The girl, apparently uninterested in her mother's telephone conversation, was watching television.

"It doesn't have to be anything that serious," the detective said. "If he breaks into your apartment or strikes you or threatens you, we might have something we can go on."

"What do you mean, you might have something to go on?"

"Well, we have to have a case. We have to have proof. If he threatens you but there are no witnesses, then it's his word against yours. If he breaks into your place while you're gone, we have to have solid evidence that he was the one who did it. I know this probably isn't much help, but it's the way the system works, and there's nothing I can do about it."

Cassandra took a moment to collect her thoughts; then she said, "In your experience, do guys like this ever give up and go away?"

"Sometimes."

"That means that sometimes they don't give up; is that right?"

"Yes."

"What happens then?"

"Well, uh, there's no way to answer that."

"You mean it just goes on forever, until everybody grows old and dies?"

"No, it usually ends when one party or the other does something drastic."

There was no need to ask him what he meant by drastic. "Do you think there's any chance that Clark will simply give up and go away?"

"I don't know. I'm not a psychologist."

"Do you think he's dangerous? Do you think he might try to hurt me or my daughter?"

"I don't know that, either. But I think you have to allow for the possibility. I think you should be very careful."

After ending the conversation with the policeman, Cassandra joined her daughter on the couch. Completely absorbed by the TV program she was watching, Lisa seemed unaware of her mother's presence.

"Is that a good show?" Cassandra asked.

"It's okay."

"Do you think you can tear yourself away from it for a moment?"

"Uh-huh," the child said, slowly shifting her gaze from the TV screen to her mother.

"I'm not going to be going to work at the insurance company anymore. That means I'll pick you up after school, and you won't have to go to the day-care center for a while."

Lisa studied her a moment; then she said, "I liked riding in the taxi. It had a radio inside that you could talk on, like a police car."

"Well, there won't be any more taxi rides for a while. Also, I'm afraid that we're going to have to eat all our meals at home. No more stopping for hamburgers and ice cream until I get another job. Okay?"

"Okay," the child said, but the perplexed expression on her face indicated that she didn't really comprehend the connection between her mother's job and stopping for fast food.

Because the insurance-company paychecks were for the period ending two weeks before they were issued, Cassandra's final check was larger than usual, which would help. Also, there was the money in her savings account, her half of the proceeds from the sale of the house in which she and John had lived. It was reserved for Lisa's education, but in an emergency she could withdraw some of it, redepositing the money when she was working again. Although she was out of work, her situation wasn't desperate. She had time to find another job.

She recalled the plan she'd come up with earlier, before Nan the Nazi had informed her that she wasn't working there anymore. A picnic wouldn't be very expensive. A little gasoline, some sandwiches and potato chips and the like. And Lisa would love it.

Cassandra was on the verge of suggesting this to her daughter when she recalled what Detective Hoskins had told her. "I think you should be very careful." Going on a picnic wasn't being very careful. Out in the country somewhere, she and Lisa would be alone, vulnerable, with no one around to help. And if Clark followed them . . .

Cassandra walked to the window and peeked out. Dusk was giving way to night. Although the streetlights provided pockets of illumination, the areas between them were filled with shadows. Was Clark somewhere out there in the darkness, watching, waiting? Releasing the curtain, she shivered.

"Is there something outside?" Lisa asked, watching her mother from the couch.

"No," Cassandra replied. "There's nothing there." And she hoped it was true.

8

"THIS LOOKS GOOD," THE WOMAN AT THE employment agency said as she studied Cassandra's application. She was blond, about forty, heavyset.

"Do you think you'll be able to find me something?" Cassandra asked. They were sitting in a small modern office with upholstered furniture that matched the brown carpet.

"I don't have anything at the moment, but suitable openings come in regularly. You won't be hard to place."

"How long do you think it might take?"

"I should have a couple of prospects for you by the end of the week. And even if the first few job interviews don't pan out for you, everything clerical or secretarial is done with word processors or VDTs these days. You've got experience with this equipment, and you're neat, attractive, personable, intelligent. Really, there shouldn't be any problem." She smiled.

When she left the employment agency a few minutes later, Cassandra felt fairly confident that she would find another job without too much hassle. Maybe it'll work out for the best, she thought. Maybe I'll make more money. Maybe I'll have a better boss.

The employment agency was located in a small building across the street from a shopping center. As she walked toward her car, which was parked in a corner of the paved lot, Cassandra realized how summerlike the weather was becoming. The day was warm and sunny, almost hot. Muggy days and mosquitoes were only a few weeks away.

Although there had been no sign of Clark, neither she nor Lisa had left the apartment over the weekend. It was Monday, and Lisa was back in school; Cassandra had begun her hunt for another job. Despite everything that had happened, her life could easily fall back into its normal routine, with everything just about as it had been. If only Clark would leave them alone.

As she climbed into her car, Cassandra realized that there truly was a way she could get her life back to normal. She would be getting a new job, one Clark wouldn't know anything about. If she moved to a new apartment, enrolled Lisa in a different school, he wouldn't know where to find her. He'd have nowhere to look.

"I'd be free of him," she said aloud. "Free of him forever."

She sat in her car without starting the engine, just considering the possibility. The more she thought about the idea, the more enthusiastic she became. I can get him out of my life, she thought. I can really do it.

Unless he followed her from the old apartment to the new one.

No, she thought, it doesn't have to work that way. There had to be some means of doing it so that he wouldn't know what was happening. Then she pushed this problem aside. It could be dealt with later.

Quickly, she started the engine and drove across the street to the shopping center. There had to be a drugstore here that sold newspapers, and she wanted to check the classified ads for help wanted—and apartments for rent.

"It's about four miles from here," Cassandra said. "The place is a little bit bigger for the same money." She was sitting with Grace on the couch in the Konecznys' apartment. Steve sat a few feet away in a recliner. Lisa and their ten-year-old daughter, Nicole, were entertaining each other in a bedroom.

"We'd hate to lose you as our neighbor," Grace said. "But I can certainly understand why you'd want to move."

"I can't believe this woman you worked for actually fired you," Steve said. "On any job I've ever had, we'd have just pitched this Clark guy out on his ass. We sure as hell wouldn't fire anybody."

Clearly, Steve, who'd never worked at anything other than construction, had no concept of what the white-collar world was like, but Cassandra decided not to attempt to explain it to him. The Konecznys' apartment was laid out like hers, but it contained more furniture, more knickknacks, more pictures on the wall. Cassandra liked to keep her environment simple and uncluttered; Grace liked to be surrounded by objects.

"I haven't said I'd take the place yet," Cassandra said. "I wanted to talk to you first. This whole thing will be for nothing if Clark is able to follow me when I move. Do you have any ideas how I can do it so that he can't follow me?"

"Gee, I don't know," Grace said.

"There is no way you can prevent him from following you," Steve said. "Your stuff would have to go by truck. A fully loaded truck sure as hell can't outrun anybody, and it's easy to keep track of."

"You mean . . ." Cassandra let her words trail off. The hope that she'd been nurturing was suddenly fading.

"The idea," Steve said, "is to fool him."

"What do you mean?" Cassandra asked.

"We've got to make him think the stuff coming out of the building belongs to someone else."

"But he's been in Cassandra's apartment," Grace said. "He knows what her stuff looks like. He'll recognize it."

"Not if we covered it and some of our furniture was moved out with it. Cassandra could stay out of sight. He'd have no reason to connect her with what was coming out of the building."

"He could come inside and check," Cassandra said. "He'd see whose apartment it was coming from."

"Not if we watch the doors to make sure he doesn't," Steve said.

"All this would take a small army," Cassandra said. "Where would I get all these people?"

"I've got some cousins that would be glad to help."

"I couldn't afford to pay them much, but if they'd be willing—"

"Pay?" Steve said. "They owe me about fourteen favors each. If they took any money from you, I'd put lumps on their skulls."

A tear ran down Cassandra's face. These people were being so good to her, even offering to mix some of their own furniture in with hers, furniture that could get bumped and scratched in the process. They were only her neighbors; they owed her nothing.

"I don't know how to thank you," she said, wiping away another tear. "I really don't."

"We'll do it this weekend," Steve said. "My cousins

will be here, or they'll find out why Grace calls me the Incredible Hulk.' He grinned.

Grace said, "I see one problem, Steve. Even if we fool this guy with the furniture, he'll still recognize Cassandra herself. All he'll have to do is follow her."

"I'll let Carl take care of that. It'll make his weekend." Again, he grinned.

Cassandra spent the week packing. Just in case Clark was watching, Steve and Grace rounded up the cardboard boxes she used. On Wednesday, the employment agency sent her for an interview at a company that made containers, including cartons like those in which she was packing her belongings. The person who interviewed her said he'd let her know.

Although she never saw Clark, he found ways to let her know that he hadn't lost interest. On Tuesday, she found a note taped to her door that said, CASSANDRA JENNINGS IS A WORTHLESS BITCH. On Thursday, a letter arrived. It said:

> *Cassie,*
> *The other part of me is taking over. Call me at 555-8238. Please. Before it's too late.*
>
> *Clark*

Cassandra warned Lisa not to mention to anyone that they were moving—not even her teacher. Cassandra thought the child could be trusted.

On Sunday afternoon, she met Steve's cousins, David and Carl Lukaszczyk. The brothers were stocky blond men in their twenties. Along with Steve and Grace, they stood in Cassandra's living room, surveying the cardboard boxes and furniture that had to be moved to her new apartment.

"One trip," David said, "if we stack it right." He'd brought a large red truck with him. When Cassandra had offered to pay for the gas, he'd refused to even discuss the matter.

"Don't forget that we've got to take some of my stuff, too," Steve reminded them.

"We should still make it," David said.

Steve nodded. Turning to Cassandra, he said, "Okay, we'll take care of everything here. What I want you to do is take Lisa and go somewhere for a few hours. Drive out to the shopping mall or see a movie or something. If this guy's watching the place, he'll most likely follow you."

Lisa stood beside a stack of boxes, watching in silence. Cassandra took her hand. "Want to go shopping?" she asked.

Lisa shrugged. It didn't matter.

At the door, Cassandra turned and said, "I don't know how I'll ever be able to repay you for this. I really don't."

Steve and his two cousins grinned at her.

Cassandra took Lisa to an enormous suburban shopping mall where they went from store to store, looking at clothes and toys and books. When they returned to their apartment, the big red truck was gone, and the place that had been their home the past few years was empty.

Standing in the middle of the living room, holding her daughter's hand Cassandra surveyed the empty room. With her things here, it had been a warm, familiar place where she and Lisa had lived, played, cried. But now it was just a stark rectangle, cold and uninviting. Suddenly, she wanted to hurry to her new apartment and surround herself with things that were familiar. She found Carl, Grace, and Nicole waiting for her in the Konecznys' apartment.

"They called just a little while ago," Grace said. "They're moving your stuff in now, and as far as they could tell, they weren't followed."

Cassandra nodded. The couch and some other things were missing from Grace's living room. Grace was sitting in the only available chair. Carl and Nicole were on the floor.

"I hope your furniture doesn't get damaged," Cassandra said.

"I'm not worried. The stuff I sent isn't all that hot, anyway. The couch is threadbare in spots. The table had a cigarette burn." She shrugged.

"Daddy put that there," Nicole offered, smiling knowingly. She was a pretty girl with brown hair and a lightly freckled face.

"You ready?" Carl asked.

"I'm ready," Cassandra replied. "What are we going to do?" When she'd asked about this part of the operation, Steve had dismissed her question, saying simply that Carl would handle it.

"Carl's a race driver," Nicole explained. "He races stock cars."

"That's just a hobby," Carl said, "a thing I do on weekends. Actually, where I learned how to make sure no one could tail me was on a job I used to have. I repossessed cars, and sometimes the people whose cars you were taking didn't like it very much. They'd come after you, try to follow you in another car. Sometimes those were very nasty people who carried guns and knives and things like that, so I got very good at losing people and making sure I wasn't tailed."

"I'll bet James Bond couldn't follow him," Nicole offered.

Getting off the floor, Carl joined Cassandra and Lisa. Grace said, "Keep in touch, okay?"

Cassandra promised she would, and then the two women hugged as if Cassandra were moving to another country instead of an apartment four miles away. A few moments later, she and Lisa and Carl were in her car, heading for her new home.

We're on our way to our sanctuary, Cassandra thought as Carl stopped for a red light. To a place where Clark will never find us.

Lisa was in the back seat, and Cassandra turned around to look at her. "Everything okay?" she asked.

"Uh-huh," the seven-year-old replied. Though apparently a little overwhelmed by all this, Lisa was coping pretty well. The light changed, and Carl turned left onto a divided thoroughfare.

"What do you do now that you're no longer repossessing cars?" Cassandra asked.

"I'm a mechanic at your friendly neighborhood Ford dealer."

A momentary doubt flickered through Cassandra's mind. Here she was, ready to begin a new life free of Clark, and everything hinged on whether an auto mechanic about whom she knew almost nothing could make sure she wasn't followed.

Carl followed the thoroughfare for a while, then made an abrupt U-turn and headed back in the direction from which they had come, closely watching the cars that were coming toward him. After a few moments, he made another U-turn and again studied the cars on the other side of the street. Suddenly, he made a sharp left, accelerated for half a block, jammed on the brakes, and turned into an alley, which he followed until it intersected with another alley. Quickly turning left, he pulled in beside a parked delivery van and waited.

After a minute or two, he said, "If anyone was following us before, they're not now."

"Are you sure?" Cassandra asked.

"I'm sure. But for your peace of mind, we'll do a little maneuver like this in another part of town before going to your new place."

"Mommy," Lisa said from the backseat, "are we trying to get away from the bad man?"

"We're just trying to make absolutely certain that he doesn't find out where our new place is. If he doesn't know where we've gone, he can't bother us anymore."

"I hope we never see him again."

"Me, too," Cassandra said, reaching back between the bucket seats and patting her daughter's leg.

As she'd planned, her new apartment was in an area served by a different elementary school. She hadn't made any of the arrangements yet for transferring Lisa to the new school, because she hadn't wanted to let anyone at the old one know she was moving. She could enroll her in the new school on Monday.

If Clark decided that the way to find her would be to follow Lisa home from school, he was going to be disappointed. Good-bye, Clark, she thought. And up yours.

After another set of doubling-back maneuvers, Carl drove her to her new apartment, which was located on the second floor of a brick building with old-fashioned metal fire escapes. The neighborhood was roughly the equivalent of the one she'd left. Nothing fancy, but the people worked for a living, and they cared about their homes. The big red truck was parked in front.

Accompanied by Carl, Cassandra and Lisa hurried up the stairs. The door to her new apartment was ajar, and she pushed it open. Taped to the wall was a paper banner that said, WELCOME CASSANDRA AND LISA. Steve and David stood beneath it, grinning. And then she saw the room. Everything was arranged. The furniture was placed appropriately, including table lamps and other things that had been in cardboard boxes. The empty cartons were gone.

"I hope we did okay," Steve said.

Cassandra saw a thing or two she would have done differently, but on the whole they'd done a darn good job. "It's perfect," she said. "Oh, thank you so much—all of you."

"Grace told us what to do," Steve said. "She and Nicole were here until it was time for them and Carl to go back to wait for you." From behind his back, he produced a bottle of champagne. "Your housewarming present."

Cassandra didn't realize she was crying until she tried to speak and found she could only blubber. Lisa stared up at her worriedly.

"Are you okay, Mommy?" the child asked.

"I'm—I'm not crying because I'm sad, honey. I'm crying because I'm happy."

The girl looked uncertain, as if not sure whether to believe that such a thing could happen. Cassandra squeezed her shoulders.

Unable to restrain herself, Cassandra ran to Steve and hugged him; then she hugged David and Carl as well. David, the younger of the two, looked embarrassed.

After the three men had left, Cassandra sat on the couch and absorbed her new surroundings. Though older than her other apartment, this place was a lot roomier. The moldings around the windows and the mopboard were thick and wide. At one time, they had probably been stained wood, but now, like the walls, they were painted off-white.

Her desk-set–type telephone sat on a small table near the door, its cord connected to the modular jack by the floor. She assumed the phone was working, since Steve had phoned Grace to let her know that everything was ready. To be sure, she went to the phone and lifted the receiver. The dial tone hummed in her ear. She replaced the receiver.

Her phone number was still unlisted, and she wondered whether she'd ever have the nerve to let her name, address, and number again appear in the phone directory. Five years from now—or even ten—would Clark still be out there somewhere, waiting, ready to hound her again as soon as he discovered her whereabouts? Would he eagerly await each new phone book so he could see whether the name Cassandra Jennings was once more being listed?

She shook her head. She had lost her job and been forced to move, get an unlisted phone, enroll her daughter in a new school, all because she'd dated a man. All because of that simple little act. There was more to it, of course. But if she hadn't gone to that party at which she'd met Clark—or if *he* hadn't gone—none of these things would have happened to her.

Fate, she thought. And yet that was too simple. It was madness, the madness of a world in which such things could happen. And the personal madness of Clark Clayton. She pushed the name from her thoughts. He was no longer a part of her life.

Lisa stood at the window, looking down into the street. "I wonder if there'll be any kids here that I'll like," she said.

"I'm sure there will be," Cassandra replied. "I saw a couple of kids on bicycles in the next block."

It would be good if Lisa had more friends, Cassandra decided. The child never mentioned anyone she particularly enjoyed associating with at school or the day-care center, and she only occasionally played with other children on weekends or during summer vacations.

Am I smothering her? Cassandra asked herself. Does

she have so few friends because I want her all for myself? Should she have been out playing hopscotch and jacks and red rover instead of watching TV and playing checkers with me? Although she was unable to answer that question, Cassandra resolved to make sure Lisa got out and played more often than she had been. There was no reason why she shouldn't, now that Clark was out of their lives.

"There's not much in the kitchen to eat, I'm afraid," Cassandra said. "How do you feel about a trip to the grocery store?"

"We could eat hamburgers," Lisa suggested hopefully, but then she frowned. "Oh, I forgot. We're not supposed to eat hamburgers anymore"

Cassandra suspected this was a calculated tactic aimed at manipulating her sympathies. Still, some fast food wouldn't cost that much, and she definitely didn't feel like cooking.

"Okay," she said. "But this is the only time until I'm working again."

"Hamburgers!" Lisa squealed, spinning around with her arms out. "I love hamburgers, and Mommy loves hamburgers, and the whole world loves hamburgers!"

"We'll get the groceries, then pick up some burgers on the way home. Okay?"

"Uh-huh," Lisa said as she stopped spinning.

Cassandra got a pen and an old envelope from her purse and went into the kitchen. The gold floor covering was worn in a couple of places, but like the rest of the apartment, the kitchen made up for any defects by being so much larger than what she'd had before. Opening one of the cabinets, she saw that canned goods had been put away. There was no paper on the shelves, something she would correct when she had time.

After checking the refrigerator and all the cabinets,

Cassandra made a list of the items she'd need and returned to the living room, where she found Lisa again staring out the window.

"Mommy," the child said hesitantly.

"What?"

"Is that him?"

"Who?"

Turning to face her mother, Lisa seemed reluctant to speak. She said: "The man . . . the bad man."

No, Cassandra thought. No, no, no. It can't be. I won't let it be.

For a moment, she simply stood there, about ten feet from the window, unwilling to move. Then, reluctantly, her thoughts swirling, she moved to the glass pane and looked out. Across the street, leaning against the door of his white car, was Clark Clayton. Looking up at her, he smiled.

Cassandra backed away. She was only vaguely aware of bumping into the table on which she'd put the bottle of champagne Steve had given her. It fell, exploding when it hit the floor, spattering carpet and furniture with froth and broken glass.

"Mommy . . . ?" Lisa said, clearly terrified. And then she ran to her mother. Cassandra embraced the child, and the two of them stood there, silently holding each other while the champagne bubbles lost their fizz and seeped into the carpet.

CASSANDRA KNEW SHE SHOULD SAY SOME-
thing to calm her frightened daughter, but she was unable to do so, for speaking would only reveal the depths
of her own terror. Lisa, more disturbed by her mother's
reaction than by Clark, clung to Cassandra's legs.

It hadn't worked. Moving, changing schools, changing
jobs, Carl's fancy driving, everything she'd done and
planned, had been for nothing. Clark knew where she
lived; he could follow her to her new job and Lisa to her
new school. The harassment would go on and on,
unending. Tears streamed down her cheeks.

What am I going to do? she asked herself. She had no
answer. She felt lost, helpless.

And she realized suddenly that her situation was worse
now than it had been before she moved. In her old
apartment, she'd had Steve and Grace for neighbors.
Here there was no Incredible Hulk next door to answer
a call for help.

"Mommy . . . ?" Lisa said softly.

"What, honey?" Cassandra said, forcing herself to muster some composure.

"Are you afraid of the bad man?" The child looked up to her mother, her eyes worried, questioning.

"I—I'm upset because he won't leave us alone."

"Does he want to hurt us?"

"I don't know what he wants, Lisa."

And that was true. What he said was basically that he wanted to reestablish a relationship with her. But his motives went much deeper than that. The true reason for his behavior was buried somewhere in the twisted workings of an insane mind. And Cassandra wondered whether Clark himself knew why he was doing these things.

Suddenly, looking down at the frightened little girl clinging to her, Cassandra felt her frustration and fear being pushed aside by anger. That son of a bitch has no right to do this to me, she thought. And I'm not putting up with it anymore.

"Lock the door," she told Lisa. "And don't open it unless you're sure it's me on the other side."

Clearly terrified, the child simply stared at her.

"Lisa," she said, taking the girl by the shoulders, "did you hear what I said?"

The girl nodded.

"Okay. Lock the door as soon as I'm out of the room."

"Mommy . . ."

"What?"

"Where are you going?"

"I'm going downstairs. I'll be right back."

After checking to make sure Clark was still there, Cassandra stepped into the hallway, waited until she heard the lock click, then headed for the stairway. Driven by her fury, Cassandra descended the steps rapidly, purposefully. In that instant, if she had owned a gun, she would have marched into the street and emptied it into Clark. She was going to put an end to this. She was going to make it clear—very, very clear—to Clark Clayton that he was never to come around her or her daughter again.

Cassandra had no idea precisely what she was going to do. If she saw a large board, she might smash the windows of his car. If she didn't find a weapon, she might attack Clark with her bare hands. It didn't matter. Whatever she did, she did, but she was going to do something.

Reaching the door, she pushed it open and stepped onto the cement stoop, her eyes scanning her surroundings. By the side of the building lay a brick, a weapon. She hurried to it and picked it up; images of herself smashing Clark tumbled through her mind. And then, as she stepped toward the street, Cassandra realized that Clark was gone.

Still clutching the brick, she stared at the spot where his white car had been parked, and her anger evaporated, leaving a numbness that seemed to reach into every corner of her body. She gazed at the street, dazed.

Finally, she walked back across the few feet of thin grass that separated the building from the sidewalk and put the brick back where she'd found it. Then she sank to the ground and sobbed.

Just inside the entrance to the building across the street, Clark watched as she cried. For just a moment, he felt the urge to run to her, offer kindness and understanding, but he knew such efforts would be wasted. There was no chance she would accept him. As she always had, she would deny him her love.

Suddenly, he was overwhelmed by his loathing of her;

B. W. BATTIN

hot, burning hatred surged through his veins like lava. Bitch, he thought. I despise you for what you did. And I renounce you.

"I hate you . . . hate you . . . hate you. . . ."

When he realized he had said the words aloud, Clark quickly checked to see whether anyone had heard him. But he saw no one. His hands were squeezed so tightly into fists that the veins were standing out on his trembling arms. Opening his fingers, he forced himself to relax.

He had driven around the block, parked his car, then entered this apartment building through the rear door. Standing in a vestibule, he was watching the woman through a window in the door. Like the others in this neighborhood, the building was old but not rundown. The space in which he stood, though unlocked, had no graffiti on the walls. Discolored by age, the glass through which he peered had survived many years without having been vandalized.

As he watched the woman crying, suffering, he felt quite pleased with himself. And there was no doubt now about what had to be done.

The woman—and that's all she was to him now, something nameless, an object—had been quite clever in her attempt to fool him. He'd driven by her apartment, seen the furniture being moved out, and he'd known. They hadn't all been the woman's things, but he'd known, anyway. And he wondered what precautions she'd taken to make sure she wasn't followed to her new home.

Had it worked, he would have been unable to find her. She'd have put her daughter in a new school, found another job, kept her phone number unlisted, and for all practical purposes, she would have disappeared. He had to give the woman credit for the attempt. It could have worked under different circumstances. Clark smiled.

He had attempted to follow neither the woman nor her

belongings today, and he hadn't bothered to watch her apartment. For he'd already known where she was going. He'd followed her the day she'd gone apartment-hunting, and again on the day she'd come back here to take the place, both times using a rented car the woman wouldn't recognize.

He watched as the woman stopped crying and stood up, her eyes scanning the area. For an instant, she looked right at him, and he was certain their eyes had met. But then he realized that she had merely glanced in his direction. She couldn't see him here.

Slowly, mechanically, the woman walked up the steps and entered the apartment building she had thought would be her sanctuary. There is no sanctuary for you, Clark thought. Not after what you've done.

Hearing a noise behind him, Clark spun around, finding himself face-to-face with a stocky gray-haired man wearing coveralls.

"Can I help you with something, mister?" the man asked.

"I, uh, I was looking for an apartment. Are there any available in this building?"

"Nope. But if you want to put your name in for the next vacancy, I'll give you a number you can call. I just do maintenance here. I don't have anything to do with renting the places out."

"Thanks, but I have to find something right away."

"In that case, you might try the place across the street. I hear there's an apartment available over there. They've got a manager lives right on the premises. First door on your left, if you're interested."

"I'll check it out. Thanks."

"Sure thing," the man said.

As Clark left the building, he glanced behind him to

see whether the man was watching him. He could see nothing but a reflection in the window of the door.

Of course, he had no intention of inquiring about an apartment for rent in the building across the street. The one that had been vacant there was no longer available. And he knew who had taken it.

That evening, Cassandra sat on the couch in her new living room while Lisa lay on the floor, both of them staring at the TV set. Cassandra knew that she was going to watch television late into the night, maybe even all night. Certain she'd be unable to sleep, she didn't want to face the terrifying thoughts that would come when she lay awake in bed.

She decided that she would not make Lisa go to bed, either. It would be better to let her fall asleep while watching TV, then carry her into the bedroom. It was not a good night for either of them to lie in dark rooms with only shadows for company.

After a few hours had passed with no further sign of Clark, she and Lisa had gone out for groceries, after which Cassandra had prepared a Spanish omelet and toast for dinner. What else was there to do? She had given up her old apartment and moved into this one, and Clark had not been fooled. She would have to decide how to deal with the situation. But in the meantime she and Lisa had to eat.

On the TV screen was one of those prime-time soap operas that had become so popular lately. Although Cassandra wondered whether Lisa should be watching this sort of thing, she lacked the energy to change the channel. She watched as an elegantly dressed dark-haired woman slipped into an office and surreptitiously began searching through someone's desk. In one of the drawers was a handgun.

Cassandra sat up straight. Should I buy a gun? she wondered.

Immediately, she dismissed the idea. She didn't know how to use one, and if she had one lying around, all sorts of horrible things could happen. Lisa could somehow get hold of it. Perhaps the most frightening possibility—because it was the most probable—was that she would actually use it on Clark. She could be charged with murder or manslaughter, go to jail; Lisa could be permanently put in her father's custody.

Cassandra saw herself in prison, other female inmates gathering around her, ripping off her clothes, ordering her to do unspeakable things. Revolted, she forced the image from her mind.

Cassandra was uncertain as to how hard all this had been on Lisa. When troubled, the child grew silent. The reaction was the same for little problems, like a disagreement with a schoolmate, and for big ones, like being pursued by a madman whose intentions were unclear.

About nine-fifteen, Lisa fell asleep. Cassandra gently picked her up and carried her into the bedroom. After tucking her in, she checked the windows to make sure they were locked.

The smaller of the apartment's two bedrooms was painted yellow. It was a bright, cheerful color, Cassandra supposed, but the room lacked something when compared to the bedroom Lisa had had when she had lived with both of her parents. That room had been intended for a child. It had wallpaper with animals on it and curtains with little cartoon figures. And it had been a sunny room that had overlooked a big flower bed.

This bedroom was as nice as the one Lisa had occupied at the other apartment, Cassandra supposed. But an apartment just wasn't the right place to raise a child.

A youngster needed a yard and a dog and a room with animals on the walls. Knowing that she was about to cry, Cassandra pushed these thoughts away.

As she looked down at her sleeping daughter, Cassandra hoped the child wouldn't awaken in the middle of the night, frightened to find herself in a strange environment. For a minute or so, she simply stood there, staring at Lisa; then she turned out the light and returned to the couch.

After midnight, Cassandra switched to a station that ran movies all night. Partway through Alfred Hitchcock's *North by Northwest*, she drifted off to sleep. When she awakened again, an old black-and-white movie was on. It took her a moment to realize it was about women in prison. She got up to change the channel, then changed her mind and turned the set off. If she could sleep sitting on the couch, she could sleep in bed.

That's all I needed, she thought sleepily. A movie about women in prison. She made her way through the apartment, checking the windows, all of which were locked. Outside, the street was hidden in shadows that the distant streetlight was unable to penetrate. If Clark was out there at this hour, watching, she couldn't see him, which she decided was probably just as well. Cassandra was already heading for her bedroom when she decided to check the door. Though certain it was locked, she needed the reassurance of finding it securely bolted.

Reversing direction, she started toward the door, and then she saw the white rectangle on the floor. Someone had slipped a folded sheet of paper under her door. She stared at it, unwilling to touch it. Finally, she reached down and picked up the paper, and when she unfolded it, and read its message, the white sheet began shaking in her hand. Made from letters cut out of newspapers and magazines, the message was brief:

I'M GOING TO KILL THE CHILD.

For a long moment, she simply stared at it, her thoughts a whirling jumble. Then she hurried to the phone and called the police department.

"Detective Hoskins, please," she said to the officer who answered.

"There's no one in Detectives right now, ma'am. Can I take a message?"

"No. I need Detective Hoskins."

"Can I ask the nature of your business with him?"

"My child's been threatened."

"What exactly do you mean by threatened?"

"I've got a note. It was slipped under my door. It says he's going to kill my child."

"Is there anyone there now, threatening you?"

"I don't know. He might be outside. It's too dark to see."

"Ma'am, I'm going to send a patrol unit around to make sure everything's all right. The officers will check the area, then stop by and make sure you're okay."

"What about Hoskins?"

"He's at home in bed at this hour. The patrol officers can get there a lot quicker than he could."

Cassandra described Clark for the officer. After hanging up, she turned out all the lights and moved to the window. Below was blackness so total it could conceal a hundred mass murderers.

She stood by the window, watching, waiting. After what seemed like a terribly long time, headlights appeared at the end of the block, chasing away the shadows as they moved closer. Another light moved around, poking its beam into doorways and the dark places between buildings. It was the police car.

The cruiser passed her building, the darkness rushing back to reclaim the street. A few moments later, the police car reappeared, pulling to the curb outside her building. Two police officers climbed out of the car and entered the building. Cassandra heard footsteps on the stairway, and she quickly opened her door.

"I'm Officer Tomley, and this is my partner, Officer Collins," one of the policemen offered as they stepped into her living room. Both men were in their twenties, tall, clean-cut.

"There's no one at all hanging around out there at the moment, ma'am," Tomley said.

"He might come back," Cassandra blurted out. "He says he's going to kill my child. He left this note." She handed it to the officer.

While Tomley gingerly held the note by its corners, both policemen studied out. "How did you receive this?" Tomley asked.

"It was slipped under my door." She told them about Clark, about the other things that had been happening.

Tomley nodded. "I understand that you've spoken to one of the detectives about this."

"Yes, Detective Hoskins."

"If you don't mind, we'll take this note with us. We'll see that Hoskins gets it as soon as he gets in."

"That's fine," Cassandra said.

Collins produced a plastic bag in which Tomley cautiously slipped the note. "Hoskins will get back to you about this," Collins said. "For the rest of our shift, we'll add this building to the list of places we keep an eye on."

Both officers smiled reassuringly.

After the policemen had gone, Cassandra went to the

bedroom to check on Lisa. The child was sound asleep. Her head, with the exception of her dark hair, was hidden under the covers.

As she watched the sleeping child, Cassandra wondered how often the officers would check the building. Every forty-five minutes? Every hour? And what if they got an important call, something that would tie them up for a long period of time?

Leaving Lisa's bedroom, she went into the kitchen and put on a pot of coffee. When it was ready, she poured some into a cup, took it into the living room, and turned on the TV, keeping the volume low enough so it wouldn't disturb Lisa. She hesitated; then, putting the cup down beside the couch, she hurried back into the kitchen and got the largest, most wicked-looking knife she owned.

Returning to the living room, Cassandra sat down on the couch, laid the knife on the cushion beside her, and picked up her cup of coffee. The police could not protect Lisa by driving by the building every so often. The only option was to guard her daughter herself.

If he tries it, Cassandra thought, he'll have to get through me. And she knew that getting through her would not be easy.

It was about ten-thirty Monday morning when Detective Paul Hoskins parked his unmarked car in the lot adjacent to the building in which Clark Clayton worked. As he followed the sidewalk to the main entrance, he noted the fenced yard to his left in which all sizes of pipes were stacked. Beyond the pipes was a huge gray structure in which they were presumably made. The policeman thought that industrial settings tended to be gloomy, and this one was certainly no exception.

Entering the brick administration building, he took the

elevator to the second floor. After examining the report filed by Tomley and Collins and the threatening note that had been slipped under Cassandra Jennings's door, he'd had the woman come in for fingerprinting so that he could compare her prints to those on the note. With the exception of some smudges in the corners, presumably put there by Tomley or Collins, the only prints on the paper were hers.

Although he had no proof that the note had been the work of Clayton, Hoskins knew damn good and well that the man was responsible for it. A precise threat had been made against the life of a child, and that gave the detective a little more maneuvering room, even if Clayton's authorship of the note could not be proved. It certainly justified another chat with him.

As he stepped into Clayton's office, the same dark-haired secretary he'd encountered on his previous visit looked up, giving him a perfunctory smile.

"Detective Hoskins to see Mr. Clayton," he said, holding up his badge.

"Uh, Mr. Clayton isn't here right now," she said nervously. "Would it be possible for you to discuss your business with Mr. Richwell?"

"Who's Richwell?"

"Uh, he's a vice-president. He's Mr. Clayton's boss."

Clearly something was going on here, and Hoskins decided that the easiest way to find out what was to talk to Richwell. "All right," he said, "I'll talk to him."

Following the secretary's directions, he took the elevator to the next floor, found the correct office, and identified himself to the vice-president's blond secretary, who had apparently been warned that he was coming, because she picked up the phone and said, "The police officer's here, Mr. Richwell."

A moment later, he was in the plush inner office,

shaking hands with a tall, dark-haired man who smiled warmly at him. When the two men were seated, Richwell said, "How can I help you, detective?"

"You can start by telling me why I was referred to you when I showed up asking to see Clayton."

"Mr. Clayton's no longer with us."

"May I ask why?"

Richwell frowned. "Is it important that you know that?"

"It could be."

The vice-president sighed. "All right. He simply stopped doing his work, and after a while he stopped *coming* to work as well. Eventually, I decided that this constituted his resignation. We're in the process of looking for a replacement."

"Do you have any idea what caused him to behave this way?"

Richwell shook his head. "He's a very bright man, and until this happened, I thought he had a really good future with us. The only thing I'm putting in his personnel file is that he resigned. If he ever pulls himself together, it may help. Someday he may need that chance."

"Do you have his address?"

"My secretary will get it for you. Would, uh, would you mind telling me what this is all about? Does it concern the company?"

"A woman filed a complaint charging him with harassment."

Richwell said nothing. He merely looked disappointed, as if someone he'd trusted had let him down.

After getting the address from Richwell's secretary, Hoskins drove to the expensive apartment complex in which Clayton lived. He located the third-floor apartment and rang the bell. When no one answered, he found the manager's apartment on the ground floor. The door was opened by a short red-haired woman in her late thirties or early forties. Her face was awash in freckles.

"Detective Hoskins," he said, flashing his tin. "I'm trying to locate one of your tenants. Clark Clayton. Apartment number 303."

"He's gone," she replied.

"Gone?"

"Gone. I saw him coming out of his apartment with a couple of suitcases, so just to make conversation, I asked him if he was going on vacation or a business trip. He said, 'Neither one. I'm moving out. Do what you want to with my stuff.' That's the last I saw of him. He didn't give any notice. He didn't even try to get his damage deposit back." She shrugged. "Of course, he forfeited most of that when he failed to give notice."

"When was this?"

"A few days ago."

"What stuff did he leave behind?"

"Damn near everything he owned. Furniture, suits and ties, you name it. The owners of the complex checked with their attorneys, who said to just leave everything where it was for thirty days, then claim it and sell it."

"Can I see the place?"

"Sure." She disappeared into the next room, returning a moment later with a key, which she handed to the detective.

Inside Clayton's apartment, Hoskins found a large-screen color TV set, exercise equipment, a closet filled with expensive suits, and some costly furniture. Sitting on the living-room couch, he considered the situation.

People did things like this. They abandoned their jobs and families and disappeared. In his years as a cop, he'd met people who thought they were under attack from aliens from space, still others who believed themselves to be Christ or God or the Virgin Mary. A bus driver once stopped his conveyance in the middle of a freeway at rush hour, announcing that it had just landed on Venus and that everyone on board should get ready to go through Venusian customs. He stepped from the bus, ran into the expressway, and was struck and killed by a truck.

Sometimes the people who did strange things were harmless. They'd had more of the modern-day world than their brains could accept, so they sought escape in fantasy. Other times, though, the craziness was more sinister, more dangerous. And that was the case with Clark Clayton. Sitting in this apartment, Hoskins could sense it, as if it were an odor lingering in the air. Clayton was no harmless crazy; Clayton was a psycho.

Before leaving, he checked over the apartment one more time, emptying the wastebaskets and going through the drawers. He found no telltale scraps of paper to indicate that a threatening note had been assembled from newspapers and magazines here. The place was neat and clean, as if its occupant would return at any moment, switch on the big TV set, work out on the exercise equipment. And yet he was certain that Clayton wouldn't be back. Clayton had a mission in which neither his career nor his possessions nor this apartment had any role.

A mission invented by the twisted logic of a psychopath.

A mission in which Cassandra Jennings had somehow become the central figure.

10

THAT AFTERNOON, CASSANDRA WAS on an expressway heading out of Chicago, toward the suburb in which she lived. Under normal circumstances, she would have been delighted at that particular moment, because she had apparently found another job. Although she hadn't actually been hired yet, the woman who'd interviewed her had all but said she would be.

It was a wonder she'd been able to impress anyone favorably after having been up all night watching television, with the big knife beside her on the couch. Cassandra knew she must look terrible.

Similar to the work she'd done for the insurance company, the job with the airline involved taking phone calls and using a VDT. The main difference was that she'd be handling reservations instead of claims. She didn't think commuting into the city would be too bad, especially if she could get into a car pool. And the job paid better than her previous one.

Again, she considered how pleased she should be by

this turn in her fortunes, but the knowledge only distressed her all the more. She knew what would happen. Clark would follow her, discover where she worked, and the same thing would happen all over again.

Another distressing aspect of all this was that to go to work at any job, she would have to entrust Lisa to a school and day-care center. At either place, Clark could find a way to get to the child. And the note had been specific about his intentions.

I want her with me, Cassandra thought. She knew that no one else would be as dedicated when it came to protecting Lisa, no matter how good their intentions.

At the moment, Lisa was with Grace. It had been the only place Cassandra could take her. She couldn't have brought the child along on a job interview. Nor could she have left her unattended in a parked car in the city, where Clark would be just one of the loonies to whom Lisa could fall victim.

Leaving the freeway, Cassandra followed a four-lane thoroughfare that led past a group of gas stations and convenience stores, then into a residential area. This, Cassandra realized suddenly, was the same route she and Clark had followed the night they'd gone into the city for dinner and a play. A simple date that had turned out to be the most ruinous night of her life.

Grace, who'd been extremely upset to learn that all their efforts had been for nothing, had urged Cassandra to find another apartment and try again, but the idea just wasn't feasible. For one thing, there was no reason to believe it would work any better the next time. Also, Cassandra simply couldn't afford to keep moving. By leaving her last apartment so abruptly, she had forfeited her modest deposit, which, under the circumstances, hadn't been much of a sacrifice. But her new landlord had required a much larger deposit, along with a month's rent to be held against possible nonpayment, all of which she would lose if she left now.

How can this be happening to me? she wondered. How can one person be able to ruin your life, then force you to live in constant fear? Governments had the power to do things like that to people, like the Nazis in Germany. In the inner city, street gangs could force people to live in terror. But this was neither Nazi Germany nor the inner city. This was happy, prosperous suburbia. And Clark Clayton was but one individual and he commanded neither a gang nor a government. How could he do this? How could he be allowed to do this?

Cassandra forced these thoughts from her mind, because if she didn't, she would begin to cry. And if she started, she wasn't sure she could stop.

She found Lisa, Grace, and Nicole on the floor playing Monopoly when she arrived at the Konecznys' apartment. Cassandra sat down on the couch to wait for the game's conclusion. It ended almost immediately. Grace landed on a property on which Nicole had put four houses; then Lisa hit one on which she'd put a hotel.

"Go into the kitchen and get yourselves a soda," Grace said to the two children as she got up.

"Can we have ice cream, too?" Nicole asked as they got to their feet.

"No," Grace said. "It's too close to dinnertime." As soon as the children were out of earshot, she joined Cassandra on the couch. "How did it go?"

"It looks like I got the job, but . . ." Making a gesture of helplessness, she let her words trail off.

"I wish there was something I could do to help," Grace said. "I'll talk to Steve tonight. Maybe he can think of something."

"You already have helped," Cassandra said. "Yesterday this couch we're sitting on was moved out of here, then back in again, just so Clark would see some unfamiliar furniture.''

"Too bad it didn't work," Grace said dejectedly. "You know, I can't figure out how he—" She stopped, because the two girls had just returned from the kitchen, soft drinks in hand.

"Lisa and I better be going," Cassandra said. "Is it okay if she takes that soda with her?"

"Sure," Grace said, and a few moments later Cassandra and her daughter were on their way to their new home. Lisa rode in silence until she'd finished her drink; then she asked, "When do I have to go to the new school, Mommy?"

"Not for a few days yet," Cassandra said evasively.

"Do you think my new teacher will be hard?"

"I guess you'll just have to go to class and find out."

What am I going to do? Casandra wondered. I have to work, and when I get a job, I'll have to send Lisa to school. I won't be able to protect her.

Cassandra stopped at a traffic light, then turned left. Again, she considered sending Lisa to stay with her father. It was the last thing she wanted to do, but if the girl's life was in danger, what choice did she have?''

"Do you enjoy the weekends with your father?" she asked.

Surprised by the question, the girl studied her a moment before answering. "We usually have fun," she said cautiously.

"Would you like to spend more time with your dad?"

Lisa shrugged, then looked away. Clearly, this topic was making her uncomfortable.

"You don't have to be afraid to talk to me about this," Cassandra said gently. "We can talk about anything, right?"

Lisa nodded. "I guess so.''

"So how do you feel about the present arrangement? Would you like to see your dad more often? About the same amount? Less often?"

"Visiting Daddy's okay, but . . ."

"But what, honey?"

"But I want to be with you, Mommy." Lisa stared at her, a worried look on her face.

"It's okay," Cassandra said, giving the girl a reassuring squeeze on the leg. "I just thought that maybe if I got a job that made me go out of town every once in a while, you wouldn't mind staying with your father."

Again, the child studied her before speaking. "Do you have to go out of town, Mommy?"

"Well, no, but some jobs are like that."

"I don't want you to go," the seven-year-old said flatly. "I want to stay with you."

Oh, God, Cassandra thought. What am I going to do? But the question seemed pointless, because the control of her life had been taken away from her. All she could do was plunge ahead in whatever direction she was pushed and wait to see what happened next.

She thought of a candy wrapper discarded on a freeway, blown this way by a bus, that way by a van, swirled in the air by the gust from a semi, totally out of control. Eventually, it would be crushed by tons of weight, pulverized until it was no more.

Cassandra was still wrestling with these things when she and Lisa reached the new apartment. She drove around the block once, looking for Clark's white car. Satisfied that it wasn't in the area, she parked and hurried into the building. As she stood outside the door, fumbling in her purse for the keys, she was afraid that Clark was about to jump out from a janitor's closet or some other place of concealment and charge at her and

Lisa. Finding her keys, she hurriedly opened the door and pulled the girl inside. Then she gasped.

"Mommy . . ." Lisa said in a weak, frightened little girl's voice. Cassandra pulled the child to her.

The apartment had been ransacked. Furniture was overturned; lamps lay on the floor; nothing in the room had been left untouched. He's still here, Cassandra thought suddenly. Whoever did this is still here.

And then she realized that wasn't so. The place was absolutely silent. The window by the metal fire escape that clung to the side of the building stood open, one curtain hanging out over the sill, as if it had been inadvertently pulled into that position by the exiting intruder. A cool breeze blew in through the opening.

Telling Lisa to stay by the door, Cassandra went to look at the window. The lock had popped out of the wood frame. On the sill were the marks of a crowbar or some other tool that had been used to force the window open. She wondered why the glass hadn't broken, then pushed the question aside. It was unimportant.

Moving through the rest of the house, she found that the contents of the refrigerator had been piled on the kitchen floor, then doused with milk and smeared with broken eggs. In her bedroom, the mattress had been shoved off the bed, her dresser and closet emptied, their contents strewn around the room. Lisa's room had been treated similarly. In the bathroom, an entire box of Kotex had been wedged into the bottom of the toilet so that any attempt to flush it would cause it to overflow.

When she returned to the living room, Lisa still stood by the door, looking frightened and confused. Her eyes scanning the room, Cassandra spotted the phone's cord, then the phone itself, which was sticking out from under a cushion from the couch. Moving the cushion aside, Cassandra saw the paper that had been folded into a long strip, then slipped under the dial. Unfolding the strip, she found another unsigned message composed in letters cut from magazines and newspapers. It read:

FIRST THE CHILD, THEN YOU, CASSANDRA.

Dropping the note, she grabbed the receiver and put it to her ear, hearing the dial tone. The phone still worked. Quickly, she dialed 911, telling the woman who answered what had happened and that she should notify Detective Hoskins. When she hung up, Cassandra realized that Lisa, who was still standing in the same spot, was crying.

"Mommy," she sobbed, "somebody ruined our 'partment."

Cassandra went to her and hugged her, realizing as she did so that unlike Lisa, she had absolutely no one to comfort her. She had to have enough courage and strength for both herself and the child. And she was uncertain just how much of those qualities she had left within her.

"None of your neighbors heard anything out of the ordinary," Hoskins said.

He and Cassandra were standing beside the overturned couch. Across the room, another detective was dusting the windowsill for fingerprints. Lisa stood next to her mother, keeping quiet but staying close.

"The woman in the apartment directly below yours says she heard a few sounds from up here, but she thought they were just the normal noises you'd expect to hear when someone had just moved in." He rubbed his cheek. "He did this slowly and quietly, I think. Nothing's smashed or anything like that. It's just messed up."

Cassandra nodded. She didn't really care how it was done. It had been done, and both she and Hoskins knew by whom. That was all that mattered. "Will you arrest him now?" she asked.

The detective frowned. "We can't find him."

"What do you mean?" Cassandra asked, not liking the sound of that at all.

"He's lost his job and moved out of his apartment. We can't locate him."

"He's out there somewhere," she said softly. "He wants to kill us."

Hoskins sighed. "I wish I could say something encouraging, but I can't. Eventually, we'll pick him up, but unless we've got some proof that he's the one who broke in or that he's the one who's been threatening you, we're not going to be able to do much. We need some fingerprints, a witness, something."

"But . . . he's done so many other things. He even made me lose my job."

"We can prove that. That's no problem. But it's circumstantial; it doesn't prove he did these other things. If this Clayton was some punk, we could pick him up and lean on him a little bit, try to scare him into leaving you alone. But he isn't a punk; he's an intelligent, educated man, and he knows a good lawyer will have him out of our hands an hour after we pick him up unless we get a hell of a lot more than the circumstantial evidence we have right now."

Cassandra watched the detective who was dusting the windowsill. "If you find his fingerprints here, will that do it?"

Hoskins nodded. "We could go to the DA with that."

She studied the detective's face. He wasn't an old man, but he looked worn, used, as if the things he did and saw in his job were draining him of something no one should be required to give up. She said, "You don't expect to find any of his fingerprints here, do you?"

"No," he said. "I think he's too intelligent to make such an obvious mistake."

"Why do you think he moved out of his apartment?"

Hoskins shrugged. "To save money, maybe. He had to figure he was going to lose his job, and that place he was in was pretty expensive. Or maybe he just wanted to avoid being picked up. He has to know we're interested in talking to him."

"What—" Cassandra fumbled for the right words. "What makes someone do things like that?"

"I don't know. The shrinks pretend to know, but I'm not really sure they do. I'm not sure Clayton knows."

"I hope you know that's more than a little frightening."

His eyes met hers, and he studied her in silence for a moment. Then he said, "I think you have every reason to be frightened."

Glancing down, Cassandra noticed that Lisa was staring up at them intently. She took the child's hand. It was cold and damp.

When the police officers had left, Cassandra set about straightening up the mess. After taking some photos of the scene, the detectives had helped her right the furniture, for which she was grateful, since things like the couch and mattress were a little bulky for a woman and a seven-year-old to handle by themselves.

She started with the kitchen, cleaning the milk and eggs off jars and bacon packages and the like. When these things were clean, she put them back into the refrigerator, then mopped up the floor. Finishing in the kitchen, she moved on to the bathroom, and removed the Kotex clogging the toilet. Although Lisa helped where she could, wiping with a sponge here, picking up an item there, most of the jobs were beyond the abilities of a seven-year-old, so the child mainly watched with a worried expression on her face.

Cassandra had just wrung out the last of the sanitary napkins when the phone rang. She hurried into the living room, which was still pretty much a mess, while a part of her mind tried to figure out who could be calling. Only Grace and the police had her number, which meant it was either one of them or a wrong number. Picking the phone up off the floor, she sat down on the couch and lifted the receiver.

"Hello, Cassie. It's me. Clark. How do you like your new place? How does Lisa like it?"

Stunned, Cassandra stared at the phone in her lap, unable to speak.

"Cassie, you there? Say something."

And then, all at once, she found her voice. "You're a psychopath!" she said furiously. "You're a sick, repulsive, demented piece of slime. If you ever come near us again, I'll kill you!"

Before he could respond, she leaped off the couch and disconnected the phone's modular plug from the wall jack. Then she simply sat on the floor, staring at the cord in her hand. Her anger drained away as quickly as it had come, leaving her with an empty, numb feeling. A few moments passed before she realized she was trembling.

How had he gotten her unlisted number? And then she knew the answer. The phone company had given her the new number before she moved in, and she'd written it down so she wouldn't forget it. The piece of paper on which she'd written the number had been by the phone. Clark must have picked it up while he was ransacking the place.

"Mommy?" Lisa was standing beside her.

"What, honey?"

"Was that the bad man?"

"Yes, honey, that was him."

"Why won't he leave us alone?"

"I don't know, Lisa. I just don't know." *I'm not sure Clayton knows*. Hoskins had said.

And then she realized that there was a way to stop Clark. Cassandra tired to push the idea from her mind, because it was a dangerous, irrational thing, but it refused to go away. She could plug the phone in again, wait for Clark to call, then accept when he asked her to go out. And when they were alone somewhere, she could kill him.

No! she thought. Don't even think such things!

Hoskings had said there was nothing the police could do without proof. If she was smart enough, careful enough, it could be done without leaving any hard evidence. Sure, the police knew that she had a strong motive for killing him, but that was circumstantial. And, according to Hoskins, a good lawyer would have his client out in an hour with no more evidence than that.

"Come on," she said to Lisa, "let's get a hammer and some nails and fix that window so no one will be able to pry it open again."

The girl followed her into the kitchen, where the tools were kept. Cassandra rooted through the drawers until she found a hammer, then began looking for the nails. The idea of killing Clark was crazy; she knew that. She wasn't even sure that she was capable of it, and she knew nothing of weapons. And if she did accomplish it and get caught, she would go to prison, lose everything—including Lisa. Even worse, she might fail in the attempt, and Clark might kill her.

And despite all these terrifying possibilites, the idea would not go away. It whispered to her, *Yes, but if you were successful, you'd be safe, rid of him. You could make him pay for what he's done to you, and then you'd be free.*

And a part of her insisted on listening.

Sitting on the bed in the small motel room, Clark Clayton stared at the rectangular box on his lap. With the exception of the essentials—clothes, toothbrush, and the like—it was the only thing he'd made a point of bringing with him when he'd left his apartment. Buying it had been a thing done on impulse. He'd seen it, wanted it, purchased it. And then he'd put it on the shelf in his closet and never used it. Not until now.

So far, he'd managed to avoid doing anything that would cause the police to expend a great deal of effort in finding him. He'd sent threatening notes on which the authorities would not find his fingerprints. He'd made phone calls, shown up at her apartment and the place she worked, and although he'd made a few mistakes, none of them had been serious enough to get him arrested. The police might have gone by his apartment to talk to him again, but he was sure that when they found him gone, they would not search for him. Nothing he'd done warranted the effort.

But tomorrow that would change, for that was when he planned to begin the woman's punishment. Tomorrow he would use the item in the box on his lap.

Putting the box beside him on the bed, he let his eyes explore the room. The motel was a dreary little place, the sort of establishment that tried with low rates to lure motorists away from the interstates. It was most likely owned by the aging woman who'd rented him the room. Someday, perhaps when the woman died, the place would go out of business, and no one would notice.

Getting up, he switched on the old TV set that occupied half the top of the dresser. When the black-and-white picture finally appeared, it was too faded and blurred to watch. He turned the set off and returned to the bed.

Along with his promising career, he'd left behind a luxury apartment and everything that went with it, including a practically new big-screen TV set. He'd given up all that for this. And he'd gladly do it again, because some things were more important than success and material conerns. Some things cut to the most secret, sensitive part of a person. They were incorporated within you, made you what you were, and made status, possessions, and such seem quite trivial by comparison.

His suitcase stood open on a chair beside the bed. Picking up the framed photo that lay atop his underwear, he studied it. You have so much to atone for, Cassandra, he thought. So very, very much.

Cassandra? Suddenly he was puzzled. That wasn't the right name, was it? And how could there be a child named Lisa? Confused, he shook his head, and a splitting pain shot through his temple. It was best not to think about these things. She was the woman; that was all. She needed no name. And the child was important to her—oh, so very, very important—which was all that mattered as far as the kid was concerned.

He put the picture back in the suitcase, picked up the rectangular box, and slipped out the object within. He held it in his hands a moment, feeling its heft and sensing the power of it. As he studied the .357's long gray barrel, he recalled the exact words he'd used to let the woman know what his intentions were.

I'm going to kill the child.

Tomorrow.

11

CASSANDRA FOUND HERSELF STARING at the worn and haggard face of a stranger in the bathroom mirror the next morning. The bags under her eyes were large and puffy, and the eyes themselves gazed at her with a frantic, confused look.

Mechanically, she applied the toothpaste to the brush and began the morning ritual. Too exhausted to stay awake again all night but unwilling to go to bed, she'd slept on the couch, the big kitchen knife beside her. It had been a fitful sleep, often interrupted by the night's soft noises, which her fearful mind had interpreted as the sounds of a madman coming to kill.

With the morning had come relief. She and Lisa had survived the night. I can't live like this, she thought. I can't.

The notion of trying to kill Clark before he could kill Lisa and her hung in the back of her mind. The perfect, final solution. She wasn't sure how she felt about the idea; her mind seemed incapable of addressing the matter. She stared into the mirror, and a tired face with toothpaste froth on its lips gazed back at her.

"Mommy." Dressed in her Smurf pajamas, Lisa stood in the doorway.

Cassandra rinsed the toothpaste from her mouth. "Yes, honey, what is it?"

"When am I going back to school?"

"I'm not sure. Maybe in a few days."

The child considered that a moment, then asked, "What are we going to do today?"

"Maybe we'll just stay home and play games, maybe watch TV. How does that sound?"

"There's nothing on TV," Lisa said. "Just dumb love stories." By that she meant soap operas.

Apparently having nothing further to say on the subject, the child disappeared from the doorway. Cassandra stared at the spot where her daughter had stood. She had no idea whether she dared enroll Lisa in school or accept a job. And yet the child had to go to school; the law said so. And to pay the rent and buy groceries, one had to work.

Cassandra slowly shook her head. She didn't have the vaguest idea what she was going to do. Her life had been reduced to getting through the next few hours, waiting to see what happened next. All control had been taken away from her.

Because the refrigerator contained neither eggs nor milk—both having been dumped on the kitchen floor by Clark—she and Lisa ate a breakfast of canned peaches and toast. After the meal, they made an attempt to play checkers, but neither of them was able to develop enough enthusiasm to make the game worthwhile. She let Lisa beat her just to get it over with, then went into the kitchen to get some coffee.

She poured the hot liquid into her cup, then leaned

against the wall and peered out the kitchen window. Her view consisted of the side of the building next door—another apartment about like the one in which she lived—and part of an alley. Suddenly, a man appeared in the portion of the alley she could see. In his late sixties or early seventies, he wore a tweed cap and was carrying a bulging plastic garbage bag. He disappeared from her view, and when he reappeared a few moments later, he no longer had the bag, which he'd presumably deposited in a garbage can.

She watched him until he was gone from her sight again, and then she continued to stare at the spot where she'd last seen him. The alley was graveled. On the other side of it was a low wire fence, and beyond that, some grass. A yard, she presumed. Having never explored the neighborhood, she had no idea what lay beyond the alley.

What if it's an asylum? she thought. Full of dangerous lunatics. The thought wasn't particularly disturbing. If they were there, they were lunatics who didn't know her, and her main concern right now was the one who did.

She was about to return to the living room when a movement caught her eye. Another man had appeared in the alley, a younger man, tall and slender, with blond hair. He looked in her direction, his eyes scanning the windows. Cassandra stepped back, out of his sight. The man was familiar. And then she knew where she'd seen him before. In the room in which she'd worked at the insurance company. A man in a blond wig. It was Clark.

Her heart pounding, she dashed into the living room and grabbed the phone. As soon as a woman came on the line at the police department, Cassandra gave her name and address, then said, "There's a man who's threatened to kill me and my child. He's here now. He's in the alley behind the building, and he's wearing a blond wig. Send someone right away. Please."

"Can you describe the man?" the woman at the police station asked.

"Yes. He's tall and thin but athletic-looking. His name's Clark Clayton. Detective Hoskins knows what this is all about. Please send me some help. He's threatened to kill us."

"All right, ma'am. I'll dispatch a car right away."

Without thinking, Cassandra hung up. And then she wondered whether she should have stayed on the line. Pushing the question aside, she hurried to the door and checked the lock. It was old and flimsy-looking. She should have replaced it, but then she'd only lived in this place a few days—a few terror-filled days.

From the hallway came a noise, a scraping sound that might have been the sole of a shoe slipping in some dirt on the floor. She listened intently, hearing nothing. Was it Clark? Was he out there with nothing but a flimsy lock and an inch or two of wood separating him from her and her child?

"Mommy," Lisa said uncertainly, "does the bad man want to kill us?"

Turning around, Cassandra found her daughter standing there, bewilderment on her face. Cassandra realized then that Lisa had been right there during the hurried call to the police station. She'd heard her mother say Clark intended to kill them.

For a moment, Cassandra couldn't move; then she thought she heard another noise in the hall. "Lisa, go lock yourself in the bathroom. Hurry."

The child stood there, watching her mother with dazed, wide eyes.

"Go on," Cassandra urged. "Go on. Move."

The girl spun around and dashed into the bathroom,

closing the door behind her. And again Cassandra thought she heard someone in the hall. Hurrying to the kitchen, she grabbed the big knife.

At the police station, Brenda Tappey, the woman who'd just taken the call from Cassandra Jennings, glanced at the big map on the wall of the communications room, noting that Jennings' apartment was in district three-Adam. Switching her headset from the phone to the radio system, she said, "Control to three-Adam."

"Three-Adam. Go ahead," a male voice replied.

"A ten-fourteen at 1627 Colmer Way, apartment 219. Be advised that the woman says that the subject is in the alley behind the building and that he's threatened to kill her."

"Do you have a description of the subject?" the male voice asked.

"Ten-four," the dispatcher said. "Tall and thin, wearing a blond wig. The woman says his name is Clark Clayton."

"Ten-four, control. We're en route from Fourteenth and Becker."

Glancing at the map, the dispatcher noted that the patrol unit was only two-and-a-half blocks from the address on Colmer Way. She flicked a switch, connecting her headset with the phone again, dialed the number for detectives, and asked for Hoskins.

District three-Adam was being patrolled that day by officers Tina Page and Gary McCraw. A brown-haired woman in her late twenties, Page had been on the force six years. Her thoughts had been on the sergeant's examination that she'd been taking in a few days when the prowler call on Colmer Way had come in.

She glanced at McCraw. A rookie, the slender young

man with thin blond hair tended to approach things with too much enthusiasm and not enough caution, but he was learning. He'd be a good cop.

As Page drove their cruiser slowly along the alley that ran behind 1627 Colmer Way, McCraw keyed the mike. "Three-Adam to Control."

"Go ahead, three-Adam."

"We're ten-fifty-six in the alley behind that ten-twenty. No sign of the subject. We'll be ten-seven."

"Ten-four, three-Adam."

Page parked the patrol unit in front of some garbage cans, and the two officers got out of the car. The apartment building at 1627 Colmer Way ran all the way to the alley, with a small set of cement steps leading to the rear entrance. Proceeding cautiously, Page and McCraw entered the building. To the right was a set of stairs, which they used to get to the second floor. There was still no sign of a tall blond man. They made their way to apartment 219 and knocked.

"Police," Page said, and a moment later the door was opened by a clearly frightened woman.

"Did you get him?" the woman asked.

Page shook her head. "There's no sign of him. Is everything all right here?"

"Yes, but he was here. I saw him. I'm positive. He's threatened to kill us, and that's the only reason he could be here."

Page knew that sometimes people tended to exaggerate the danger to themselves, but there was no doubt in her mind that the woman facing her now was desperate.

"We came in from the alley," McCraw said. "We'll check the front of the building; then we'll check back with you."

The officers went down the stairs at the other end of

the building, then stepped out into the paved parking area that served the apartment house.

"Nothing out here," McCraw said.

Page started to agree with him; then she saw something move to her left. For a moment, she stared in that direction, uncertain what she'd seen. She had a view of the parking area, the building next door, the street. And then she realized what had caught her eye. The windows of the building next door—the movement had been reflected in the glass.

"There's something between the buildings," she said, pointing in the appropriate direction.

Hurrying to the corner of the apartment house, the officers spotted a tall blond man moving away from them, toward the alley.

"Hold it, mister," Page shouted. "We're police officers."

The man bolted. Oh, Christ, Page thought. And then she and McCraw were chasing him.

As he reached the alley, Clark Clayton glanced behind him, spotting the two police officers. They were a hundred and fifty feet or so behind him; he still had a chance to get rid of the .357, which was jammed into his belt and dug into his flesh as he ran. If he could dispose of it, the police would have nothing on him that a good lawyer couldn't handle.

He ran down the alley, forcing his legs to work, hoping to put as much distance as possible between himself and the officers. He passed garbage cans and backyard gates and telephone poles. The alley apparently separated a street that held, primarily, apartments from one that contained mostly houses. The houses, which lay to his left, would provide the best chance for him to get out of the sight of the pursuing officers long enough to rid himself of the gun.

Realizing the police might be keeping an eye on the woman's apartment, he had decided that the best place to wait for his opportunity to kill the child would be where officers in a cruising patrol car would be unable to see him—in the building. He'd approached it from the rear, hoping that doing so would reduce his chances of being spotted. And he'd worn the wig, because even if the police were keeping an eye on the place, they wouldn't be looking for a blond man.

He should have given up on her sooner; he knew that now. But vengeance hadn't been what he'd wanted; it was merely what he was left with.

His plan had been to find a place to hide, then wait. A janitor's closet or a storeroom. And he'd discovered just the right place, the door leading to the basement. It was right by the front entrance, which Cassandra would have to use to get to her car. It was also locked, though circumventing the lock would have been no problem for a mechanical engineer, a person who'd been in charge of product development for a major plumbing manufacturer—if only he'd had time. But before he could deal with the basement door, he heard someone knocking on a door on the floor above him, and then a voice had announced that it was the police.

Looking behind him, he saw that the officers were keeping up with him. Too many weeks had passed since he'd used his exercise equipment. He was no longer in top condition. His leg muscles were starting to protest, as were his lungs. He couldn't go much further. He had to get out of the officers' sight, get rid of the gun.

There was a low fence on his left, and he decided to hurl himself over it and scramble between a detached garage and the house. He swerved toward the fence, and suddenly a big black dog was there, barking furiously, daring him to try it. The monster's eyes were blazing, its white teeth flashing as it barked at him. Startled, he lost his footing in the loose gravel, fought for balance, then fell, sliding as he hit. The barrel of the gun dug painfully into his thigh.

Knowing that he didn't even have time to brush the gravel from his scraped palms, Clark was instantly on his feet and running, thankful that he hadn't knocked the wind out of himself and that the .357 magnum hadn't gone off. Ahead was another yard. For a second, he didn't think he could make it, but then he was there, and he dashed through a vegetable garden that someone had been readying for spring planting.

Passing between two tall bushes, he cut through the front yard on his right, then headed back toward the alley. Glancing over his shoulder, he saw that he had finally succeeded in getting out of view of the cops. But where to put the gun? Ahead was another backyard, then the alley. Where? he asked frantically. Where? And then the ground disappeared from beneath his feet.

For a moment, he was confused, uncertain what was happening. Suddenly, his body slammed into the ground, and he was lying in the moist earth, struggling for breath. Turning his head, he saw a medium-size tree lying on its side, a big burlap-covered ball around its roots. Forcing his body to turn, he saw the hole in which the tree was about to be planted. No one was around. Quickly, he pulled the gun from his belt and shoved it into the hole. Because it was too deep for him to reach the bottom, he pulled himself over to the pile of soft earth that had been dug from the ground and, using his hands, pushed some of it into the hole, covering the gun.

He tried to sit up, and dizziness swept over him. He couldn't run anymore. Neither his lungs nor his legs would tolerate it.

Suddenly, the two police officers were there. Breathing heavily, they pulled him roughly to his feet, mumbled things about keeping silent, having an attorney. It seemed unreal, a scene from some cop show on TV. This sort of thing simply didn't happen to a bright young executive in charge of product development.

But then he recalled that he wasn't that bright young executive anymore. He'd given all that up for something far more important, for the chance to undo the most profoundly terrible thing that had ever happened to him.

As the officers handcuffed him, he realized that he didn't know precisely what that terrible thing was. Although he found that realization disturbing, it did nothing to diminish his determination to continue with what he was doing.

The child, then the woman, would have to die.

When the phone rang, Cassandra was nervously pacing the living room, wondering what had happened to the two police officers.

"We've got Clayton," Detective Hoskins told her. "The officers spotted him outside your building. He ran, but they caught him."

"What happens now?" she asked.

"He's contacted a pretty expensive lawyer, and we just don't have that much on him. His prints weren't on any of the threatening notes, and he didn't leave any in your apartment when he broke in. He'll make up some more or less plausible excuse for running from the officers, and his lawyer will have him out in a couple of hours."

She started to ask the policeman what she should do, but then she thought better of it. He didn't know, either. There was nothing she could do. Clark would come back, continue to torment her, maybe kill her and Lisa. And all she could do was wait for it to happen.

"Thank you," she said into the telephone.

"I'm sorry there isn't something more I can do," Hoskins said.

"I know," she said. "I know."

As she hung up the phone, the idea of killing Clark swirled through her thoughts again. I'm not capable of the act, she thought. I just couldn't do a thing like that.

It wasn't that she didn't hate Clark enough to slay him. If she could wish him dead, he would have died days ago. But wishing wasn't the same thing as being there with your intended victim, raising the knife or slipping the poison into his drink or squeezing the trigger. It took a certain something inside to plot someone's death, then coldly go about it. Whatever that something was—be it a positive quality like courage or a negative one like the lack of something warm and human—she was sure she didn't possess it.

So what do I do? she wondered, feeling hopeless, lost.

There was only one thing she could do. She had two hours before Clark would be able to follow her. She had to take Lisa to stay with John. It didn't matter what she wanted or what Lisa wanted. It was the only way to ensure the child's safety, and right now that was the most important thing.

Lisa sat on the couch, watching television. Since she had learned that the "bad man" had threatened to kill them, the girl had withdrawn into herself. Lisa had emerged from the locked bathroom moody and silent. Rather than face what was happening, the child had escaped into some internal place where, at least emotionally she could be safe.

"Lisa."

Keeping her eyes on the TV screen, the girl said nothing.

Cassandra sat down beside her. "Honey, we have to talk."

Slowly, Lisa's head turned, her eyes meeting her mother's. The child's eyes provided no clues as to what was going on inside her head. It was as if invisible shades had been drawn over them, letting Cassandra see only their shape and color, nothing more.

"Honey, I think you should spend a few days with your father."

"Because of the bad man?"

"Yes," Cassandra said, relieved to hear the child speak. "Because of him."

"Because he wants to kill us?"

"He might just be saying that to scare us, honey. We can't be sure."

Lisa just stared at her.

"Come on, honey. Let's get some of your things packed."

"Aren't you going to stay with us?"

"I—I can't, honey. I don't think I'd be too welcome there." Cassandra led Lisa into the child's bedroom, got the small blue suitcase the girl used from the closet, and opened it on the bed. Lisa watched sullenly as her mother began putting child-sized garments into the case.

Twenty minutes later, they were in the car, northbound on the interstate, heading for Milwaukee. Cassandra wondered if she should have called first instead of just showing up, saying, "Here, take this child. I'll be back for her when it's safe."

But she hadn't wanted to call. It would have given John and Janice too much time to think of questions to ask her. And she wanted to get Lisa away from the apartment as quickly as possible. Hoskins had said two hours, but anything could happen.

As she drove, she continually checked the rearview mirror, just in case.

They had just crossed the line into Wisconsin when Lisa said, "How long do I have to stay with Daddy?"

"Until—until everything's okay again."

"You mean, until the bad man goes away?"

"Yes. Until we're sure he can't hurt us."

"How long will that take?"

The only answer was the truth. "I don't know, honey. I just don't know." Cassandra kept her eyes on the road. She knew that if she looked at the child, she would cry.

They drove the rest of the way in silence. When they reached the Milwaukee suburb in which Lisa's father and his second wife lived, Cassandra left the freeway, followed a thoroughfare for a couple of miles, then turned onto a street of relatively new white frame houses. John's house was on the left, a single-story home with a brown shingle roof and a front yard that was all lawn, with no trees.

Lisa said, "I don't want to stay with Daddy."

"I don't want you to have to stay with him, either, honey. It's only so the bad man won't know where to find you, so he can't hurt you."

"I want to stay with you."

Reluctantly, Cassandra slowed the car. I don't want to do this, she thought. But she knew she had to.

"Please, Mommy," Lisa said, tears streaming down her cheeks.

Abruptly, Cassandra stepped on the gas, pulling past the house with the brown roof and no trees in its front yard. It had just occurred to her that she was free of Clark, and as long as she didn't go back to the apartment, she would remain free of him. There would be no more danger, no more reason to leave Lisa with her father.

"Are you going to let me stay with you, Mommy?"

Cassandra hesitated, then committed herself. "Yes."

Lisa broke into a smile. She leaned toward her mother as if to hug her, then apparently thought better of trying to hug someone who was driving a car.

Uncertain where she was going, Cassandra simply drove. When she came to a sign indicating Interstate 94 to Madison, she got on the expressway. She had the card her bank had sent her that would allow her to get money at other banks all over the country. Though by no means new, her car was reasonably sound. It would get her wherever she decided to go.

She hated the thought of leaving furniture and clothes and everything else in the apartment, but when measured against her life and Lisa's, those things were merely objects, all of which were replaceable, even if doing so would not be easy. Then she thought of the things that were not replaceable, like the scrapbook in which she'd taped a lock of Lisa's baby hair. Maybe she could get Grace and Steve to rescue some of the more important items for her.

"Mommy."

"Yes, honey."

"Where are we going?"

"I—I don't know, honey." She needed time to think.

12

CASSANDRA CLOSED THE DOOR OF THE phone booth, reached for the receiver, then hesitated. She needed a moment or two to think about what she was going to say.

It was early morning. The phone booth stood outside a small grocery store that hadn't opened yet. Across the street was a gas station, and next to that stood a store with a sign above the entrance identifying it as Denney's Feed and Farm Supply. She was in Iowa.

After reaching Madison yesterday, she had left the freeway and headed west, passing through Dubuque and Waterloo. When she reached Interstate 35, she headed south. She'd driven well into the night, and finally, too tired to continue, she'd pulled into a cheap motel on the outskirts of town, where she and Lisa had spent the night. Because her room had no phone, this morning she'd driven along the town's main drag until she found the booth.

Cassandra wasn't sure at what point in her journey

she'd realized where she was going, but by the time she reached Interstate 35, she had a destination. A place where people knew her, cared about her. And a place that was a long, long way from Chicago.

From her purse she got a small notebook in which she kept addresses and phone numbers. Although it customarily stayed by the phone, Cassandra had slipped it into her purse when she was moving out of her old apartment. Except for her car, she noted sadly, all of the possessions she had brought with her were in her purse. Opening the notebook to *R,* she located the number, then slipped the appropriate amount of change into the phone, dialed the operator, and asked to place a collect call to Sue Riley in Albuquerque, New Mexico.

"Yes, operator," Cassandra's sister said, "I'll accept the charges." And as soon as the operator was off the line, Susan said, "Cassandra, what are you doing in Iowa? Is something wrong?"

"I'm sorry I had to call you collect," Cassandra said. "Nothing here is open yet, so I couldn't find any change. I'll pay you back as soon as we get there—uh, that is, if it's okay with you if we come."

"Cassandra, tell me what's going on. You're making me very worried."

Cassandra told her the whole story. When she finished, she said, "I hate to impose on you like this, but if you wouldn't mind giving us a place to stay for a while—"

"Cassandra Marie, you know you wouldn't be imposing! You're my sister, and sisters can't impose."

"Will Rob mind?"

"Rob will be delighted to see his favorite niece and sister-in-law. Now, what about money? We could probably wire you some if you need it."

"I've got enough money to get there, I think. If not, I can use my magic bank card that's good anywhere."

She told her sister that they'd probably be arriving in Albuquerque the next day. She had to find a map somewhere to be sure. After ending the conversation with Susan, she checked her notebook for Grace's number and placed another collect call. When Grace accepted the call, Cassandra again found herself apologizing and promising to pay for the call. Then she told her former neighbor what she'd done.

"Good for you," Grace said. "You and Lisa go out there to the Sunbelt and make a new life for yourselves. Forget all about this Clark jerk and enjoy the sunshine."

"I hate to ask you this after all you've done, but if I mail you the key to my apartment, could you rescue some of my stuff? If you could, I'd—"

"We'll take care of it. What do you want us to do with the furniture?"

"I just meant my personal things. I can't ask you to—"

"One of the Hulk's numerous cousins has an empty garage. We'll put the heavy stuff in there until you can let us know what to do with it. The other things we'll send to you. What's your sister's address?"

Cassandra gave it to her, and when she left the phone booth, she was crying. As she slipped behind the wheel of her car, Lisa said, "What's wrong, Mommy?"

"Nothing's wrong, honey. I'm just crying because I know some people who are so very, very nice to me."

Lisa cocked her head, frowning. "Is that like crying because you're happy?"

"Yes, something like that." Taking a tissue from her purse, she dried her eyes. "I talked to your aunt Susan, and she says she and your uncle Rob would love to have us come visit them in New Mexico for a while."

"When are we going to eat breakfast?"

"As soon as we find a restaurant that's open."

* * *

That evening, while Cassandra and Lisa were watching television in a motel room in Guymon, Oklahoma, Clark Clayton was driving by the building in which they'd lived for only a few days, looking up at the dark windows of their second-floor apartment.

This was the second night in a row that the woman hadn't been there. He'd called her new unlisted number repeatedly, on one occasion letting it ring a hundred times. No one answered. No one was there.

Where had the woman gone?

Clark stopped at a traffic light, waited for it to turn green, then gunned the big Oldsmobile around the corner. He'd checked her old apartment, thinking she might have moved in with some friends there, but there had been no trace of the woman, her kid, or her car.

He was afraid she had moved out while he was in the hands of the police, taken her things and gone. The only way he could find out for sure was to do something he didn't want to do. He had to break into her apartment. It was taking a big chance, because if the police were watching and caught him, he could be charged with burglary. And it might take more than an expensive lawyer to get him off.

Still, it had to be done. He pulled into a residential street about two blocks away from the woman's apartment, parked his car, and got out. He didn't want the car where a passing police cruiser might notice it.

When he reached the building, he strode inside and up the stairs as if he had legitimate and important business there. There was only one lock on the door of the woman's apartment, an old model with no provisions to prevent its latch from being slipped with some thin, flexible object. Alone in the hallway, he quickly removed a credit card from his wallet, slipped the latch, and stepped into the room, closing the door behind him. He wondered absently why he hadn't entered the place this way the last time he was here instead of prying open a window. But the reason was simple: he hadn't thought of it. He switched on the light.

Everything was here, furniture, TV set, telephone, all of it put back the way it had been before he'd trashed the place. Moving from room to room, he found clothes in the closets, food in the refrigerator, toiletries in the bathroom. He sat down on the couch. Where had the woman gone? Why hadn't she taken anything with her?

Had she simply abandoned this place, he wondered, the way I abandoned mine? Have we both cut ourselves adrift from the ordinary world to walk in our own private dimension in which we'll face each other as equals and resolve once and for all what must be settled between us? Although there was a storylike quality to this notion that appealed to him, he dismissed it as nonsense. His purpose was vengeance, the payment of a long-overdue debt. It was the woman's turn to be the one who suffered.

But where had she gone? How would he find her? And then he realized there was indeed a way he might get the answer to these questions. He would try it tomorrow.

Getting up, he considered again trashing the place, then dropped the idea. The neighbors would be on the alert now for any sounds coming from the apartment. And although he didn't know why he believed it, he was convinced that the woman would never come back here.

Tomorrow, he thought. Tomorrow I may know where she is. Switching off the light, he left the apartment.

"Cassandra!"
Susan came dashing out of the house as Cassandra

climbed out of her car, which she'd just parked in the driveway. Susan hugged her tightly, then stepped back, saying, "You look good, kid. You do. Despite everything that's happened to you."

Two years older than Cassandra, Susan had the same dark curly hair and brown eyes as her sister. The most apparent difference between them was their weight; Susan was about thirty-five pounds heavier.

Lisa had emerged from the car and was standing by her mother. Sinking down so she was about on the child's eye level, Susan put her hands on the girl's shoulders. "I can't believe how much you've grown," Susan said. "My gosh, the last time I saw you, you were about this tall." She indicated the appropriate height with her hand. Looking up at Cassandra, she said, "Do you realize it's been three years since we've seen each other?"

"I know," Cassandra said, regretting that it had taken something so drastic to get the two of them together again.

"Need some help with your bags?" Susan asked, removing her hand from Lisa's shoulders and straightening up.

"The only suitcase we've got is a small one with some of Lisa's things in it. When we left the apartment, I was taking Lisa up to stay with John so she'd be safe. We got all the way to Milwaukee, then decided to keep on going." She shrugged. "I don't know when we decided we were coming here."

Susan shook her head. "I can't believe what you've been through. This guy, this Clark, must be some kind of a—the only word that comes to mind is fiend."

It was an apt description, Cassandra decided. Opening the trunk of her car, she got their one suitcase, which Lisa insisted on carrying. It was early afternoon, sunny and almost hot. And bright. Cassandra had been squinting ever since she got here.

Susan's house was a large stucco home, sort of earth-colored, with silvery shingles on the roof—presumably to reflect some of the intense summer heat. It was crammed into a neighborhood of similar homes. Her first impression of Albuquerque was a seemingly endless collection of subdivisions.

Inside, the house was a mixture of Susan's midwestern background and the Southwest. Early American furniture that would have been at home in at least half the houses in Illinois stood beside large Indian pots. Midwestern-looking landscapes hung beside small Indian rugs and diamond-shaped objects made of yarn and sticks that Susan identified as *ojos de Dios*—eyes of God.

After showing them the room they'd be sharing, Susan took Cassandra and Lisa into the large, efficient kitchen, and the three of them sat at the table and drank iced tea.

"I'm going to need to get some things," Cassandra said. "I picked up a toothbrush and some other stuff like that on the road, but I'm going to need some clothes. The ones I have on are starting to stick to my body."

"I'm afraid most of mine would be too large for you," Susan said. "Why don't we do this. I'll give you a robe to wear while I throw these things into the washing machine. Then tomorrow, after you've had a chance to rest, we can go shopping."

"Thanks. That would be just perfect."

Susan studied her a moment, then said, "What about money, Cassandra? If you've got problems in that area, I might be able to help."

"I'm okay for the moment. My half of what John and I got for the house is in a savings account. It's for Lisa's education, but in an emergency I can withdraw some of it. And this, I think, qualifies as an emergency."

"Can I have more tea?" Lisa asked.

"Sure," Susan said. She got a pitcher of it from the refrigerator and filled the child's glass. "More ice?"

"No, thank you," Lisa said.

Susan put the tea back into the refrigerator and returned to the table. "Have you given any thought to what you're going to do, Cassandra? Do you think you'll ever go back to Chicago?"

Cassandra realized suddenly that she hadn't even considered what would happen after she arrived in New Mexico. She'd decided to come here, and that was as far as her thinking had gone. Now that she thought about it, though, one thing was certain—she did not want to go back to Chicago. There was loneliness in Chicago. And terror.

"I think I'd like to stay here," Cassandra said. "This looks like a fairly large city. I should be able to get a job doing something. And I saw a lot of apartments."

"Take your time," Susan said. "You don't have to rush into making any decisions. And you don't have to rush to find an apartment, either, if you're sure you want to stay here." She placed her hand on Cassandra's. "I speak for Rob, too, now, okay? You're welcome to a bed and three squares a day for as long as you need them."

Cassandra nodded. Her eyes were growing moist.

"Don't worry about Danny and Nicky, either. It's a four-bedroom house, so nobody ever uses the room you and Lisa are in except company. And you're company. No, not company. Family. And that's better than company."

"Thanks, Susan." They fell silent then, until Cassandra said, "Where are Danny and Nicky?"

Susan checked her watch. "They'll be getting home from school in about ten minutes. That is, if they don't stop for some baseball on the way.'' She smiled. ''Rob usually gets here about five-thirty. They're all excited about seeing you.''

I'm free, Cassandra thought. It's over. I'm going to make a new life here for Lisa and me, and Clark Clayton will never be able to bother us again.

She wondered what Clark was doing at the moment. Was he watching her apartment? Had he discovered yet that she was gone? But then, the answers to these questions were unimportant, for she had seen the last of Clark Clayton.

''I think I'm going to like it here,'' Cassandra said.

''Good,'' Susan replied, smiling.

Clark Clayton drove slowly down the block. This was the suburb to which the woman had driven that Sunday afternoon to pick up the child. Clark remembered that afternoon well. The woman had just slept with him, then rejected him—teased him with her love, then snatched it away. Using a rented car she wouldn't recognize, he'd followed her here, his emotions a mixture of confusion and hurt and anger.

On his left was a house with a brown roof. It was the one he sought, the one in which the woman's former husband lived. There was no sign of her car, but then it seemed unlikely that the woman would run to her ex-husband. It was more probable that she had left the child here, but Clark doubted that, as well. The woman was too attached to the child to part with it.

He had come here because a divorced couple who'd had children, though separated and free to remarry, still remained legally tied to each other in a number of ways— things like child-support payments and visitation rights. The woman couldn't simply disappear; the ex-husband would have to know where she was.

Clark drove to the end of the block, turned around, and returned to the house with the brown roof. Parking his car at the curb, he strolled up the walk to the front door and rang the bell. A blond woman opened the door.

"Uh, excuse me," he said. "I think I'm a little lost. By any chance, do you know where the Landry residence is?"

"Landry?" the woman said, frowning. "I don't know of anyone around here with that name. I'm sorry." She was about thirty, tall and thin, with short, straight hair.

Clark shrugged. "Oh, well. I guess I'll just have to keep looking."

"Don't you have an address?"

"No, I'm afraid not. All I was given was a set of directions. You know—turn left here, right there, so many houses from the corner, that sort of thing."

"I guess I can't help you, then."

Clark thanked her and headed for the car, his purpose accomplished. Although the blond woman had told him nothing useful, he had learned all he needed to. For one thing, there was nothing to indicate that he had been wrong in believing that the child was not in the house. There had been no toys on the floor, no sounds of kiddy shows playing on the TV. But the most important thing he learned from his visit to the front door had been on the mailbox: the family's name. Browning.

He started the car, then headed for the freeway that would take him back to Illinois. Although the next step involved the woman's former husband, it could be handled in Chicago. There was no need to stay longer in Milwaukee. On the way out of town, he stopped at a pay phone at a gas station and copied down the number of John Browning.

Early that evening, at a phone booth across the street

from a bowling alley in surburban Chicago, Clark placed a long-distance call to Wisconsin.

"Hello." It was the woman with straight blond hair. He recognized her voice.

"May I speak to Mr. Browning, please?"

"Yes, just a moment."

A few moments passed; then a man said, "Hello."

"Mr. Browning?"

"Yes."

"Uh, this is Walter Thorson with the Creighton Employment Agency in Chicago. I'm trying to locate your former wife, Cassandra Jennings."

"I—I'm afraid I don't understand. Why are you asking me where she is?"

"Well, we have a job for her, a very good one for someone with her qualifications. But I'm afraid we can't locate her."

"What do you mean, you can't locate her?"

"She doesn't answer her phone. I even went by her apartment, but no one was there. I've been trying to find her for about two days now, and if I don't get in touch with her pretty quick, she'll lose the job."

The line was silent for a moment; then John Browning said, "How did you get my name?"

Prepared for the question, Clark replied, "We get a complete background synopsis from all our applicants, because sometimes the little things you learn can be very important in placing someone."

"I see."

"So, uh, can you help me? I really need to get in touch with her."

"No, I don't know where she might be."

There was concern in his voice, most likely because if the mother was missing, so was Browning's daughter. And Clark believed him; the man did not know the whereabouts of his ex-wife. Clark ended the conversation and hung up.

Emptying his mind, he watched the neon sign on the bowling alley. FAMILY FUN, it flashed at him in big green letters. For several minutes, he remained in the booth, his eyes fixed on the sign. Suddenly, he slammed his fist into the phone, causing the receiver to fly off its hook. Furious, he stepped from the booth, then turned and kicked it as hard as he could, denting a metal corner and shattered an adjacent piece of glass.

I can't let her get away, he thought. I gave up everything because of her. And then he realized that this could have been her plan, that the woman could have been manipulating him all along. First she teased him with her love; then she arranged things so that he'd give up his job, his apartment, his belongings. And now even vengeance was denied him.

Almost drunkenly, he walked to his car, which was parked about ten feet away at the curb. Everything—the street, the car, the bowling alley, with its flashing green sign—seemed confused, distorted, surreal. He had to think. This couldn't be the end of it. The woman had to be found, had to be punished.

Climbing into his car, he rested his head on the steering wheel, wishing the jumble of thoughts in his brain would stop swirling.

13

"HI," THE GIRL SAID SHYLY. A THIN child with red hair and freckles, she stood on her side of the block wall that separated Aunt Susan and Uncle Rob's backyard from hers.

"Hi," Lisa replied, and immediately fell silent, waiting for the other child to make the next move. She was kneeling by a bed of pretty yellow flowers, and when the red-haired girl had spoken to her, she had been on the verge of bending over to smell them.

Lisa had come out back simply to enjoy the early-afternoon sunshine and the beautiful blossoms that Aunt Susan tended so lovingly. Although it was Saturday, she and her aunt were the only ones at home. Her mother, as usual, was out looking for a job. Uncle Rob was doing something with his lodge brothers—whoever they were—and Nicky and Danny were playing baseball or riding their bikes or whatever boys did.

"What's your name?" the red-haired girl asked.

"Lisa. What's yours?" She moved to the wall.

"Elizabeth. Are you visiting the Rileys?"

Lisa nodded. "They're my aunt and uncle. We'll be staying with them until my mom finds a job. Then we'll move into a apartment."

"Where are you from?"

"Chicago . . . but my mom says it's not exactly Chicago. It's a place real close to Chicago."

"I'm not from New Mexico, either. My dad says a lot of the people here moved from somewhere else."

"Where are you from?"

"Duluth."

"Where's that?"

"Minnesota."

Although Lisa was uncertain exactly where Minnesota was, she decided not to ask. "How long have you been here?" she asked.

"About two years. How long have you been here?"

"About a week."

Abruptly, Lisa found herself thinking about her previous home and about the weekends she spent with her father. She wondered whether she would have to go all the way back to Wisconsin to visit him now. She wasn't even sure whether her father knew where she was. Although she wanted to stay with her mom, she didn't want to lose touch completely with her dad. She decided to ask her mother about this.

"My mom and dad moved here to get away from the cold weather," Elizabeth said. "Why did you move here?"

The main reason, Lisa knew, was to get away from the bad man. But she was uncertain whether she should mention anything about that, so she said, "I don't know. I guess my mom just decided to come."

Both girls were silent for a moment, then Elizabeth

said, "I'm going down to Kelly's house to play. She's got a hopscotch in her driveway. You wanna come?"

"How far away is it?"

"Just down the block."

"I'll have to ask my aunt."

"I'll wait here," Elizabeth said.

Although Lisa wasn't sure whether she wanted to accompany Elizabeth to Kelly's, that was apparently what she was going to do. Briefly, she wondered how you so often ended up doing things you had never decided to do, but then she pushed the thought away. Those things just happened.

As she headed inside to ask her aunt's permission, her thoughts again turned to the community in which she'd grown up. She wondered what Nicole was doing now, and then she realized it was silly to wonder about such things, because the older girl had never really been her friend, anyway. She really hadn't had many friends, now that she thought about it. Except for her dad, there was no one back home she would really miss. And she wondered whether Elizabeth would be her friend—her first friend in her new home.

She found her aunt in the living room, sitting in a chair and reading a book. "I met a girl next door— Elizabeth. She wants me to go to Kelly's with her. Is it okay?"

Lowering her book, Aunt Susan hesitated, then said, "Kelly Murphy?"

Lisa shrugged. "I don't know. She said it was just down the block."

"That would be the Murphys. Okay, you can go, but don't go anywhere else without letting me know, okay?"

"Okay."

'And don't stay too long."

"I won't."

As she headed back to tell Elizabeth that it would be okay to go to Kelly's with her, Lisa decided that it was a good thing her mom had come here. Everything she saw seemed bright and cheerful compared to Chicago, and she was apparently about to make her first friend. And best of all, she and her mom wouldn't have to worry about the bad man ever again.

"It's okay," she said as she hurried into the backyard. "I can go."

In suburban Chicago that afternoon, Nicole Koneczny stood facing the front of her apartment building with her eyes closed.

"Eighteen . . . nineteen . . . twenty," she counted loudly; then she shouted, "Here I come, ready or not."

As she turned from the wall, she heard a trash can bang, a sound that had to come from the alley. The only problem was that if she went that way, all the kids who had taken off in other directions would get home free. On the other hand, a lot of the hiders always got home free, anyway, and the alley was as good a place as any to start. She headed in that direction.

"Excuse me," a man said from behind her.

Startled, Nicole spun around to find herself looking at a thin man with red hair.

"Hi," the man said, smiling. "I'm a police officer, and I want to find out if you can help me."

Instantly wary, Nicole recalled her mother's warnings about strangers who might approach her, pretending to be what they weren't.

"If you're a policeman," the child said, taking a step backward, "how come you're not wearing a uniform?" Glancing behind her, she measured the distance to the apartment's entrance. If she had to, she could make a dash for it.

The man laughed. "I'm not wearing a uniform because I'm a detective."

"Let me see your badge," Nicole said. She was beginning to believe that the man was indeed a policeman and that he might commend her for being cautious, doing everything just right.

"Sure," the man said, producing his badge. It was silver, and in its center, in blue letters, was a single word: POLICE.

"Allee, allee, oxen-free!" a boy shouted as he dashed behind her and touched the spot on the wall that had been designated as home.

"It doesn't count, Eddie," she said. "I'm talking to a policeman."

His interest in the game abruptly forgotten, Eddie came over to see what was happening. He was a somewhat chubby boy with curly brown hair that usually hung in his eyes. "Are you a policeman?" he asked.

"That's right," the man said, again showing his badge.

"Are you working on a case?" the boy asked.

"I wouldn't be here otherwise," the cop said, and as he spoke, the three other hide-and-seekers showed up and gathered around to find out what was going on.

"My name's Detective Lumley," the man said. "I'm looking for someone, and I'm hoping that maybe you can help me. Do any of you know Cassandra Jennings? She has a little girl named Lisa, and she used to live in this building."

"I know her," Nicole said excitedly. She was the only one of them who lived in the building.

"We need to find out where she went. It's urgent that we locate her.

"Is she a crook?" a blond boy named Jerry asked.

"No, nothing like that. We need her help for something, but she moved, and we don't know where she

165

went. I was thinking that maybe she told someone living here where she'd gone."

"My mom knows where she went," Nicole said. "Mrs. Jennings called her, and she wrote it down. Do you want me to get it?"

The man looked delighted. "It would sure be a big help if you would."

Proud to be doing something as important as helping a police detective on a case, Nicole turned and started to dash into the building.

"Wait," the policeman said, and she stopped. "Uh, don't mention this to anyone, okay?"

"Not even my folks?"

"Not even them. I'll explain why when you get back," he said reassuringly.

Unsure about this, Nicole hesitated, but then she brushed her uncertainties aside. Her mother had always told her that police officers were her friends and that she should turn to them whenever she needed help. She hurried into the building. As long as she was doing what the police told her to do, everything was all right.

In her apartment, she discovered that one of her parents had apparently stepped out for some reason while the other was in the shower, since the only sign of activity was the sound of running water coming from behind the closed bathroom door. Or, as sometimes happened, they were both in the shower—although why two people would want to be in a small, hot, sticky place at the same time was something Nicole had never understood.

The phone was on the wall in the kitchen. Below it, on a small table, was the pad on which her mother had written down Mrs. Jennings's new address. Taking another sheet of paper from the pad, Nicole copied down the information, then hurried back to her friends and the waiting police detective.

"Albuquerque," the man said, studying the slip of paper.

"I think she's got some relatives there or something like that," Nicole offered. "My folks would know for sure. I can ask them if you want me to."

The man shook his head. "All of you listen to me now. This is important." He paused, making sure he had everyone's attention. "This is a very important and secret investigation. I want all of you to promise me you won't tell anyone that I was here looking for Cassandra Jennings—not even your parents."

"But . . . why?" Nicole asked.

"Because if you tell someone—even your mom and dad—that person will tell someone else, even if you ask them not to. Without thinking about it, your mother will run into one of the neighbors and say, 'Did you hear that the police were investigating Mrs. Jennings?' And sooner or later the wrong people will hear about it. Do you understand?"

The children nodded solemnly. This was serious business, police business.

"Now, do you promise me that this will be our secret?" He was looking at Eddie.

Eddie nodded. "Yes, sir."

Shifting his gaze to Jerry, then to the others one at a time, he made each one promise to keep the secret. When it was Nicole's turn, she hesitated, uncomfortable with the notion of withholding something from her parents. It wasn't exactly the same thing as lying, but—

"Do you promise?" the policeman asked again.

"I promise," Nicole said.

"Good," the policeman replied. "You have helped me a lot. When this is over and it's not a secret anymore, the chief of police will send each of you a letter thanking you for helping with an important case. Then you can tell your parents all about it.''

Bubbling with pride and thrilled to know something their parents didn't, the children watched the police officer walk across the street and get into his white car.

"He's got an unmarked car," a dark-haired girl named Mary said.

"Hey," Eddie said as the white car drove away and the man waved, "what do you think Mrs. Jennings did?"

"She might not have done anything," Mary said. "She might *know* something that the police need to know."

"Yeah," a freckle-faced girl named Jane put in, "maybe she was a secretary for some gangsters or something."

"He never asked us for our names or addresses," Nicole said.

The others looked at her, puzzled.

"Don't you see? How's he going to get the chief to send us letters if he doesn't know who we are or where we live?"

"He can find that out," Jerry said, looking at her as if she were stupid. "He's a detective, and detectives know how to find out whatever they need to know."

Nicole considered that. If detectives knew so much, how come he didn't know where Mrs. Jennings and Lisa were? But then that was how they found out stuff like that, by asking people.

"Come on," Eddie said, "let's finish the game. You're still it, Nicole."

Pushing her doubts aside, the girl returned to the wall and covered her eyes with her arm. "One . . . she said loudly. "Two . . .''

As she counted, dark uncertainties swirled in her mind.

That evening, Cassandra made two long-distance calls.

The first—and by far the easiest—was to the police department back in the Chicago suburb she had fled a week ago with her daughter. Detective Hoskins had been unavailable, so she'd left him a message informing him what she had done. After hanging up, she took a few minutes to collect her thoughts. The next call was one she was not anxious to make.

Alone in her sister's kitchen, she sat at the table, the sounds of the television set softly drifting in from the den, which was in another part of the house. She heard a child's voice—Nicky's or Danny's—then the deeper tones of a man's voice as Rob said something. Cassandra was unable to make out the words.

Lisa, who was also in the den, had spent the afternoon playing with some neighborhood children. Cassandra was pleased. Being abruptly uprooted could be hard on a child, and Lisa had just moved twice—once to another apartment and immediately after that to a place more than a thousand miles away. Lisa was beginning to make some friends here. That was definitely a good sign.

The girl still wasn't in school. Cassandra had held off because until she had a place of her own, she would have no idea what school Lisa would be attending. It seemed pointless to enroll the girl in the school serving this neighborhood, then promptly transfer her to another. The child had had enough major changes for a while.

Not wanting to do what she knew she must, Cassandra studied the table's imitation wood surface, then her hands, then the counter with its single row of Mexican tiles above the splashboard. Finally, her eyes moved to the phone. Made of beige plastic, it hung on the wall, and it waited for her.

Reach out and touch someone, Ma Bell said. But in the commercials, the person "touched" was always happy about it. Good old Granny or your pal from college or someone else who'd be delighted to hear from you. Her ex-husband would not be pleased to learn that she'd taken his only child far away without telling him and that she had decided to call because she wanted to let him know where to send the child-support payments.

Come on, she told herself. You weren't afraid to rush out into the street, hoping to find a weapon you could use to bash a psychopath who'd threatened to kill you. So why are you afraid to call a man, thirteen hundred miles away, someone you used to live with and who's never harmed you—not physically, anyway?

But it was a stupid question, for the big problems forced you to deal with them. It was the little ones that made you fidget and sweat indecisively. She reached out and touched the phone.

The connection felt its way along wires and microwave relays and lasers that traveled through flexible glass strands until the phone in Albuquerque was linked to one in suburban Milwaukee. Janice answered.

"Is John there? This is Cassandra."

"Cassandra?" Janice replied, pronouncing the name as if she'd never heard it before. "Uh, yes. Just a moment. I'll get him."

As she waited, Cassandra realized that Janice's reaction hadn't been a snub. It had been more like surprise or excitement.

"Hello, Cassandra?"

"Yes. I'm—"

"Where the hell are you?"

"In Albuquerque. I'm—"

"Albuquerque? What the hell are you doing there? Is Lisa with you? Is she okay?"

"She's here, and she's fine."

"I've been trying to find you. Your number's been

changed to one the phone company won't give out, and this morning I drove down to Chicago, and some young couple was moving into your apartment. They said they'd never heard of you."

Cassandra realized he was referring to the building in which Grace and Steve had been her neighbors. He didn't know she'd moved to a place four miles away. There was so much he didn't know.

She had wrestled with what to tell him, finally concluding that, as Lisa's father, he had a right to know the truth. Besides, a lie, once told, fed on itself. It grew, forcing seemingly unrelated events to be altered so they conformed to it. A single deception had the potential to develop into a whole network of untruths.

Her fear, of course, was that John would decide that Lisa was unsafe with her and try to take the child away. But if that occurred, she would have to deal with it at the time. She had decided to tell John the truth, and she still believed that decision was the correct one.

"Do you have any idea how worried I was?" John asked. "My daughter had just disappeared, and I had no idea what had happened to her."

She told John the truth.

"My God," he said after hearing the whole story. "You mean the police couldn't do anything about this guy, anything at all?"

"Not enough to do any good."

"Why didn't you call me? I could have helped."

"How could you have helped?" Cassandra asked, annoyed because of his presumption that he was so much better able to handle things than she. "What could you have done that I was incapable of doing?"

"I . . ." Apparently having no immediate answer for that, he let his words trail off. Finally, he said, "You should have brought Lisa up here to stay with me. She would have been safe up here."

The accusation hung in the soft background hiss coming over the long-distance connection. *You care more about having the child with you than you care about her safety.* And Cassandra realized there was a certain amount of truth to that. Still, she had to defend herself.

"Albuquerque is a lot farther away from Clark Clayton than Milwaukee," she said flatly.

"And a lot farther away from me."

"I hardly arranged all this to get Lisa away from you."

"It could have been handled better, Cassandra. It really could have."

A few silent moments passed during which Cassandra imagined she could feel the loneliness of the telephone wires suspended across some unpopulated corner of Kansas or Nebraska or whatever desolate place lay between her and John.

"Our custody settlement states that I have visitation rights," he said. "I think you may have violated the court order by taking Lisa that far away."

"You've still got visitation rights," she said. "You can fly out and see her anytime."

"That's big of you, Cassandra. That's really big of you."

"Look, John, I have legal custody of the child. That means that she has to go where I go, and there's nothing in the divorce settlement that says I can't live in Timbuktu if that's where I want to go."

"You owed it to me to tell me," John said, sounding more hurt than annoyed now.

"I owe you an apology for that, John. I know I do. It's just that everything happened so quickly, and when I got out here, I had to start looking for a job, and—and

I knew that there would be a hassle when I called you, so I put off making the call. I'm sorry.''

"What's your address?"

She gave it to him, then said, "John, please don't tell anyone where I am. I don't want to take any chances that Clark Clayton might find me. If he learns where we are, he's just crazy enough to come after us.''

"I won't tell anyone," he said.

With that the conversation died. What needed to be said had been said, and only silence was being transmitted between Albuquerque and Milwaukee. John broke it. "Can I speak to Lisa?''

"Yes, I'll get her.''

After the girl had spoken to her father, Cassandra sent her back to the den and ended the call. Then she sat alone in the kitchen and cried.

In suburban Milwaukee, John Browning sat in his kitchen, trying to sort out everything he'd just learned. To give him privacy, Janice had gone into the living room. He would have to tell her about this, and together they would have to figure out what, if anything, they were going to do.

At least now he knew why the man from the employment agency had been unable to locate Cassandra. He had forgotten to tell her about the call, he realized. But then what good would it do her to know that she might have a job in Illinois when she no longer lived there?

Getting up, he headed for the living room. He would have to continue sending Cassandra child-support payments; only now they would go to New Mexico. And he didn't like it. It wasn't that he resented supporting the child he'd fathered, but if he never got to see that child, he would feel as though he were being cheated.

"Janice," he said as he entered the living room, "we need to talk."

It was nearly dawn when Clark Clayton's flight taxied away from the terminal building at O'Hare. From his window seat, he looked out at the lights along the taxiways and runways. The plane stopped to wait for an incoming flight whose landing lights were becoming larger, brighter, lower.

He closed his eyes, replaying his encounter with the children. He saw himself in the red wig he'd worn as a precaution—because no one was on the lookout for a red-haired man and because he didn't want the woman's big muscular neighbor to recognize him. Clark took satisfaction in the knowledge that the girl who'd given him the information he so desperately sought was probably the muscular guy's daughter. Clark smiled. A fake badge and a little moxie was all it had taken to track down the woman.

The incoming jet touched down, shrinking as it roared down the runway. A few moments later, Clark's plane was speeding down the same runway.

As the panorama of lights that was metropolitan Chicago disappeared from beneath the jetliner, Clark pulled out the small carry-on bag he'd pushed under his seat. Removing the framed photo from it, he studied the face surrounded by dark curls. I'm coming for you, he thought.

Again, he smiled.

14

THE BOY SAT IN THE CHURCH, CONfused because it was afternoon and before this he'd always come here in the morning. Also, this was the first time he'd sat in the front row; usually, his family occupied one of the middle pews. And directly in front of him was a big box that his mother had peered into and then cried.

Near the box was the minister, who was saying things the boy didn't understand. There was nothing unusual about that, but this time his words seemed different somehow. And he kept mentioning the boy's father. The boy looked at his mother, who sat beside him, and he wished she could notice him and offer to explain what was happening. But she didn't notice him. She hardly ever noticed him.

Again, he wondered why the minister kept talking about his father, who was away on a business trip. He often went on trips, but this time he would be gone a long, long time. That was how his aunt had put it. A long, long time. And then she had cried.

He wished his daddy would hurry up and get back. His daddy was fun. He liked to tickle the boy and give him rides on his shoulders and tell him stories. It was never as much fun when just his mother was there. She never played with him. Sometimes she wouldn't even answer him when he asked her a question—especially if she was watching TV.

Bored with what was going on around him, the boy reached for one of the hymnals from the rack in front of him. Usually, the rack was on the back of a pew, but because he was sitting in the front row, it was attached to the low wooden wall that separated the part of the church in which people sat from the part where the minister stood. As he pulled the book from the rack, it slipped from his fingers and fell to the floor with a low thud.

For a moment, the boy thought no one had noticed; then he saw that his mother was looking at him. It was that look that meant he was in trouble, and the boy was suddenly afraid. The last time she had given him that look, she had slapped him so hard that he'd been carried backward by the force of the blow. He was unable to recall exactly what he'd done, but he'd never forgot what she said she'd do the next time he angered her.

"I'll hold your hand down on that electric burner and turn it on," she said, pointing at the stove.

Quietly picking up the hymnal and replacing it in the rack, the boy avoided his mother's eye. He wished more than anything else in the world that it was his mother and not his father who took long business trips.

But then he realized that wasn't really what he wanted.

He didn't wish his mother would go away. He only wished that she'd treat him like his father did. That she'd love him like his father did.

That she'd love him at all.

Suddenly, the minister wasn't talking about the boy's daddy anymore. He was saying:

". . . begun our descent into Albuquerque. The weather there is sunny and warm, and we don't expect any delays getting into Albuquerque International."

Clark Clayton opened his eyes and looked out the window at the brown parched land below.

In the Chicago suburbs, ten-year-old Nicole Koneczny lay in bed that Sunday morning, still troubled by the same questions that had kept her awake for quite a while after her mom had kissed her good night.

She was bound by two incompatible commitments, and she was unable to resolve the conflict. Nicole had promised her parents that she would never deceive them, that she would always be open and honest. And yet she had come into their home—no, sneaked into their home—to do something behind their backs. And now she was keeping what she had done secret, as if she were ashamed of it.

She had also told the police detective—Lummer? Lubby?—that she would not reveal to anyone, even her parents, that he was trying to find Mrs. Jennings and Lisa. "This is a very important and secret investigation," the detective had said. "I want all of you to promise me you won't tell anyone . . ." And Nicole had promised.

"When this is over and it's not a secret anymore, the chief of police will send each of you a letter thanking you for helping with an important case. Then you can tell your parents all about it."

And what would happen then? Would her parents understand? Would they be proud of her for helping the police, or would they feel that she had betrayed their trust?

And hanging in the back of her mind were dark disturbing questions she really didn't want to consider at all. Would the chief of police really ever send her a letter? If not, if the man had lied about that, then what else had he said that was untrue?

The girl rolled over and buried her face in the pillow, forcing herself to think about something else. School would be getting out for the summer before long, and her mom and dad had yet to decide where they would go on their vacation. Her dad kind of wanted to rent a cabin on a lake up in northern Wisconsin or Minnesota, and her mom was hinting that she wanted to visit her aunt and uncle in California. Nicole wanted to go to California. If they went to a lake, her dad would spend all his time fishing, which Nicole found boring. California, on the other hand, was not just the place where one found her mom's relatives. It was the place where Disneyland was located. And Nicole had never been to Disneyland.

She was still pondering the delights of the California amusement park when her mom, wearing a nightgown, padded past the open bedroom door on her way to the bathroom. Nicole heard the sounds of the plumbing being used; then her mother reappeared, and this time she stepped into Nicole's bedroom.

"Morning," Grace Koneczny said, sitting down on her daughter's bed. "You almost ready for breakfast?"

Nicole nodded. Sunday was hot-cakes day. The meal was one of her favorite's, but today she didn't have much appetite.

"Mom . . ."

"What?"

"Have you heard anything from Mrs. Jennings and Lisa?"

Her mother eyed her curiously. "Not since they called from Iowa. Why?"

"Oh, I was just wondering."

And then it all wanted desperately to come out. Her folks could be trusted, and once she'd told them, there'd be nothing left to worry about. It would be done, and there would be no taking it back. And no more keeping secrets from her mom and dad.

"Mom," Lisa said, "I—" Abruptly, she stopped as all her doubts crashed in on her.

"Do you promise?" the policeman had asked, looking Nicole in the eye.

"I promise," she had replied.

"What is it, honey?" her mom asked, looking at her strangely.

"Uh, I was just wondering. If we go to California this summer, can we go to Disneyland?"

Grace Koneczny laughed. "Is that what you're so worried about?"

Unwilling to lie, Nicole said nothing.

"Well," her mother said, smiling, "we haven't decided for sure where we're going this summer. But I'll tell you what. If we do decide on California, I'll do my best to see that Daddy takes us to Disneyland. Okay?"

"Okay," Nicole said. Knowing it was expected of her, she worked up a smile.

"I'm going into the kitchen and get started on the Hulk's breakfast."

Nicole watched as her mom left the room. She knew

she should be pleased, because her chances of getting to Disneyland had just improved a little. But she wasn't pleased. She had come within a whisker of telling her mother everything, and at the last moment she had been unable to do so. And having come this close, then having failed, she knew that she was unlikely to ever be able to tell her parents. Which meant she had no way of relieving her guilt.

Nicole Koneczny again rolled over and buried her face in the pillow.

Clark arrived in Albuquerque too early for most of the city's residents to be up and about, especially on what for the majority of them was a day off. A sleepy-looking taxi driver put the larger of Clark's two suitcases in the trunk of his cab. The smaller bag, the one with the picture in it, Clark placed beside him on the taxi's rear seat. As the driver pulled away from the terminal building, Clark removed a piece of paper from his pocket. It had been torn from a notepad, and on it, in a child's handwriting, was his destination, which he read to the cabby.

"Is it far?" Clark asked.

"About twenty minutes with traffic as light as it is at this hour on a Sunday morning," the driver replied. He was a chubby fellow with a dark complexion, and Clark noticed that he had a small blue cross crudely tattooed on the back of his hand.

"You from around here?"

"No, Illinois."

"This must seem pretty dry compared to Illinois."

"Yes," Clark said. "Yes, it is."

Apparently having lost interest in making conversation, the cabby fell silent, and Clark looked at the city. He had passed through Albuquerque once when he was in the navy and had been transferred from Norfolk, Virginia, to San Diego. For all practical purposes, though, he was totally unfamiliar with the town. Spread out all over the place, it was a fairly big city with freeways and high rises and wide thoroughfares. And to the east was a tall, rugged-looking mountain that he was certain would dominate the view from anywhere in town.

The cabdriver's estimate of how long it would take to reach the address Clark had given him turned out to be quite accurate. Twenty-two minutes after leaving the airport, the cabby was driving slowly through a residential area, noting the house numbers.

"Next block," he said, increasing his speed slightly.

The neighborhood was new—middle-class, and upper-middle class homes with three or four bedrooms, walled yards, and trees, most of which were still too young to provide much shade.

"Point the place out to me, but don't stop," Clark said.

"Whatever you say," the driver replied, apparently not surprised by the request. He stopped at a stop sign, then drove slowly into the next block, watching the house numbers on the right. "There it is," he said. "The one with the silver roof."

Ths stucco house was like all the others in the neighborhood. It proclaimed success but not wealth. It was the home of a reasonably prosperous salesman, perhaps, or a junior executive. He realized suddenly that it was the sort of place in which he would have lived if he'd had a family and a mortgage. But then he'd given all that up because—because he'd had to.

Suddenly, his eyes were drawn to the double-wide cement driveway. He'd seen a big red station wagon there, but now he was able to see what was on the other side of the station wagon. A small blue Ford with Illinois plates. He had found her.

"What now?" the cabdriver asked.

"Take me to a motel, one that's not too expensive."

"There aren't any motels right around here. They're all on Central Avenue."

"No problem," Clark said.

First he would get settled into a motel; then he would rent a car. He hadn't rented one immediately because, not knowing his way around the city, he'd felt it would be better to let a cabdriver find the address for him, then take him to a suitable motel. He watched carefully so he could find his way back to the house with the silver roof.

Because it was impractical to look for work on Sunday, Cassandra had taken the day off from job-seeking. She sat in a comfortable recliner in Susan's living room, looking through a seed catalog, one of many from which her sister ordered bulbs and flower seeds.

At the moment, Cassandra had the house to herself. Susan was at a meeting of her garden club, and Rob was spending the afternoon on the golf course. Their boys were at a Little League game. Neither of them was playing, but a pal of Nicky's was the star pitcher for one of the teams. Lisa and Elizabeth Schultz, the girl next door, were down the street playing with the Murphy girl. Except when the other girls were in school, Lisa spent almost all her time with them. For a child who'd had almost no friends a little over a week ago, Lisa had become quite gregarious.

I'm glad that we came here, Cassandra thought happily. I think New Mexico is going to be very good for us.

Her only immediate problem was finding a job. So far she had absolutely no prospects. Albuquerque was one of those Sunbelt cities to which people were migrating. The new arrivals who just happened to have Ph.D.s in nuclear physics or chemical engineering or something like that could go to work doing secret government research at Sandia Laboratories, one the the city's major employers. The other newcomers had to compete with one another for the less high-powered jobs. Unlike Chicago, where the woman at the employment agency had been quite encouraging, here the attitude of people at the agencies was: We'll call you if anything comes up, but don't hold your breath.

So Cassandra kept looking, and hoping. Eventually, people who kept trying found work, even in Albuquerque. And she had to remember that she'd only been at it a week, even though after a week of job seeking she felt as though she had spent an entire lifetime filling out applications that no one would ever read. The hard part, she knew, would be keeping up her spirits. Looking for work was a process in which you had to face a lot of rejection, which could be pretty damn hard on your self-esteem.

Putting the seed catalog on the coffee table, Cassandra picked up a news magazine. Members of the Riley clan went to the living room to read and to the den to watch TV. Susan was the main reader in the family; Rob and the boys liked television, especially sports—and most of all football—from what Cassandra could gather. She was reading an article about the hopelessness of trying to balance the federal budget—and was wondering why she was reading it—when the front door opened and Susan came in.

She sat down on the couch, setting her purse beside her. "I've got a proposition for you," Cassandra's sister said. "Or rather Marge Sellers does. Have you ever done any house-sitting?"

Cassandra shook her head.

"Well, I don't really think it requires any experience. Anyway, Marge lives in the next block, and she's a member of my garden club. At the meeting today, she told me that she was going to be out of town for a month and the woman who usually house-sits for her is in the hospital. She wanted to know if I knew anyone who might be interested, and I told her I'd ask you. The sitter gets the use of everything in the house and ten dollars a day. You don't have to do it if you don't want to—I mean, I'm not trying to run you out of the house or anything—but I thought you might be able to use the money, and I know Marge would be relieved to have someone reliable staying in her house."

"Oh, I'd like to do it," Cassandra said. "I could stop sponging off you and Rob, and—"

"You're not sponging," Susan said, interrupting her.

"Well, I feel like I am. And I'd like the chance to earn some money, too. The only problem is that I'm looking for a job, which means that I couldn't stay at the house all the time."

"Marge understand that. Her main concern is that someone is there at night."

"Does Marge know that I have a child?"

"No problem there, either. She raised three of her own and loves to have her grandchildren visit her."

"Well," Cassandra said, pausing to consider all this; then she made her decision. "I guess you can tell Marge that she's got a house sitter."

Susan nodded. "I'm glad it's just a block away. After not having seen you for so long, I'd hate to have you way over on the other side of the city somewhere."

Cassandra said she wouldn't have liked that, either.

She was pleased with the way this had worked out. Despite Susan's protestations to the contrary, she felt as if she were freeloading. Now she would be able to get out of Susan's house, earn a little money, and still be only a block away. It was perfect.

"I'll call Marge and let her know," Susan said, rising.

"When's she leaving?"

"In just a couple of days. As you can see, she was pretty desperate to find someone."

"Where's she going?"

"Spain. Every year she and some friends of hers take a trip. They've been in England and Japan and Australia, and I forget where else. Anyway, this year it's Spain."

"Must be nice."

"Maybe when Rob and I get finished feeding and educating two boys, we can do something like that." She headed into the kitchen, where the phone was located.

And Cassandra decided that would be a goal of hers. Someday she and some friends, or maybe even a grown-up Lisa, would save their money and take vacations to exciting places.

And she realized suddenly how nice it felt to be able to do normal things again, to plan and dream and wish. Now that she was free of Clark Clayton, she could do anything. She'd eventually find a job here, maybe a job that she could really enjoy, one in which she could advance. And maybe she'd even meet the right man. Maybe she'd take those exciting vacations with her husband.

Or her lover.

Although she didn't know how that happened to slide into her thoughts, it seemed wickedly delicious. Cassandra and her lover jetting off to Paris or London or Tokyo.

Sure, it was just foolishness, a silly dream. But that she was again able to relax and tease herself with such notions was absolutely marvelous.

Feeling a silly grin spread across her face, she raised the middle finger of her right hand and jabbed it in a northeasterly direction—toward Chicago.

"What was that all about?" Susan asked, returning from the kitchen.

"I was just saying my final farewell to Clark Clayton."

Facing Chicago, Susan made the identical gesture. "Oh, by the way, Marge Sellers says you're hired."

For a moment, the sisters simply looked at each other, and then they both broke into laughter.

Standing in front of the motel, Clark Clayton stared at the street. It was night, and he'd neither rented a car nor tried to see whether he could find his way back to the house with the silver roof. After the cabby had brought him here, he had taken his bags to his room, and then exhaustion had caught up with him.

Except for the nap he'd taken on the plane, he hadn't slept last night. He hadn't had a good night's sleep since he had discovered that the woman was missing. Unable to resist the appeal of the bed, he'd lain down, intending to sleep an hour or two, no more. But when he'd awakened, it was dark out.

Now he needed to eat. Other than the snack he'd been served on the plane, he couldn't recall when he'd last eaten. Looking down the street in both directions, Clark saw a visual cacophony of neon sighs, none of which indicated a restaurant. Arbitrarily, he turned left and began walking. He would have to come to a restaurant eventually.

The evening was surprisingly chilly, considering how warm the day had been—at least that portion of it he'd seen. He was glad he'd slipped on a jacket before leaving his room. The street stretched out before him, a canyon with walls of winking, dancing neon.

He'd been walking about ten minutes when he finally found a restaurant. It was a small stucco building, and it was apparently nameless, since the sign said only, AMERICAN AND MEXICAN FOOD. Clearly, the establishment would never make anyone's list of choice eating spots. Through the window, Clark could see a number of empty booths and a counter at which a single customer sat. It was a place of worn plastic seat covers and menus reproduced on a Xerox machine.

Two or three blocks ahead, Clark saw the golden arches, along with other familiar eating places: Arby's, Wendy's, Burger King. Although he would prefer any of those places to the establishment before which he stood, they were still two or three blocks away, and he was tired of walking. He stepped into the nameless restaurant. A bell above the door tinkled.

He sat down in one of the empty booths. A moment later, a waitress appeared and handed him a menu, which turned out not to be photocopied. It was typed on a sheet of paper that had been slipped into a see-through plastic holder.

"Would you like some coffee while you're waiting?" the waitress asked. Pale-complexioned and without makeup, she appeared to be in her thirties, although she could have been almost any age. Her nearly colorless blond hair was tied in a short ponytail.

Clark told her he would like some coffee. While she was getting it for him, he examined the menu, which also failed to name the place. On one side of the page were the American offerings—burgers, chili, chicken-fried steak—and on the other were the Mexican choices—enchiladas, tamales, burritos. When the waitress brought the coffee, Clark ordered the American dinner number five, hamburger steak with hash brown potatoes and mixed vegetables.

While he waited, the only other customer—a man wearing a jacket with the Coors beer logo on the back—paid his bill and left. A few minutes later, Clark's dinner arrived. It tasted as he'd expected it to, as it did at countless truck stops and bus stations and little restaurants like this one all across the continent. It was a fading part of Americana, he supposed. Someday it would be entirely replaced by the golden arches and the other chains. To Clark, this was neither a pleasant nor a sad thought; it was merely an observation.

He was about halfway through his meal when he heard the rumble of motorcycles outside. Then the door opened, and two men and two women entered, the four of them dressed in grubby jeans and blue denim jackets. The women were young, probably in their late teens. The men were in their twenties. One had a thick black beard, and the other had about three or four days' growth of blond hair on his face. The foursome slid into a booth on the other side of the small room. They began talking in low tones. One of the girls giggled.

As he finished his meal, Clark glanced toward the table at which the four people sat and found himself staring into the eyes of the bearded man. The curly hair so completely covered the man's face that it was like looking into the eyes of a big shaggy dog. Except, Clark realized suddenly, it was not the sort of dog you would pet. This was a hungry dog, one that scrutinized him with calculating hunter's eyes.

"Anything else?" a woman's voice asked.

Startled, Clark looked up and found the waitress standing beside his table. He'd been unaware of her arrival. "No," he said. "Just a check."

She gave it to him, and he followed her to the cash register, where she took it back from him. Opening his wallet and removing a ten, he was careful not to reveal how much money he carried. The billfold contained a little over two thousand dollars, all the money he'd had in the bank, less the cost of his plane ticket. It wasn't his total worth, but the rest of it was in stocks, which couldn't be immediately converted into cash.

As he accepted his change from the waitress, he wondered whether he should have bought travelers' checks. The first flight on which he'd been able to book a seat had been the one he took; there had been plenty of time to get travelers' checks. Only he hadn't thought of it. His mind had been awhirl with the knowledge that he'd found the woman, that he would have the chance to settle that long-overdue debt. And the repayment of that debt was all that mattered. When he'd done what he had to do, the tormenting emptiness that had haunted him all of his life would finally be filled in, closed, made right.

That it had come down to a matter of vengeance was the woman's fault. He'd given her the opportunity to make up for what she'd done, and she'd rejected him. For that she would pay. Then she would die. And her ability to reject him would die with her.

As he walked past the table at which the four motorcyclists sat, the man with the beard grinned at him. Preoccupied, Clark barely noticed.

Outside the restaurant, he turned right and headed back toward his motel. Although the four-lane divided thoroughfare was brightly lit, the side streets were dark except for puddles of illumination provided by sparsely placed street lamps. Reaching one of the side streets, he stopped to check for traffic, and he thought he heard the sound of someone hurrying across the street, concealed by the darkness that cloaked most of the block. He peered into the blackness, seeing nothing.

As he stepped off the curb, bright lights suddenly appeared to his left, followed by the blaring of a horn. Quickly stepping back, he watched as a green car swung in off the thoroughfare and passed in front of him, its driver eyeing him defiantly. He was a young man whose dark hair was cut in the close-cropped style of the fifties. His expression said, *Get out of my way, and that includes other drivers and pets and children and you, you asshole.*

Feeling a little unnerved, Clark watched as the car's one functioning taillight receded down the block. There was no sign of whoever he'd heard crossing the street a few moments ago—*if* he'd heard anyone. He was no long sure that he had; besides, it really didn't matter, anyway. He crossed the street and continued walking toward his motel.

He was in the middle of the next block when he stopped, suddenly alert, his heartbeat quickening. Had he seen something at the end of the block? Had a head peeked around the corner of the building, then quickly pulled back out of his sight? It's all right, he told himself. This is a brightly lit street with a lot of traffic. Nothing's going to happen to you here.

Even if someone had peeked around the corner of the building, it was entirely possible that it had nothing to do with him. Perhaps someone was waiting for somebody to pick him up or something like that. He started forward again, his eyes fixed on the end of the block. He was only vaguely aware that he was passing the mouth of an unlighted alley. Suddenly, he was yanked off balance, pulled into the darkness, and a hand was clamped over his mouth.

Someone was holding him from behind, someone

strong. In the dim illumination seeping into the alley from the street, he could see a shape in front of him. And then he realized that it was someone wearing a ski mask. The figure was holding something with a sharp point against Clark's stomach.

"You could die right now," a whispery male voice said. The pointed object pressed painfully against Clark's flesh. His stomach involuntarily tried to shrink back from it.

"If you want to stay alive, don't do anything stupid," the voice whispered.

With the hand clamped over his mouth, Clark could neither speak nor move his head. With his eyes, he tried desperately to communicate: *I won't, I promise. I won't. I won't. I won't.* But then he realized that in the darkness of the alley his assailants couldn't possibly see his expression.

The man in the ski mask suddenly increased the pressure on the object pressing into the soft flesh of Clark's belly, and if Clark's mouth hadn't been covered, he would have gasped. The man quickly slipped the wallet out of the rear pocket of Clark's pants. And then the knife—or ice pick or screwdriver—was withdrawn. *It's going to be all right,* Clark thought. *They're not going to kill me. I'm going to see sunshine and clouds and rain again.*

As all the things Clark would again see swam joyously through his brain, the man standing in front of him pocketed the wallet. Then his fist buried itself in Clark's stomach. Clark was unable to breathe. The powerful hands still held him, still covered his mouth, although the effort was wasted, for had the person behind him let go, Clark would have collapsed in the alley, gasping for breath.

The fist rammed into his midsection again, and for a

moment Clark thought he was going to throw up, hamburger steak and potatoes and mixed vegetables squirting out from around the hand covering his mouth. But then a blackness darker than the alley filled his vision. A streak of white light flashed before his eyes, then another.

Clark was unaware of being released, of falling on the alley's sandy surface, of the heavy boot that was viciously and repeatedly driven into his body.

15

UNIDENTIFIED SWISHING AND RUM-
bling noises slowly worked their way into Clark's consciousness. After listening to the sounds for a while—he
was uncertain how long—he realized that they were
being made by the passing traffic on a nearby street.
Then he vaguely became aware of the hard, gritty surface on which he lay. The next sensation Clark experienced was pain.

It was an ache in his gut, his crotch, his legs. He tried
to move, and nearly unbearable agony ripped through
his midsection. Just lie still, he thought. Just lie still for
a while.

Everything came back to him in a rush. He was in
Albuquerque. He'd eaten at a small restaurant. He'd
been on his way back to the motel when he was grabbed,
dragged into the alley, then beaten and robbed. Abruptly,
all his mental processes seemed to stop while he concentrated on that word. Robbed.

His wallet had been taken, which meant he had no

money, no credit cards, no identification. And he was in a city where no one knew him. No, that wasn't true. One person here knew him. But he had come here to punish that person, then kill her.

He moved himself just slightly, and again almost every part of him hurt, but not as bad this time. If he took his time, he would be able to get up. Clark let another minute or two pass; then he slowly, painfully, sat up. After resting a few moments, he got to his feet, using the wall of the building for support. When he was standing erect, he stood there, the pain rising and subsiding, and then without warning he threw up.

When his stomach had emptied itself, he tried moving, discovering that although he was somewhat unsteady, he was able to walk. If he went slowly, he could make it back to the motel, or at least to someplace where he could call the police.

Police? The word seemed to rattle around inside his head. That's what the Clark Clayton who was a junior executive at a company in Illinois would do, but he was no longer that man. He had come here for revenge, and although he didn't know precisely how he was going to do it, it would ultimately result in the deaths of a woman and a child. He had come here to murder.

The police didn't know that. At this particular moment, he was the victim, an innocent visitor from Illinois. The police would have to help him. But . . . He let the thought float away as he leaned against the wall at the entrance to the alley, trying to find the strength to continue walking.

But what? he wondered. And then it came back to him. He didn't want the authorities to know he was here. The woman might have contacted them, asking them to keep an eye out for him. And even if she hadn't, they would be looking for him soon enough. The police were definitely to be avoided.

Which meant that he had to make it back to the motel without collapsing on the sidewalk or getting picked up as a drunk. Steeling himself, he began walking again. Though still shaky, he was moving better now.

I'll make it, he thought. I have to make it.

He wondered who had robbed him. The four people in the restaurant? Had the two men robbed him while the women watched for any signs of trouble? He realized that it could have been one of the women he'd seen peeking around the corner of the building at the end of the block. But he would never know for sure who had done it, and the knowledge would be of no value in any case. It would not help him accomplish what he had come here to do.

A young couple holding hands was approaching Clark on the sidewalk. They were teenagers, Clark saw. A boy with shaggy dark hair and a blond girl whose hair was a mass of tight curls. As he neared them, he tried to move as naturally as possible. When they were about fifteen feet from him, the teenagers exchanged looks, then abruptly changed directions and darted across the street in the middle of the block, causing the driver of a green van to honk at them.

He encountered no one else on his painful slow journey back to the motel. When he was locked safely inside his room, he sat down on the edge of the bed, knowing that he should check himself over for damage and that he should take a bath. But instead of doing those things, he lay back on the bed and closed his eyes. A moment later, he was asleep.

Clark awoke about dawn. For a while, he lay on the bed, watching as the room brightened. Like his Illinois motel room, it was inexpensive, although this one was a little nicer. Here there was no path worn into the carpet by the door, and the TV set was color.

He felt terrible. The odor of vomit hung vaguely about him, and his mouth tasted rancid. He moved, only a little, and discovered how stiff and sore he was, especially his midsection and his legs. Girding himself for the pain, he eased his body to the edge of the bed and sat up with his legs on the floor. Although it hadn't hurt as much as he'd thought it would, he wasn't sure he could stand up.

Trying it, he managed to stand. Forcing his legs to walk, he moved unsteadily into the bathroom. In the mirror, he saw that his face had not been injured, although the image in the glass was haggard and somewhat dazed. The first thing he needed to do was take a shower and wash away the filth of the alley and the lingering aroma of vomit.

As he undressed, he discovered the marks of the beating he'd received. His stomach and his legs were covered with bruises that came in various shades of red and blue and yellow. The attack had been vicious. His assailants hadn't just wanted to rough him up; they'd wanted to hurt him. They could have killed him.

As he stepped under the hot, cleansing spray of the shower, he realized that things could be worse. At least none of the brightly colored bruises would show when he was dressed. If they were visible, they would cause people to notice him, remember him, and considering his reason for being here, he clearly had to avoid calling attention to himself.

However, the events of last night had created some very serious problems for him, and as he gingerly lathered his body, Clark considered them. He had no money, no credit cards, no identification. Which meant he had no way to rent a car. Not to mention no way to eat. And, uncertain what his plans were, he'd only paid for one night at the motel. By lunchtime, he would have to be out of the room. He had neither food nor shelter. The one-time junior executive on the way up had become a derelict.

His bank account in Illinois was empty, and his car was in the parking lot at O'Hare. He supposed he still owned the things in his apartment, things like the big-screen color TV, the exercise equipment, and clothes. But those things, like his car, were more than a thousand miles away. His only other assets were some stocks, the certificates for which were in a safe-deposit box in Illinois, as unreachable as his car and clothes and TV set.

What am I going to do? he asked himself. And then he found himself waiting for an answer, as if some voice were about to speak to him. But the only sound was the steady hiss of the shower.

After brushing his teeth, he put on clean clothes. Though still sore, he felt much better than he had a while ago. He was even hungry. How am I going to eat without money? he wondered.

Sitting down on the edge of the bed, he tried to think, to figure out some reasonable plan for dealing with this situation, but his brain seemed incapable of functioning. His gaze drifted around the room, coming to rest on the clothes he'd worn last night. When he emerged from the bathroom, he'd tossed them on the room's only chair, which stood next to the dresser.

Quickly getting off the bed, he checked the left front pocket, in which he often stuffed bills he'd received in change, because doing that was easier than fitting them into his wallet. For a moment, he thought the pocket was empty, but then his fingers pushed into a place where the cloth had been folded over, and he felt the money. Excitedly, he removed the bills and counted them, discovering that he had seventeen dollars. In his other front pocket, he found twenty-four cents.

Seventeen dollars wasn't much money, but it was one hell of a lot better than no money at all. At least now he could eat breakfast, and his body, which had thrown up the only decent meal he'd eaten in the last couple of days, badly needed the nourishment. He wondered why his attackers hadn't bothered to search his pockets. But then maybe muggers never took the time to go through their victim's pockets. Having never experienced one before, he didn't know what was normal procedure for a mugging.

Pocketing the money, Clark picked up the smaller of his two suitcases, took it to the bed, and sat down. He opened it and removed the framed photo. For several minutes, he examined the face in the picture; then he returned it to the case. It was the face of the enemy now. He would no longer accept the woman's love even if she offered it. The hurt caused by her heartlessness had damaged his core. Irreparably. Such cruelty could not be forgiven. It had to be punished.

These thoughts rekindled his resolve. Things were going to be different but not impossible. He would find a way to accomplish what he had come here to do.

Throwing his toiletries and dirty clothes into the suitcase, he left the motel. The first thing he had to do was find a place to put his suitcase. When he reached the street, a man was standing at the corner, apparently waiting for a bus. Clark quickly walked the quarter of a block to where the man stood.

"Excuse me," he said. "Which way to downtown?"

The man was a squat fellow with dark hair. He eyed

Clark with just a trace of suspicion in his expression; then he pointed to Clark's left. "That way," he said.

Clark crossed the street and waited for a bus to come. While he stood at the yellow-painted curb, he recalled meeting the woman at a party. He was unable to recall whose party or who had been there. When he'd noticed her standing with two other women, the three of them deeply engrossed in their conversation, he'd nearly dropped his drink. It had taken a good half an hour or so for him to work up the courage to talk to her. But when he approached her, she'd seemed taken with him.

When he got home, he looked her up in the phone book, but he was too confused and afraid to call her. For the next few weeks, he tried to figure out what the woman's sudden appearance meant, finally concluding that he was being given a second chance, a once-in-a-lifetime chance, and that everything that had happened might somehow be undone, made right.

I should have known better, he thought bitterly. The only second chance had been hers, the opportunity to hurt him again. But this time it would be her turn to suffer. He would see to that.

A bus stopped and picked up the man across the street, then continued on its way, leaving behind a black cloud of diesel smoke. As he watched it grow smaller, Clark saw a bus approaching on his side of the street. It was marked DOWNTOWN.

As he climbed aboard, Clark asked the driver whether she was going anywhere near the bus station.

"I pass within a block or so of it," the driver said as she steered her bus away from the curb.

"Would you let me know when we get there?" Clark asked.

"Sure."

After putting his suitcase in a locker at the bus station, Clark had breakfast in a small restaurant, then walked through downtown Albuquerque until he came to a small park. He sat down on a bench and tried to figure out what he was going to do. After several hours of considering and rejecting ideas, he concluded that he had to have help. Somewhere in this sprawling city of strangers he had to find someone who would help him.

As she did most nights, Wendy Harrison was sitting at a table in the dimly lit bar. Only two couples were using the wide dance floor, shuffling almost aimlessly to country music coming from the jukebox. This was Monday night, and Monday nights were slow. Wendy took a slug of her beer and mentally shrugged.

On the other side of the dance floor, a stocky blond man was sitting at a table with a woman who wore her brown hair in what Wendy thought of as the mop-top style, sort of the way the Beatles wore it when they first became popular. The man and woman were engrossed in their conversation, unaware of Wendy or anyone else. The woman was a stranger, but the man was Jeff Albert. Two nights ago, Jeff and Wendy had slept together.

It had been a one-night stand with neither of them expecting anything else. Although she was only twenty-seven, Wendy had been married twice and divorced twice. And since the end of her second marriage, she had slept with a lot of men. One of them, a guy named Tim, had asked her why she slept around so much, and she'd told him it was her hobby, sort of like stamp collecting. She'd laughed, but Tim had looked away and said nothing.

She didn't really like to talk about it. If sleeping around was what she did, then it was what she did. It didn't need to be talked about or analyzed or understood. It was the way things were for her, and that was all she—or anyone else—needed to know about it.

Absently, Wendy touched her curly blond hair. She had a round face, at 135 she was about ten pounds overweight, in part due to her nightly consumption of beer, she supposed. When she looked in the mirror, sometimes she thought herself attractive, although she usually saw a plain woman with very white skin and very little shape.

She knew that it was stupid to think about it as much as she did. You could change your hair or your clothes or your makeup, but you couldn't change what God gave you. It was like hanging a fancy picture on a cracked wall. When you got done, you still had a cracked wall.

For a few moments, Wendy watched a slowly moving couple so tightly squeezed together they might as well have been making love right there on the dance floor. Then she let her eyes wander to the bar, where a wiry dark-haired man sat, nursing his beer. Wendy had never seen him before, but she could surmise some things about him.

For one, he didn't belong here. Unlike everyone else in the place, who wore jeans and western shirts, he was wearing slacks and the kind of shirt you could probably wear a tie with if you wanted to. And there was an awkwardness about him, an uncertainty, that indicated he was uncomfortable in this environment.

Wendy considered moving to the bar to see whether she could strike up a conversation with him. And she immediately rejected the idea. It was one thing she had never done. The men she met approached her. It was a matter of pride. It was okay to go to a place like this and have a beer or two and see what happened but not to make passes. When you started throwing yourself at strangers, you'd lost your self-respect.

Suddenly, the man at the bar turned, and their eyes met. Wendy smiled pleasantly, then looked away. She took a swallow of beer. A moment later, the man from the bar was standing beside her table.

"Are you waiting for someone?" he asked hesitantly, as if uncertain whether this was the right thing to say.

Wendy shook her head, pleased that he had approached her.

"Uh, may I join you, then?" he asked.

"Sure," Wendy replied.

He sat down, and for a moment his eyes explored her face; then he asked, "What's your name?"

"Wendy. What's yours?"

He hesitated, looking uncomfortable. "Clark," he said finally.

Wendy had seen this reaction before when she'd asked a man his name. It usually meant the man was married—and the name he gave you was quite likely invented. "Where are you from, Clark?"

"Illinois."

"Cornfield, Illinois, or the Chicago part of Illinois?"

"The Chicago part. How about you, Wendy? Are you from Albuquerque?"

"I've lived here for the past two years. I was born in a little town in southern New Mexico you never heard of. My dad was working on a construction job there. He also worked in Grants at the uranium mines for a while. He just sort of followed the work, so I moved around a lot as a child." She waved her hand in the air. "Damn! I've known you for less than a minute, and here I am already telling you my life story. I'm always doing that to people."

Clark smiled. "I don't mind."

"Well, I do. I'm getting tired of hearing it. Why don't you tell me your life story. I haven't heard that one."

Although the smile stayed on Clark's face, all the sincerity abruptly drained from it.

"I'm sorry," Wendy said, feeling awkward. "When I meet people, sometimes I talk too loud and ask too many questions. I guess I'm just covering up my nervousness."

"It's okay. Really. I, uh, I haven't had a terribly exciting past. I've always lived in the Chicago area. When I graduated from high school, I joined the navy, and when I got out of the navy, I went to college. When I got out of college, I got a job. I'm thirty-three years old, and I've never been married." He shrugged. "That's it."

"What kind of work do you do?"

"I work for a company that makes plumbing supplies. I'm in product development."

"Is that what brought you here—your job?"

He frowned, and for a moment he looked at her without speaking. "No," he answered finally. "How about you—what do you do?"

"I'm a security guard at a big shopping mall."

He smiled. "Really?"

"Really. Why? Don't you think a woman can be a security guard?"

"It's not that. I, uh, just meant that I thought it sounded interesting. Have you ever arrested anybody or anything like that?"

"A couple of shoplifters once. Of course, I don't really arrest them. I just hold them for the police."

Wendy began to relax, to be comfortable with this man, and as far as she could tell, he was beginning to feel at ease with her too. They talked about music, cars, TV shows. And although the college graduate from Chicago and the high school dropout from New Mexico didn't have the same tastes, they seemed eager to learn about each other.

And as Wendy talked to the thin but muscular man with the intense blue eyes, she had to remind herself not to let herself become too attracted to him. For tomorrow he would be gone.

And it was hard not to be taken with Clark. Probably because she had never met anyone quite like him before. Most of the men she knew were truck drivers or electricians or mechanics, people who worked hard, drank lots of beer, sometimes got into fights, and liked to watch the same kind of trashy stuff on TV that she watched. But Clark was different. He was a suit-and-tie sort of person from Chicago. He went to plays, read books, and Wendy was sure he would be right at home in a fancy restaurant.

"Have you ever sniffed wine?" she asked him suddenly.

"Sniffed wine?"

"You know, like you do in the restaurant when the waiter brings you a bottle."

Clark laughed. "I've been to a couple of expensive restaurants where I had to go through the motions, but as long as it doesn't taste like someone peed in it, I really can't tell a good wine from a bad one."

Wendy started to laugh. Something about what Clark just said had struck her funny, and she was unable to stop.

"Peed in the wine," she sputtered, and then Clark was laughing, too.

Later, they left the bar together and drove off in Wendy's battered yellow Datsun, whose left-front fender, acquired in a junkyard, was blue.

16

SITTING AT THE TABLE IN WENDY'S tiny kitchen the next morning, Clark watched as she tended the things she had cooking on the small gas stove. He recalled the last time he'd slept with a woman who'd made breakfast for him the next morning. A woman who'd shared her body and food with him, then rejected him.

He didn't think Wendy would do that. But if she did, it wouldn't be the same. It would be a normal man-woman thing, one person telling another that last night had been for fun, that a more involved relationship hadn't been sought, wasn't desired. What *the* woman had done went much deeper, was so much more painful.

Glancing over her shoulder, Wendy smiled at him. He smiled back. She had made love last night with determination, as if she were driven to perform, to enjoy it, to make sure the man enjoyed it. But *had* she enjoyed it? Clark wasn't sure. He'd never made love with anyone like Wendy before.

He'd really never met anyone like her before. Although she had her hang-ups—quite likely including sex—she was nonetheless one of the most open people Clark had ever met. Wendy was not a person of secrets or deceptions. What you saw was what you got, everything out in the open, nothing held back.

He, on the other hand, had held a great deal back, and he found that he was feeling guilty about it. He could hardly tell her that he had come here to murder someone, but he could tell her more than he had.

"Here it is," she said, setting a plate in front of him. On it were scrambled eggs, bacon, and toast. She got her own plate and sat down, facing him.

Neither of them had been very talkative this morning, and they ate in silence. Wendy's apartment was a small flat-roofed stucco structure behind a house of the same style, which was quite common here, Clark had discovered. According to Wendy, both buildings were rented.

"I have to leave for work in half an hour," she said.

Clark nodded, uncertain what to say. Unless she invited him to stay here, he would be back on the street with only a few dollars in his pocket. And why would she invite him? As far as she knew, he was a mechanical engineer from Chicago. He'd picked up a woman in a bar, had a fling, and shortly he would go home.

"Will I see you again?" Wendy said softly, almost sadly.

"I . . ." Having no idea what to say, he let his words drift off.

Wendy stared at her plate.

"I—I don't have anywhere to go," he said finally. "There are some things I haven't told you about myself. I walked away from my job in Illinois, so I don't work there anymore. I don't work anywhere. I came here because I have to do something. The night before last, I was robbed by two guys. They dragged me into an alley and took my wallet. So I don't have any money."

Now Wendy was looking at him as if he were a puzzle and she were trying to solve it. "I saw the bruises," she said. "I didn't ask about them because I figured you'd tell me if you wanted me to know about it."

"They wore ski masks," he added for no reason in particular.

"Why did you come here?" she asked. "What is the thing you have to do?"

"I can't tell you that.",

Wendy nodded slowly. "It's okay. You don't have to tell me unless you want to."

A few awkward moments passed during which neither of them seemed to know what to do next. Finally, Wendy resumed eating her breakfast, and Clark did the same. His eggs had gotten cold, his toast soggy.

When they'd finished eating, Wendy gathered up their plates and took them to the sink. She turned on the water as if she were going to wash them, then turned it off again. Suddenly, she hurried over to Clark and kissed him gently.

"Would you like to stay here?" she asked.

"Yes," he replied softly. "And not just because I'm in need of a place to stay." He'd started out speaking the words because they were necessary; then he'd realized that he was telling her the truth.

Wendy hugged him.

"Watch this," Cassandra said as she and Lisa pulled into the driveway. She pushed the button on the device attached to her sun visor, and the garage door began opening.

"Daddy's got one of those," Lisa said, clearly unimpressed.

Cassandra drove into the two-car garage, the other half of which was occupied by Marge Sellers' tan Volvo. As they got out of the car, Lisa said, "Mommy, am I still going to be able to play with Elizabeth and Kelly while we're here?"

"Of course you can, honey. We're only about a block from your Aunt Susan's house, and Kelly's house is maybe half a block—almost exactly as close as it was before. Besides, on the days I'm busy, you're going to be staying with Aunt Susan, anyway, so not much is going to change for you."

Tomorrow was going to be one of those days she'd referred to. Cassandra had signed up with a firm that provided temporary office help, and she would spend the day at a warehouse, entering numbers of parts into a computer. She would sever her relationship with the temporary-help outfit as soon as she found a full-time job, but in the meantime it was a chance to earn some money from time to time.

I'm going to make it here, she thought as she and Lisa entered the house. Everything's going to work out.

The house was similar to Susan's. Although it seemed bigger, it wasn't. The difference, Cassandra supposed, was that only one person lived here. Without children or the clutter that families generated—even the tidiest of them—a house expanded, became more spacious.

"What do you think?" Cassandra asked as they entered the living room.

"It's okay," Lisa replied noncommittally.

The furniture was sort of good-quality American nondescript. Cassandra's first impression when she'd come here yesterday to meet Mrs. Sellers was one of overwhelming neatness. Everything washed, shined, vacuumed, dusted, ordered. Marge Sellers might enjoy having her grandchildren visit, but Cassandra was certain that she didn't waste any time before getting things back in order after they'd gone.

"Be very careful here," Cassandra warned. "This house doesn't belong to us, so we have to be sure we don't make any messes or break anything."

"I'll be careful," Lisa promised.

They explored the house. It had a big greenhouse window in the den—one of Cassandra's jobs would be watering the many plants it held. The backyard, though a little smaller than Susan's, was even more splendid. Flagstone walkways led between bed after bed of flowers, all of them carefully chosen for color, shape, and height. It was gorgeous. Posted in the kitchen was an elaborate set of instructions telling Cassandra when and how to water the different varieties of plants.

Standing on the covered patio, Cassandra said, "I'm going to like this. We can sit out here on hot afternoons and look at flowers. We can even have lunch or dinner here."

"Hamburgers?" Lisa asked hopefully. "Or pizza?"

Cassandra laughed. "We'll have both hamburgers and pizza on the patio before we leave here."

"Promise?"

"Promise. Come on," she said, taking her daughter's hand. "Let's go for a walk in the garden."

"We just looked at the garden."

"So let's look at it again."

Lisa shrugged. "Okay."

As they walked through Marge Sellers' beautiful yard, Cassandra thought about how good it was to be forever rid of Clark Clayton. It was the first time she'd thought of him in a couple of days, and she immediately pushed him from her mind. He would never find her, never bother her again. He was no longer important.

"What kind of flowers are those?" Lisa asked, pointing to some pink and white and red blooms in a shady spot under a tree.

"I think they're impatiens."

"They're beautiful," Lisa said.

"Yeah," Cassandra said, giving the child a hug, "they sure are."

It was about midnight when Wendy turned off the light and slipped into bed beside Clark, her smooth flesh pressing lightly against his.

Clark had spent the day watching television and occasionally dozing. Not having fully recovered from the beating the two muggers had given him, Clark had needed the rest. Another day or two of regaining his strength would probably be in order. But what would he do after that? He couldn't stay here forever, the guest of a blond security guard who'd taken him in as if he were some stray animal. He had things to do. He had come here for a reason.

But he had no money, and no way of getting any. If he left here, he would have nowhere to stay, nothing to eat. One solution would be to get a job, a low-paying job of the variety that didn't check references or require credentials. Every city had that sort of work; all he had to do was find it—and hope Wendy would continue to let him stay here until he got paid.

"Do you think I'm attractive?" Wendy asked, her hand finding his beneath the covers.

"Yes."

"But I'm so—so flat-chested and so shapeless."

"To me you're beautiful, Wendy." Again, he found himself saying what he had to say, then discovering that it was the truth.

"Are you sure you're not saying that just because you need a place to stay?" Then before he could answer, she quickly said, "No, don't answer that. I'm sorry I said it. I didn't mean to."

"It's okay, Wendy. And I meant what I said. You *are* beautiful to me."

Suddenly, she rolled over and began kissing him almost frantically. She had done the same thing last night. It was her way of indicating she was ready to have sex.

"Wendy . . . don't attack me."

She stopped and rolled away from him. "Don't you want to make love tonight?" she asked, sounding hurt.

"It's not that. It's just that you come on too strong, too—too all at once. It's better if you go slowly. Let me show you."

Clark put his hand on her shoulder, discovering that she was rigid. He was trying to think of something to say when she relaxed and let him pull her gently to him.

"Show me how to do it your way," she said.

He kissed her, softly teasing her lips with his, then moved to her neck. When she moaned, he moved lower.

In the morning, they slept late, because it was Wendy's day off.

Uncertain whether Wendy was awake, Clark focused on the bright light seeping in around the curtains, trying to figure out what time it was. He guessed it was about ten or ten-thirty.

"Good morning," Wendy said sleepily. She'd been curled up beside him; now she slipped an arm over him, pulling her body tightly against his.

"Good morning," Clark replied, and then they both fell silent.

He was drifting off to sleep when Wendy said, "I've been married twice."

"What?" Clark said, pulling himself back to wakefulness.

"I've been married twice."

Clark knew he was supposed to respond, but all his sleep-dulled mind could come up with was "Oh."

"About the only good thing I can say about either marriage is that there weren't any kids. I mean, it's good because a divorce is always so messy when there are kids."

"Do you think you'll ever get married again?"

"I don't know," she said sadly. "I guess I'd like to be married if it would work, but after two flops I'm a little afraid."

"How come you never had any children?"

"Can't. There's something wrong with me. Inside."

Clark could tell that admitting this was painful for her. She seemed to want him to know everything about her, even those things it hurt to talk about. And despite her own complete openness, she had never questioned him about his reason for being here, about the secret things he'd said he had to do.

And he found himself wanting to tell her, to tell her everything. But of course he couldn't do that. What he had to do was his private thing. No one else, not even Wendy, would understand.

"They used to hit me a lot," Wendy said.

"Who?"

"My husbands. Both of them. Especially the last one, Ronny; he'd beat me up pretty good sometimes."

"I'm sorry," he said. "I know what it's like to be mistreated."

"Who mistreated you?"

For several moments, Clark simply lay there, saying nothing. Then he slipped out of bed and opened his suitcase, which sat on an old wooden chair. Wendy had driven him to the bus terminal to retrieve it from the locker: the only time he'd left the apartment since coming here. He removed the framed photo and handed it to Wendy.

"She did," he said.

Sitting up in bed, Wendy examined the photo. "Who is this?"

"I simply call her the woman." And then, although he hadn't intended to say more, he added, "It's because of her that I came here."

Wendy watched him, apparently waiting to see whether he was going to offer any further explanation. When he didn't, she studied the photo for a few moments, then handed it back to him. After puttting it back into the suitcase, he returned to the bed. Wendy slipped her arms around him.

"It's okay if you don't want to tell me," she said softly. "I don't mind."

"I'm sorry. I just can't tell you any more than I have."

They stopped talking, and after a few moments, Clark was again drifting into sleep. Just as he was entering into complete slumber, he thought he felt Wendy hug him a little tighter and whisper, "Love me."

"I do," he said. But he was uncertain whether he'd actually spoken the words or merely thought them. A moment later, he wasn't sure Wendy had said anything at all.

Later that day, Wendy drove him around the city, which was even more spread-out than he'd imagined; a hot and dusty place of freeways and high rises and urban sprawl.

"That's where I work," Wendy said.

To Clark's right was a complex of connected stores and shops surrounded by a sea of parked cars. He surveyed it as Wendy drove past, but his thoughts were elsewhere. He touched the piece of paper in his shirt pocket, the piece of paper with the woman's address on it. He was glad he hadn't put it in his now-missing wallet.

"That's Sandia Crest up there," Wendy said, indicating the mountain at the eastern edge of the city. "It's about a mile higher than the city. The TV and radio stations have their towers up there, and there's a tram you can ride to the top—you know, one of those things that hangs from a cable."

"Hmm," Clark said. And then he reached a decision. "There's a place I'd like to drive past if it isn't too much trouble."

"Sure. Where?"

Taking a piece of paper from his pocket, Clark read her the address.

"That's not too far from here," Wendy said. She changed lanes, then turned left at the next intersection with a traffic light. Ten minutes later, she was driving slowly along a block Clark had seen before, on the morning he'd arrived here.

"Okay, that's the house," Clark said, "the one with the silver roof." The woman's car wasn't there.

"Do you want me to stop?"

"No, don't stop."

When they reached the end of the block, Wendy said, "What now?"

Clark didn't answer. Did he want to get her involved in this? Doing so would be a risk. Although he trusted Wendy, he'd only known her a couple of days. And what he had come here to do was the kind of thing you kept to yourself. Still, he needed someone's help. Without it, he would be unable to do what had to be done.

"Go around the block," he said. "Park somewhere

close enough to see the place but far enough away so we won't he noticed."

Wendy did as instructed, pulling to the curb partway down the block from the house with the silver roof.

"I just want to watch the place for a while," Clark said.

"Is this where she is, the woman in the picture?"

"Yes."

After they'd parked there for about ten minutes, there was still no sign of the woman's blue car. Clark said, "I don't want to get you involved in this. You—"

"It's okay. I'm not worried."

"You should be. You could get into a lot of trouble."

She searched his face for a few moments; then she said, "Do you want my help?"

Clark nodded. "I want it, but it's a lot to ask. You don't know how much. You might be arrested if anyone finds out."

Wendy frowned. "What are you going to do?"

"Punish—" He stopped, suddenly certain that this woman he'd known only a couple of days couldn't possibly understand, certain that she would think him some kind of lunatic, a monster.

"Punish the woman in the picture?"

"Yes," he said.

Several silent minutes passed during which Wendy seemed to be exploring something within herself. And when she did finally speak, her words were entirely unexpected.

"My—my father used to make me have sex with him," she said, her voice flat, emotionless. "It started when I was twelve. On Friday and Saturday nights, he used to go out and get drunk. When he'd come home . . ." She let her words trail off.

Clark explored her face. It seemed to be slack, devoid of feeling, but he could tell that she was ashamed of what she'd just admitted to him, because she was keeping her eyes averted from his.

Suddenly, Clark heard himself saying, "My father died when I was very young. My mother was very cruel. She poured boiling water on my hands once. Another time she wouldn't let me use the bathroom. She made me hold it and hold it, and then when I couldn't hold it anymore and wet my pants, she beat me. She died of cancer while I was in the navy. She left everything to the Cancer Society.

"But none of that was what really hurt," he said, only vaguely aware of the tears running down his cheeks. "What hurt was that she never—ever—loved me."

Wendy was crying, too. They hugged each other, sobbing, and Wendy said, "Oh, God, Clark. You had it even worse than I did. My—my daddy wasn't trying to be mean. He was sick, that was all. Even when he did what he did, he still loved me. I know, because sometimes he hated himself afterwards. He just couldn't stop."

And then she was crying so hard that she was unable to speak. For a while, they simply sat there in the car, hugging and crying, letting out the things that had hurt them both deeply.

"I'll help you no matter what you're going to do," she said.

"Even if I have to kill someone?"

"You think I'm afraid of going to jail? You think my life's so great and wonderful that jail would be that much worse?"

Uncertain how to respond to that, Clark said nothing.

"Are you going to need to watch her house?" Wendy asked.

"Yes. I need to find out what her schedule is, where she goes. I need to figure out exactly what I'm going to do."

"She might recognize you."

"I know, but I don't know what to do about it."

"I could do it. I'm going on night shift the day after tomorrow, and I'll be free during the day."

"Wendy," he said, looking into her eyes. "when this is over, when I've done this thing that I have to do . . ."

She nodded. She understood.

What he was doing was essential. It was the only way he could ever be right with himself, with life, with the universe. But once it was done, the two of them could build a life, could be together always.

"Yes," he said, "I think you should do the watching."

Again, she nodded.

And then they kissed.

17

SITTING BEHIND THE WHEEL OF HER yellow car with the blue fender, Wendy watched the house with the silver roof. She was parked on the same side of the street, with two houses between her and the one she watched. So far there had been no sign of a blue car with an Illinois plate or a woman who looked like the image in Clark's metal-framed photo.

Although the temperature was pleasantly in the mid-seventies, the sun had heated the interior of the car enough to make it uncomfortable, even with the windows open. And it was only midmorning, which meant that it was going to get still hotter in the car and that Wendy was going to be a sticky mess by the time she went home.

Somewhere in some deep recess of her mind, Wendy wondered why she was doing this. And she worried about what Clark had said about murdering someone, presumably the woman whom she had agreed to watch. But she paid little attention to these misgivings, because she was in love. How can I be? she wondered. All this is happening too fast. How can I know after only a few days that I'm in love?

But she was in love. More in love than she had ever been in her life. If Clark left her, she would be devastated. He was more suitable, more right, for her than anyone she'd ever even hoped to meet. He was the end of the old Wendy, the Wendy of bad marriages to men who beat her. And he was the end of the one-night stands, which, she realized now, had only been a search for love, an attempt to quench her overwhelming need to be wanted.

She would do anything to ensure that she never lost Clark. She would watch this house for him. She would even kill for him. She'd had a taste of what it was like to be the new Wendy, and she would do anything to avoid ever again being the old Wendy. If Clark betrayed her, left her, she might kill herself. And she might kill him.

Kill? The word circled in her brain, a scrap of paper swirled aloft by a dust devil. Was she truly capable of murder?

And then she saw herself as a gangly fifth-grader. It was recess, and the kids were choosing up sides for softball, girls and boys all playing on the same teams. The teacher had appointed Jack Tarker and Anna Apodeca team captains. As each captain took turns calling out names, the group of unchosen kids was shrinking, quickly being reduced to the least popular, the poorest players, the most worthless in the eyes of their classmates.

Wendy found herself standing with a short boy whose face flaked, as if it had dandruff. They looked at each other, the last two to be chosen. Momentarily, one of them would be named the most unwanted child in the class.

The young Wendy was unable to understand why the teacher would allow such a cruel event to occur again and again. And yet the teacher not only allowed but encouraged it. And Wendy had been taught to believe that the teacher was a good person, a fair person, which meant the fault had to be Wendy's. But the child had no idea what she could do to make herself more popular, or a better softball player. And she didn't understand why the other children judged her so harshly just because of a game.

Kill.

The word had come into her mind in those days. Once, Wendy had been waiting in the car while her mother ran some errand, and Jack Tarker had come walking through the parking lot. Jack Tarker, who had curly brown hair and who was the best marble shooter and softball player in fifth grade. Jack Tarker, who was almost always the captain of the team and who always chose her last. Realizing that he was going to walk in front of her car, Wendy slid over into the driver's seat and tried to figure out how to start the engine. She hadn't been able to do so, but she knew that if she had, she would have run over Jack Tarker. And she would have been glad.

Kill.

The word had come into her mind another time when she was in elementary school. A cruel girl named Kathy liked to taunt her. On the playground one day, Kathy, accompanied by two other girls, had approached Wendy while she was using the swings.

"Get off the swing," Kathy ordered. She was a tall girl with brownish-blond hair and an upturned nose. And she was big-boned and athletic, always one of the first to be chosen to play softball.

"There's two swings nobody's using," Wendy said. "You don't need all three of them."

"There's three of us," Kathy said.

"I was here first."

Kathy and her two friends closed in on the swing, and Wendy knew that if she didn't comply with their wishes, they'd grab it as she swung by, spilling her on the ground. Dejectedly, she got off the swing, which was immediately claimed by one of Kathy's companions.

As Wendy started to walk away, Kathy blocked her path. "Where do you think you're going, bubble butt?"

Wendy didn't answer.

"There's only one thing I want to know," Kathy said. "Why'd she give you such a funny look?"

"Who?" Wendy asked, wondering if she had done something to annoy the teacher.

"Mother Nature!" Kathy exclaimed, and her friends roared.

Desperately wanting to get away from these girls, Wendy ran, tears of hurt, shame, and anger flowing down her cheeks. And behind her, Kathy yelled, "What's wrong, crybaby? Gonna run home to your mama, crybaby?"

"Run home to your mama, fart face," one of Kathy's friends exclaimed.

I'm not mean to them, Wendy thought. Why do they hate me? What did I do to them? But these attempts to analyze the situation did nothing to assuage Wendy's anguish. Tears, hot and mean, bubbled up and ran down her face. When she reached the school building, she noticed a brick lying beside a small pile of sand, the remnants of some childish construction, probably a space station or a fort or the like. As she stared at the brick, her tears of shame and frustration became tears of anger. She picked up the brick and walked slowly back toward the swing.

Kathy and her friends were standing near the swings, engrossed in conversation. They hadn't wanted the swings, Wendy realized; they'd only wanted to make her leave them, to impose their will on her, to belittle her. Kathy's back was to her as she approached. Although Wendy could hear what they were saying, she paid no attention. Their words were unimportant.

She was about three feet from Kathy when she raised the brick and took aim. One of the other girls screamed, and Kathy spun around. The brick, which would have hit her squarely in the back of the head if she hadn't moved, flew past Kathy's face, missing her by less than an inch.

All the girls were silent. Kathy stared at her, her eyes showing confusion and fear. Wendy simply stood there, part of her realizing she'd been lucky the brick had missed. But another part of her was disappointed. That part had wanted to see Kathy lying on the ground, blood seeping from her mashed head. Kathy and her companions backed away. And they avoided Wendy from then on.

Kill.

The word had come into her mind more than once when her father had come home drunk and forced her to have sex with him. Her bed had been attached to one of those bookcase headboards. It had sliding doors to cover the two side compartments, and in one of the compartments she'd placed a sharp knife. Twice when he was forcing himself into her, his alcohol breath choking her, she'd reached back, touched that sliding door.

What stopped her was fear. But not fear of killing. She'd been afraid that he'd realize what she was doing before she was able to bring the knife out and bury it in him. And if that had happened, she was sure her father, who was much stronger than she, would have used the knife on her. But on those occasions that she'd reached back and touched the sliding door, she'd wanted desperately to plunge the knife into him. Again and again and again.

A woman in a compact car drove by the spot where Wendy was parked. The woman had dark curly hair, and for just an instant Wendy thought it was *the* woman, the one in Clark's photo. But it wasn't. The face was wrong, and the car had been white, with a New Mexico plate. Wendy watched as it turned right at the corner and disappeared.

Although Clark had declined to let her bring the photo with her, she remembered it well. And she realized something about it that Clark apparently didn't, not fully, anyway. The picture in the metal frame was old, the woman's clothes about twenty years out of style. Clearly, this was not the woman he'd followed here from Illinois.

Apparently, she looked like the photo, which meant that she looked now as the woman had then. The woman in the picture would be about fifty now. Her face would look nothing like the one in the photograph.

So who were these two women? And how had Clark merged them into one? Wendy was fairly certain she knew the answer to the first question, and she had more or less reasoned out the second. The woman in the photo was Clark's mother, his cruel mother who had abused him and refused to give him her love. And the other woman was someone he met, someone who just happened to look like his mother. Apparently, she, too, had hurt him, refused to love him.

This next part Wendy didn't completely understand, but she was fairly certain she was at least close to having it figured out. Somehow, probably because she looked so much like his dead mother, Clark had decided that this woman *was* his mother. From her he'd tried to get the love his real mother had never given him. And when he couldn't get it, he'd decided to get even, something he'd been unable to do with his real mother.

Even though she didn't fully comprehend all this, it made a certain amount of sense. She certainly understood the desire to get even. She rarely saw her father, but when she did, she experienced conflicting emotions. A part of her wanted to forgive him, to love him. But another part still wanted to slide open the compartment in the bookcase headboard, get the knife . . .

And Wendy thought that if she met someone who looked like her father, who behaved like him, she might react very much as Clark had.

She also believed that the only way for Clark to resolve all this was for him to complete what he had come here to do. Only then could he push this matter aside and lead a normal life. And Wendy knew that she would do whatever she could to help him. Even kill.

And Wendy realized suddenly that she *wanted* to harm this person who had hurt Clark, in part because this woman had been cruel to the man Wendy loved but also because this woman was a rival. If Clark had wanted her love as much as Wendy suspected, then he might still want it. And Wendy could think of only one way to make sure she never offered it to him.

Abruptly, Wendy began digging in her purse, removing a piece of paper, a pen, and a small pair of scissors, with which she cut off a snip of her blond hair. Setting it carefully aside, she began writing on the paper.

"I don't understand why she isn't there," Clark said. He and Wendy were in her car, on their way to the shopping mall at which she worked. Two days had passed since Wendy began watching the house with the silver roof.

"I don't think she was just stopping here on her way to somewhere else," Clark said. "I'm sure this was her destination."

"Maybe she got a place of her own," Wendy suggested. She signaled, then changed lanes. The afternoon rush was still under way, and traffic was heavy.

"Maybe," Clark said, frowning. Thinking he could phone, claiming to be a prospective employer, he'd asked Wendy to go to the door on some pretext or another and get the name from the mailbox, as he had in suburban Milwaukee at the home of the woman's ex-husband. Wendy had done so, finding no name on the box—or anywhere else on the front of the house.

There were other ways to learn the name of the people in the house with the silver roof, such as asking the neighbors, but not without arousing suspicion. Clark could not afford to do anything that might let the woman know that a stranger was interested in her or the people with whom she was staying, for she would immediately suspect who that stranger was. And Clark wanted her calm and unsuspecting, for if she was unprepared, she would be vulnerable.

But first he had to find her, which was why he was accompanying Wendy to the shopping mall. Because Wendy went to work at six in the evening, she had to abandon her vigil before five, and Clark wanted to check out the place at night. When they reached the mall, he would take her car. Once it was fully dark, it would be safe for him to do his own watching.

The mall's parking area was uncrowded. At this time of day, people were headed for home and dinner; shopping could wait for another time. Wendy pulled into a vacant space and switched off the engine.

"Wanna come in and see where I work?" she asked.

"Okay." It wasn't dark yet, and he didn't want to arrive at the house with the silver roof until it was.

The mall was enormous. On its two levels were a number of large department stores, along with countless smaller shops that sold things like books and shoes and toys. Wendy took him to a short hallway at the end of which were two doors, one labeled REST ROOMS, the other marked EMPLOYEES ONLY. She opened the latter one and led Clark down a set of cement stairs, turning on the lights when she reached the bottom.

They were in a corridor that ran to the right, abruptly ending after only fifteen feet or so where a wall had been built across it. The only things here were three lockers, a wooden bench, and one closed door. Wendy spun the numbers on a combination padlock, then opened one of the lockers.

"You mean a place this size has only three security guards?" Clark asked, indicating the three lockers.

Wendy laughed. "No, this is the women's locker room. A lot of the security officers come here in street clothes, then change into their uniforms. So when the management started using women security officers, they decided they needed a separate locker room, and this was what they came up with."

"How many female guards do you have?"

"There used to be three of us, but two of them quit. Now there's just me."

Wendy had no need to change clothes, since she was already dressed in her brown uniform. Putting her purse in the locker, she closed the door and secured the lock.

"What's in there?" Clark asked, inclining his head toward the closed door to the right of the lockers.

"Nothing. There used to be heating equipment and stuff like that in there, but they put in a whole new system when they expanded the mall. They changed everything around down here. This hallway used to be about twenty times as long as it is now."

Clark tried the closed door, finding it locked. "Do you have the key?"

"Sure, but it's just an empty room. There's nothing inside to see."

Clark examined the door. It was heavy, apparently designed to deaden sound. "I'd like to see it, anyway, if you've got time."

With a shrug, Wendy produced a ring of keys, inserted one of them into the lock, and opened the door. Reaching into the room, she flipped on the light.

Clark stepped through the doorway. As Wendy had said, there was nothing here but a large empty room. The spots where various pieces of equipment had stood were marked by outlines on the floor. In places, large bolts protruded from the cement. The concrete walls apeared to be quite thick; apparently, this place had been designed so the noise made by the equipment wouldn't disturb the shoppers on the levels above.

Rising up from the floor were a number of short pipes, most of them capped. Clark examined them, finding one that he was sure was a gas line. "Where does this line come in from?" he asked.

"I don't know," Wendy said, apparently puzzled by his interest in all this. "There are lots of pipes running along the ceiling out in the hallway. Maybe it's one of them."

Clark left the room, and scanned the hallway ceiling, seeing a number of pipes but not the one he sought. Then he noticed the metal plate on the floor about two feet in front of him. Squatting, he lifted the plate, discovering a valve. It was what he'd been looking for.

An idea was taking shape. He was pretty sure he knew how he was going to punish the woman. Although it was a complicated plan, it would be very effective.

Wendy had just finished relocking the door to the room. Suddenly, she stepped over to Clark and slipped her arms around him, pulling her body tightly against his. "I love you," she whispered.

"I love you, too," he said gently, feeling the emotion spreading warmly throughout his body.

"I wish I didn't have to go on duty in a few minutes. I'd make love to you. Right here and right now."

Clark hugged her. Although he didn't speak, he shared her wish. Wendy was becoming less frantic in her lovemaking, more sensuous. And he approved of the change.

"I, uh, I made you something while I was watching the house. I guess I was embarrassed to give it to you. I was afraid you'd think it was silly."

Reaching into her shirt pocket, she pulled out a folded sheet of paper. For a moment, she looked at him like a child who was trying to work up the courage to offer the teacher an apple; then she handed it to him. Unfolding it, Clark found a lock of blond hair taped to the paper. Written in pen was the message:

> *A piece of me to have with you always.*
>
> *Wendy*

"Thank you," he said, meaning it. "I will keep it with me always."

They simply stood there, hugging, until Wendy had only seconds to report for duty. Then they dashed up the stairs, Wendy hurrying toward the security office, Clark heading for the car.

THE ATTRACTION

He watched the house with the silver roof until after one in the morning, seeing no sign of the woman or her child or her blue car. He was feeling frustrated when he picked Wendy up at the mall. But the next day his luck changed.

18

"IT'S SO DAMN DISCOURAGING," CAS-
sandra said. She and her sister were sitting at the
table in Susan's kitchen, drinking iced tea.

"I thought I'd get a little work from this temporary-
help outfit," Cassandra went on, "but I spent one day
working at a warehouse, and that's the last I heard from
them."

"Looking for work's always like that," Susan said.
"But if you just keep trying, something always comes
your way."

Suddenly, Cassandra found herself envying her sister.
Happily married and with a nice home and no major
financial worries, Susan was content being a wife, mother,
grower of flowers and member of the garden club. Unlike Cassandra, she had never seen her marriage slowly
disintegrate. She had never been a single parent. She
had never had to survive on child-support payments and
the salary from one of the low-paying jobs in which
working women so often found themselves. Cassandra

pushed these thoughts from her mind. She should be happy for her sister, not jealous of her.

"How's Lisa adjusting to her new surroundings?" Susan asked.

"She absolutely loves it here. I think that if I told her we had to leave New Mexico, she'd demand a new mother."

"Is she still getting to know the neighborhood children?"

"She and the little girl next door to you and Kelly Murphy have formed their own little clique. She's with them now. They're inseparable."

"I haven't seen Lisa since the day you spent working at that warehouse."

"They always get together at the Murphys' place—I suppose because it's about halfway between here and the house we're staying in."

"It's good she's making friends."

Cassandra nodded. Everything was good here—if only she could find a job. But then, Susan was right. If you just kept trying, sooner or later something would come your way. After finishing her iced tea, Cassandra left her sister to begin cooking the Riley clan's dinner.

As she stepped outside, Cassandra found herself shading her eyes against the intense brightness. Although she was becoming accustomed to the intensity of the sunlight here, stepping from the shaded interior of a building into the brilliance of a New Mexico afternoon still caused her a few moments of discomfort while her eyes adjusted. She'd occasionally experienced the same phenomenon in Illinois—coming out of a movie matinee, for example—but it hadn't been nearly as bad there. Slipping behind the wheel of her car, she discovered the upholstery was so hot that she was barely able to sit on it.

As she drove away from Susan's house, Cassandra passed a yellow compact, which she wouldn't have noticed at all if it hadn't been one of those odd two-tones created when portions of its body were replaced using parts of another color. In this case, a blue fender.

As she glanced at the car, her eyes met those of the woman sitting in the front seat—a woman in her late twenties with curly blond hair. The blond woman immediately looked away. Absently, Cassandra wondered why strangers went to such great lengths to avoid even the slightest eye contact with each other. But it was a question whose answer she had no real interest in, and it drifted from her consciousness as quickly as it had entered.

As she passed the Murphy house, Cassandra looked for Lisa and her friends, but she saw no sign of them. They were most likely in the backyard, she decided. When she pulled into the driveway of the house she was sitting, the yellow car with the blue fender drove by. Cassandra was only vaguely aware of it.

Wendy was stunned by the resemblance between the woman she'd just seen and the face in Clark's photo. She'd expected a similarity, but this was more than that. The woman she'd just seen *was* the woman in the picture.

But of course she wasn't. The woman in the photo was dead; if she were alive, she would be much older than the person who'd emerged from the house with the silver roof, then driven to another home in the next block. Still, it was Wendy's logical mind that kept her cognizant of this. There was another part of her mind, a less rational part, that told her it was the same woman, preserved unchanged from the time when the picture was taken.

And for Clark that was exactly what had happened.

His mother, looking exactly as she had when he was about thirteen, had suddenly been given back to him.

Wendy drove until she spotted a phone booth at a gas station. Parking her car beside the booth, she slipped into the enclosure and dialed her phone number. When Clark answered, she said, "I've found her. She stopped at the house I've been watching, then drove to another place in the next block. I think that's where she's staying, because she put her car in the garage. She used the automatic opener."

For several long moments, Clark said nothing, and when he finally did speak, his voice sounded whispery and distant. "Go back and keep watching," he said. "Let me know if she goes anywhere else. We have to find out what her schedule is."

Wendy did as instructed. Although she saw no further sign of the woman, just before she had to leave to get ready for work, a child came down the block and entered the house. A little girl with dark curly hair. The woman's daughter.

The next day, Wendy was back, watching the house. The morning passed, became the noon hour, then the afternoon, without any sign of the woman or child. It was another bright day, with the sun again turning the car's interior into an oven.

"Follow the child," Clark had told her.

And then he'd fallen silent. He'd sat in the living room, staring at nothing, and whatever had been going on inside his head had been private, not to be shared. Wendy had gone to work, returned, and still he was sitting, thinking, staring. He hadn't come to bed with her.

And Wendy had lain awake, worrying. She hated to see Clark focus all his attention inward like that. It made her afraid of losing him. He was so absorbed by his thoughts that he was unaware of her presence, and for Wendy that was a cold, empty, frightening feeling.

This morning, things had been better. Clark had conversed with her. It had been talk about the weather and things like that, but at least he'd been aware of her presence. In time, she hoped, he would tell her what he'd been thinking. For if two people were in love, *truly* in love, they openly shared themselves, holding nothing back.

Perspiration trickled down Wendy's cheek, and she blotted it away with a facial tissue, which was becoming soggy. She didn't have another. I'll sit here in this hot car for you, Clark, she thought. I'll do anything for you. But please don't do what every other man I've ever known has done to me. Please don't betray me.

Immediately, she tried to dissolve the thought, to make it go away as if it had never existed, for if Clark were to use her in this scheme of his and them dump her, Wendy would be devastated. She would be hurt as she had never been hurt before. And she knew that if Clark did that, she would probably kill him.

And then these things instantly vanished from her mind, because the child had just emerged from the house. Glancing disinterestedly toward Wendy, the girl with the dark curly hair skipped down the block. Wendy turned the car around and followed the kid. At the end of the block, the girl stopped, cautiously looking in both directions, then crossed the street and entered the walled backyard of the corner house. Wendy parked across the street.

A few minutes later, three girls—the one she had followed and two others—emerged from the backyard. They moved to the paved driveway, where they held a hurried discussion; then they began taking turns hopping on the driveway's cement surface. They were playing hopscotch.

That game was replaced by jumping rope, and then the girls disappeared into the backyard. Although Wendy could hear an occasional squeal from the other side of the wall, the girls did not reappear. When it was time for Wendy to leave, the girl with the dark curly hair was still in the walled backyard.

Over the next few days, Wendy continued to watch the child. On Saturday, the girl spent most of the day with her two friends. Prior to the weekend, they had only gotten together in the afternoon, presumably because of school, although as far as Wendy could tell, the girl she was watching had yet to be enrolled in school.

"I think kids are more set in their ways than grown-ups," she told Clark. It was the first of her two days off, and they were sitting on her couch. It was evening.

He nodded. "I've decided what I'm going to do."

Wendy waited, saying nothing.

"After you hear what I've got in mind, you may not want to be involved in it. If that's the case, I'll understand."

"I won't back out," she said softly. "I've given myself to you completely. Whatever happens, we're going to do it together. We'll always do everything together."

A tear ran down Clark's cheek. "I love you, Wendy. But I have to do this. I have to."

"I know," she said, her own eyes growing moist.

And then he told her what they would have to do. Although a part of Wendy was horrified, she didn't listen to that part, because it had nothing to offer but more of the same old empty life that had become intolerable. Instead, she concentrated on her love for Clark, on the knowledge that once this thing was behind them, they would be free to get on with their life together, both of them free forever of the past.

The thought that they might get caught did not occur to her, because she would not let it.

When Clark had finished explaining his plan, Wendy said, "And when all this is over with, we kill the woman."

"Yes," Clark said. "When everything else is done, we kill the woman."

"We start tomorrow."

"Yes, tomorrow."

They embraced.

Sitting on the kitchen floor, the boy watched his mother. A slender woman with dark curly hair, she stood at the counter, the only sound the constant chop-chop-chop as she cut up carrots and onions and other vegetables on a big cutting board. The boy had a toy truck, which he pushed silently back and forth. He knew better than to make noise.

Putting down her knife, the woman turned and moved to a metal cabinet that stood against the wall, her gaze passing over the boy as if he weren't there. But that was usual. She noticed him only when he did something to call attention to himself, and that normally meant he was in trouble.

He had seen other boys with their mothers. He'd seen the little looks of affection their moms gave them; he'd heard the warm comments their moms made, simple things like "You're going to be big and strong when you grow up" or "You've got your dad's blue eyes." Other kids took these things for granted. Sometimes they were even embarrassed by them.

The woman put the vegetables and some meat in a pot, which she put on the stove. Then she turned her attention to the ingredients she'd been putting into a large bowl. Working up his courage, the boy asked, "What are you making?"

"Cookies," his mother replied as she added another ingredient.

And suddenly the boy recalled a scene he'd witnessed at Billy's house. Billy had asked his mom the same question, and when she said cookies, he'd rushed over to her, hugged her, saying, "Can I have some when they're done?" Then, before she could answer, he'd quickly added, "I love you a lot, Mommy." His mom had stopped what she was doing, picked him up, kissed him. A little bit later, they'd all had milk and freshly made chocolate chip cookies.

Suddenly, the boy was sure that what had worked for Billy would work for him. He stood, hesitated, then stepped toward his mother, intending to do just as Billy had done. As he neared her, she turned, and for just an instant the boy thought she was going to hug him, but then he realized that she had the bowl in her hands, that she was moving it . . .

"Goddammit!" the woman screamed as she collided with the boy. And then something heavy hit his shoulder. There was a crash, and something thick and sticky was all over him, running down his neck seeping into his pants.

The boy was yanked forward, shaken. "What the hell's the matter with you?" his mother demanded. "Do you see what you did?"

The boy simply hung his head and waited for whatever was going to happen.

"Do you?" she screamed.

Abruptly, he was being dragged upstairs. Too afraid to consider what might happen, he simply surrendered to the superior force. Shoving him into the bathroom, his mother ordered him to take off his clothes. He did so mechanically while she turned on the shower. When he was fully undressed, steam was pouring from around the shower curtain.

"Get in," his mother ordered.

The boy hesitated. "T-too hot," he said, his voice a strange squeak.

The woman slapped him. "Get in."

Trying to find someplace his mind could go to escape what was happening, the boy obeyed, stepping under the scalding hot spray.

"Scrub," the woman commanded, handing him a washcloth.

The boy scrubbed. His skin, already reddened from the intense heat, grew still redder when he rubbed it with the cloth. The hot spray hurt, but instead of pain, the boy told himself it was love he was feeling, that it was penetrating his body, filling him. And he thought he heard a child crying, a boy. But how could that be, with so much love in this steamy space, so much hot, penetrating love?

But then he screamed, for looking at the spot he'd been rubbing with the washcloth, he saw white gleaming bone. The cloth was stripping his flesh from his body, peeling it back, globs of it falling, floating toward the drain. . . .

Again, he screamed.

"Clark!"

And then he wasn't in the shower anymore, but spinning in some surreal place between the shower and another world, another life.

"Clark! Wake up!" Wendy's voice. He fought his way toward it.

"It's okay," she said. "You were having a bad dream."

And Clark was in bed. Wendy was beside him. The dream faded. "It's okay," he said. "I'm awake now."

Wendy hugged him. "You're trembling," she said.

Suddenly feeling cold, he pulled his body tightly against hers, trying to borrow some of her warmth. It was a long time before he could go back to sleep.

19

STEP ON A CRACK, BREAK YOUR MOTH-
er's back, Lisa thought as she skipped along the sidewalk, carefully avoiding the joints in the cement. It was
a lovely sunny afternoon, but then every day here was
beautiful and sunny. As far as Lisa could tell, it never
rained, never even turned cloudy. Aunt Susan said sometimes there were dust storms in the spring, but Lisa
found it hard to believe that the weather here wasn't
always perfect.

She was on her way to Kelly Murphy's house. Mrs.
Murphy had promised to set up her home-video camera
so they could play TV cooking show. Mrs. Murphy was
going to let them actually make a cake, and Lisa was
sure that she and Kelly and Elizabeth were going to
have more fun than they'd ever had before in their lives.
It was all she'd talked about when she got home last
night. It was all she'd talked about today, too. Her mom
had probably been glad to see her leave so she could
have some peace.

Ahead, parked on her side of the street, was the small yellow car with the blue fender that she'd noticed around the neighborhood lately. As usual, it was just sitting there with a woman inside. Although Lisa found this mildly curious, she'd never considered what the woman might be doing. Grownups did a lot of things she didn't understand, and no doubt this was one of them. Absently, she wondered whether the woman could be a private detective, like on TV, watching a house or something like that. Probably not, she concluded, and dismissed the matter as unimportant.

Lisa was unable to decide what name to use for the cooking show. Lisa Jennings was an okay name, she supposed, but she wasn't certain it sounded like a TV name. The names she'd considered and dropped included Daniela Daniels, Jane Grace, and Tyra Taste. She guessed it pretty much came down to a choice between her real name and Crystal Cooke. But which one? Would she be able to decide, or would she simply blurt out one name or the other right there on the air?

And then she felt foolish for thinking of it as being on the air. It was just on the Murphys' viedotape recorder. It wasn't really on TV.

She was approaching the yellow car now, and for just a moment she thought she saw two heads through the rear window. But looking at the car more closely, she just saw one person inside, the same blond woman who was always there. Abruptly, the door opened, and the woman climbed out. Lisa hesitated, then continued walking toward her.

"Excuse me," the woman said, smiling. "Do you know where the Butlers live?"

Lisa shook her head. "I haven't lived here very long. I don't know anybody."

"Maybe you've seen their house. It's two stories, and it's yellow."

When Lisa reached the spot where the woman stood, she stopped. The house the woman was describing sounded more like the homes in Illinois than any of the places she'd seen around here. "No," she said, "I haven't seen any houses like that."

The woman shrugged. "I guess I'll never find it."

Uncertain whether the conversation was over, Lisa hesitated, then smiled politely—the way her mother had taught her—and started to continue on her way.

"Can I give you a lift?" the woman asked. "I'm going the same direction you are."

Instantly, her mother's admonition never to accept a ride with a stranger came crashing into her mind. "No, thank you," she said, and continued walking toward Kelly's house.

"Good for you," the woman said. "I bet your mother told you to never ride with a stranger. You're doing the right thing. Your mom will be proud of you."

Lisa relaxed. The woman understood. Her mom had probably told her the same thing. Or maybe she was a mom herself and had told her little girl never to ride with a stranger. From behind her came the sounds of a car door closing, an engine starting. As the car moved slowly past her, Lisa waved, and the woman waved back.

Suddenly, Lisa realized that the car's rear door was opening, and the notion started to take shape that she should shout a warning to the woman, tell her that her door had accidentally come open. But the thought never formed in Lisa's mind, and the words of warning were never spoken. Because she had just been yanked off her feet.

Stunned, she tried desperately to make sense out of what was happening to her. She heard the car door slam shut and the motor speed up. She was in the car. She had been pulled into it by someone, someone who still held her. She was partially on the seat, partially on some-one's lap.

And then her mind sorted everything out. She was being kidnapped. There was only one thing she could do, and she put every bit of strength she had into doing it.

Kicking as hard as she could, striking blindly with her arms, she screamed. Not words, just a loud, terrified, desperate shriek.

Suddenly, an arm clamped down tightly on her body, and a hand was clapped across her mouth. Lisa bit it.

"Goddammit!" a man said, and then something was stuffed into her mouth, reducing her scream to a muffled groan. With two hands now free, the man quickly subdued her. Held so tightly that she could neither kick nor hit her abductor, Lisa stopped fighting. Her eyes filled with tears, which ran down her cheeks. She could hear her heart beating madly, almost as if it were out of control.

Lying face up, she could see the man holding her, but through the tears he was just a blur. Lisa's mind, no longer in a total state of panic, began posing important questions. Why were these people doing this? What were they going to do to her? But these questions could only circle aimlessly inside her head, for she had no answers for them.

They drove for a while—Lisa was uncertain how long—and then the surface on which they were riding abruptly changed. The car began swaying and bouncing; small stones hit its underside. Since she had looked up and seen the blurred face of her captor, Lisa had kept her eyes closed, although she was too terrified to analyze why she was doing so. She only knew that she didn't want to look into the eyes of the man holding her. Finally, the car stopped.

The woman got out of the car first. Then, opening the door, the man picked Lisa up and carried her while he stepped from the car. When he put her down, he held her so that her back was to him. Lisa opened her eyes.

They were out in the country somewhere, but not the sort of country she'd been used to in the Midwest. This was a rocky and mountainous place with trees that looked more like bushes than trees. Piñons and junipers, her aunt had said they were called. The man pulled the gag from Lisa's mouth. It was a handkerchief.

The woman had just removed the car's license plate. Now she put on another one with a different number. "What do you want to do with the stolen plate?" she asked.

"We'll drop it in a garbage can somewhere," the man holding Lisa said.

Opening the trunk, the woman tossed in the plate, then took out a large cardboard box, which she put on the ground. Next she got a can of spray paint and some other things from the trunk and moved to the front of the car. Quickly, she taped some paper around the headlight; then she began painting the blue fender yellow.

"Hey, it matches pretty good," she said.

"It should," the man replied. "It's supposed to be exactly the same color that was put on at the factory."

"I know, but this car has spent a lot of years sitting in the sun, and that can really fade the paint."

"You see," the man said softly, "you were kidnapped in a yellow car with a blue fender. In a moment, this car will be solid yellow. And it has a different license number than the other car did. This way we're safe, just in case someone saw us when we pulled you into the car."

Lisa didn't understand why he was explaining all this. She wanted to ask him why they were doing this to her, but she was sure that if she opened her mouth to speak, no words would come out. The man was holding her by the shoulders. As he'd spoken to her, his grip had relaxed somewhat. Now it relaxed some more.

Lisa considered trying to wriggle out of his grasp, maybe kick him or something, then try to run. But she wasn't sure it would work, and she was afraid of what the man might do to her. The woman had finished painting the fender. It was a little shinier than the rest of the car, but otherwise it looked about the same. The man pushed Lisa over to the box, which was so large it had nearly filled the trunk.

"You're going to get into the box," the man said. "Then we're going for a drive, and when we stop we're going to carry the box with you inside. If you damage the box in any way or if you make any noise or do anything else to attract attention, I'm going to kill you."

He put his hand in front of her so she could see it. He was holding a gun.

"Do you understand?" he asked.

Lisa nodded. She still hadn't clearly seen the face of the man who was threatening to kill her.

"If you cause any trouble, I'll shoot the box full of holes. I'll kill you. And then I'll kill your mother, too. Do you understand?"

Again, Lisa nodded.

"I know where to find your mother. It would be real easy to use this gun on her. But there's no reason for anything like that to happen. Not if you're good."

Lisa stared at the box. She wanted to run, to dash into the trees that looked like bushes and get away from this man. Then she could warn her mother, and the police would protect them, and . . .

But the man would shoot her before she got more than ten feet away. And even if he missed, she had no idea which way to run. She had no idea where she was.

"Into the box," the man said.

"Can't," Lisa said, and then she realized she had spoken the word only in her mind.

"Get in," the man said, giving her a shove.

But Lisa was terrified of that box. Nothing was going to convince her to get into it. It was a cardboard coffin, and once she was enclosed within it, she would never see her mother or her friends or anything again.

Savagely, the man grabbed her and put her into the box on her side. "Remember what I said," he warned.

He flipped one of the cardboard flaps closed, then another, and another. Looking down at her through the narrow rectangle that remained open, he said, "Look at me."

Obediently, Lisa turned her head and looked into the face of her captor.

"If you're quiet, you and your mother will be all right. It's up to you." And then he closed the last flap, shutting out the light.

As Lisa lay in the darkness, smelling the cardboard, the box was lifted, then set down. There was a thunk. She was in the trunk. A moment later, the car's doors were opened and closed, the engine started, and Lisa was being gently rocked and shaken as the car made its way along a dirt road. The rocks thrown up by the tires sounded like bullets hitting the bottom of the car.

But Lisa was only vaguely aware of these things, because she kept seeing the face that had peered into the box before the fourth flap had been closed. It was a face she'd seen before. In Illinois.

It was the bad man.

Her face was wet with tears. Afraid that the wetness would seep through the cardboard and damage it, causing the bad man to kill her and her mother, Lisa tried to stop. But the harder she tried, the more she cried.

THE ATTRACTION

*   *   *

In the Chicago suburbs, ten-year-old Nicole Koneczny was standing over the kitchen garbage can into which the peelings were dropping as she pared potatotes. A few feet away, her mother was readying the meat for a pot roast.

"Is this enough?" Nicole asked, indicating the three peeled potatoes on the counter.

"For the Hulk," Grace Koneczny said. "Now you'd better peel some for the rest of us."

Getting another potato from the bag on the counter, Nicole began scraping off its skin with the peeler. She had known three potatoes weren't enough, but her thoughts were not on what she was doing. She was thinking about the promise she had made to the policeman.

Time had diminished its force somewhat; she no longer felt as bound by a pledge made to a stranger—even if the stranger was a police officer—as she did to the commitment she'd made to her parents. She had promised them that she would always be honest and open, that she would keep no secrets from them. That she had told them nothing about her encounter with the detective was a constant source of guilt.

Had she told them immediately there would be no problem. But if she did so now, she would have to explain why she had broken her promise to them. Her mom and dad would think she didn't trust them. And yet only telling them could make the guilt go away. Nicole didn't know what to do.

"Hey," her mom said, "you've scraped away half that potato. You're just supposed to get rid of the skin. We eat the other part."

"I'm sorry," Nicole said, and she found herself hoping that her mother would realize that something was wrong, that she'd look into her eyes and make her tell.

But her mom had shifted her attention back to the pot roast she was preparing.

And then it all rushed to the surface. Suddenly, Nicole was tingling with the desire to tell. She *had* to tell.

"Mom."

"Mmmm."

"I—" The words she'd been so anxious to speak only a second ago wouldn't come.

"What is it, honey?" her mother asked, turning to face her. And when Nicole didn't respond, her mom stopped preparing the pot roast and dropped to the girl's eye level. "Come on," she said gently. "Out with it."

"There's something I haven't told you about."

"What?" Grace Koneczny smiled. "You can tell me. You know that."

Nicole told her, and when she was finished, the guilt was gone. She should have done it much sooner; she knew that now. Still, there was one nagging doubt.

"Should I have done what the policeman said?" Nicole asked. "Was it okay that I told you?"

Her mother, who was frowning, didn't seem to have heard her.

"Mom?"

"What, honey?"

"Was it okay that I didn't do what the policeman said?"

"Yes. You did the right thing, Nicole. I'm glad you told me." She smiled, but it was a thing done mechanically, for she was still absorbed in her thoughts.

"Are you sure you're not mad at me?"

"I'm sure. You go ahead and finish peeling your potatoes. I'm going to make a phone call."

"Who are you going to call?"

"The police. I want to make sure that man was really a police officer."

Nicole watched as her mother looked up the number, then picked up the wall-mounted telephone's receiver and dialed. Now, she thought unhappily, the policeman will know I didn't keep my promise.

But then he might nōt have been a policeman. Although she was uncertain why a man would come around pretending to be a cop and asking questions about Mrs. Jennings, it was plain that her mother found that prospect very disturbing.

Forgetting about the potatoes she was supposed to be peeling, Nicole listened as her mom began talking to the police.

Cassandra was watching television in the den when the phone rang. Moving the recliner to the upright position, she got out of the chair and quickly moved to the table on which the phone had been placed. Its long cord was a messy tangle that Cassandra kept forgetting to straighten out. She lifted the receiver.

"Cassandra, it's me, Grace. I got your number from your sister."

"Grace, I'm sorry I haven't called you, but—"

Grace cut her off. "Is everything okay there?"

"Yes, everything's fine," Cassandra answered, an uneasy feeling settling over her. "Why?"

Grace was silent a moment, as if she were searching for the right words; then she said, "I, uh, I think there's a chance that man who was bothering you knows where you are."

"Clark?" A sudden emptiness seemed to hit Cassandra's stomach, then spread outward.

"Yes," Grace said. "I can't be sure, of course, but—but Nicole may have told him where you are. It wasn't her fault," Grace added quickly. "She thought he was a policeman."

"What—what happened?" Cassandra asked. Her legs felt weak, and she sat down in the small upholstered chair that stood by the table.

When Grace had finished telling her about the man who'd pretended to be a police officer and how Nicole had given him the information he sought, Cassandra said, "When was this?"

"Right after you left. Everything's okay there, isn't it? I mean, nothing's happened, has it?"

"We're fine. Lisa's playing with her new friends, and I'm sitting around the house, waiting for someone to call and offer me a job at one of the jillion places I've applied." And why was she saying these things? What good would it do her to have a job and what good would it do Lisa to have friends if Clark had found them? He'd ruin it. He'd ruin everything.

"Cassandra," Grace said slowly, "do you think that maybe he's watching your sister's house, that he doesn't know where you are?"

"He might not be here at all," Cassandra said. "Once he found out how far away we were, he might have given up." But she didn't believe that. Clark would follow her to China, to the North Pole, anywhere.

"That makes sense. It's possible that the guy wasn't even Clark." But the tone of her voice made it clear that Grace didn't believe that any more than Cassandra did.

When the conversation ended, Cassandra hung up the phone, and then she simply sat there, feeling numb. Her world, all her hopes and plans, had just been smashed. Instead of a paradise where she would find a job and Lisa would go to school and they'd live happily in the perpetual sunshine, New Mexico was just another place where a madman could torment her.

And then, with a terrifying jolt, she realized that Clark had done more than just torment her. He'd threatened to kill her daughter.

Lisa was at the Murphys' house, playing with her friends—playing TV cooking show with the Murphys' home-video equipment. Instantly, Cassandra was on her feet, scurrying toward the garage. She had to make sure Lisa was all right. In the garage, she pushed the button on the wall that operated the automatic door. A motor came to life, and the door began rising, letting the afternoon's glare into the dimness of the garage.

Cassandra was behind the wheel before she realized that she hadn't brought her purse, which meant she didn't have the car keys. And why was she going to drive, anyway, when the Murphys' house was only half a block away? Getting out of the car, she hurried into the brightness outside. And then she was racing toward the Murphys' house.

Reaching the end of the block, she dashed across the street and into the path of a van. The driver hit the brakes, then the horn, then swore at her. As she ran across the Murphys' front lawn, Cassandra realized she could have phoned to check on Lisa, but it was too late to worry about that now. Stepping onto the porch, she pressed the button that rang the doorbell. The door opened almost immediately.

"Yes?" a woman said. She was tall and thin, with long dark hair.

"Hi, uh, I'm Cassandra Jennings, Lisa's mother. Can I see my daughter a moment?"

"But . . ." the woman looked confused. "But Lisa never showed up. The other girls were wondering where she was. They tried to call her, but Mrs. Sellers' number is unlisted."

For a moment, Cassandra simply stared at the woman; then she turned and rushed away from the house. The only other place Lisa could be was Susan's house. And as she ran along the sidewalk, she tried to convince herself that Lisa was there, that she had decided to visit her aunt instead of playing with her friends today.

But she wouldn't have missed playing TV cooking show today for anything, something inside Cassandra said. But she didn't listen, because Lisa had to be at Susan's. The alternative was unthinkable.

Cassandra was out of breath when she reached her sister's door. She pushed in the doorbell button with all her strength, as if by doing so she could make it convey the urgency of the situation. To Cassandra, the few moments it took Susan to come to the door seemed like a lifetime.

"Susan," she said desperately as her sister opened the door, "tell me Lisa's here. Please tell me she's here." But she could tell by the look in her sister's eyes that Lisa wasn't inside. The color drained from Susan's face.

"She was supposed to be at Kelly Murphy's," Cassandra said. "But she's not there, and there's nowhere else she could be except—except here."

"Cassandra," Susan said, "I talked to Grace before she called you, so I know what she told you. You don't think . . ." She let her words trail off.

Cassandra just stood there, unable to think, unable to move.

"We'd better call the police," Susan said.

And that snapped Cassandra out of her daze. There was something she could do, some action she could take that might help. She dashed into the house and dialed 911.

20

CITY NOISES, LIKE BUSES AND MOTOR-
cycles and horns honking, were penetrating the car's
trunk and the cardboard carton in which Lisa lay on her
side with her legs pulled up.

The box was uncomfortable. It was too short for her
to stretch out in, and her legs were beginning to ache.
Also, every time the car hit a bump, she bounced. The
floor of the trunk on which her box rested was hard; her
only cushion was a single thickness of cardboard.

She didn't know why the bad man was doing this to
her. When she tried to figure it out, the only conclusion
she could come to was that the bad man did bad things
and that this was a bad thing. She wasn't even sure
there was a reason. Maybe bad men didn't need reasons; they just naturally did bad things.

Such thoughts were just confusing her. She was accustomed to having only minimal control of her life. All
she had to do was be alive, the world would take care of
the rest. Her mom or a teacher or someone would al-

ways be there to guide her, to see that she was okay. In a way, that was still her situation, but with one big difference. Instead of her mom or a teacher, the bad man would decide what was going to happen to her. The bad man or the woman helping him.

Shifting her position, Lisa realized that the bottom of the box was damp. For a few moments, she was unable to figure out where the wetness had come from, but then she realized that her panties were moist as well. She had wet her pants. Not much, probably not enough to seep through the box. Still, it seemed absolutely horrible to have wet her pants without even knowing it, and she began to cry, her body shaking as she sobbed.

Mommy, she thought, please help me. Please. Oh, please. But her thoughts weren't reaching her mother. They were trapped with her in the big cardboard box.

Abruptly, Lisa stopped crying, because the car had just stopped, and so had its motor. The doors opened, then slammed closed, the car shifting as the man and woman got out. Lisa heard the trunk being opened. Bright light shined in through the narrow cracks between the flaps at the top of her box.

"Remember what I said," the man whispered. "If you yell or try to get out of the box, I'll kill you. And then I'll kill your mother."

The box was lifted from the trunk, and Lisa was being carried. She heard car sounds—engines, doors slamming, brakes squeaking—and then the box was bumped against something, and the noises changed. There were people sounds now, footsteps, a man talking, other people talking, and from somewhere rock music. And there were odors here, too—popcorn giving way to cookies, then something sweet like candy or bubble gum.

"I wonder what the hell they bought," a man's voice

said, "an assemble-it-yourself piano? The box is big enough."

Lisa wanted desperately to kick her way out of the box, to tell these people that she was being kidnapped, that they had to save her from the bad man. But she didn't do it, for she believed the bad man when he said he'd shoot her, even with all these people around. He'd shoot her; then he and the blond woman would escape and kill her mom.

The sounds and smells of this place were familiar. She was pretty sure that she was in a shopping center, a mall. Which meant that the real world, the normal world, people who could help her, were separated from her by only the thickness of the cardboard. She could tear it with her hands.

Lisa wished the man would accidentally drop the box or that someone would trip him. She'd be thrown out, and it wouldn't be her fault. The man would have no reason to shoot her or kill her mom. It would be just an accident, not something she did on purpose.

The man stopped and said, "There's no chance anyone will be down there, is there?"

"I told you, it's the women's locker room, and I'm the only woman left on the security staff, and only security guards have lockers."

A door was opened, and Lisa had to brace herself as the box tilted in one direction, then another. Because the man had used the words "down there," Lisa knew she was being carried down some stairs. At the bottom, the box was set down a moment; then another door was opened, and the carton was moved again, but only a few feet this time. It was put down again, a door closed, and then the flaps were suddenly opened. The bad man and the woman were looking down at her.

"You can get out of the box," the man said.

Lisa did so. She was in a large room with cement walls and floor. In places, things like big screws were sticking out of the floor. There were a lot of pipes. Some ran along the ceiling; others stuck up from the floor along the wall. While Lisa had been taking in her surroundings, the woman had left the room. Now she returned with a big wrench in her hand. The man took it from her and began doing something to one of the pipes that stuck out of the floor.

"Okay, that's got it," he said after a moment. "When the time comes, all we'll have to do is turn on the valve."

The two of them looked at Lisa for a moment; then the woman said, "You're going to have to stay here. Later on, I'll bring you something to eat."

With that, they opened the door and left. Lisa could hear the door being locked from the other side, and then there was only silence. If they were saying anything, the words didn't penetrate the cement walls or the thick door.

For quite a while, Lisa simply stood there, staring at the cement on which she stood. Although she felt tears welling up, she didn't cry. She supposed that you could only cry so much, even in a situation like this. After a while, you ran out of tears.

Finally, she began to explore her prison. The door was metal, but when she tapped on it, there was almost no noise, as if the inside of it were made of feathers or something like that. To the left of the door were two light switches. One was already pushed up. She hesitated, knowing switches didn't always do what you expected them to, but then she flipped up the other one. Above her, more lights came on.

Leaving the door, she moved to the pipe the man had done something to. The other pipes sticking up from the floor all had covers screwed onto them, but this one didn't. The pipe was about two feet high; she bent over and looked into it, seeing only a black hole. She smelled just the hint of a familiar odor, but she was unable to identify it.

Lisa walked through the rest of the room, but there wasn't much to see. It was just a big empty place. As she sat down with her back against the wall, Lisa recalled something the woman had said. Although Lisa didn't recollect the exact words, they'd given her the impression that the woman worked here. It had been a mistake to let her hear that; it was something she could tell the police.

And then she remembered a show she'd seen on TV. A man had kidnapped a woman. But he'd been careless; he'd let her learn too much about him. And that was when the woman had realized that he was going to kill her. He was being careless because it didn't matter.

Lisa wished she hadn't recalled that show. Suddenly, the tears that hadn't wanted to come were streaming down her face. She wasn't supposed to be here. She was supposed to be playing with Kelly and Elizabeth. She was supposed to be making a cake while pretending that it was a TV cooking show.

Lisa wondered whether she would ever see Kelly and Elizabeth again. She wondered whether she would ever see her mom again. Or her dad back in Wisconsin.

It was so quiet in the cement room that her sobs echoed off the walls and she could hear her tears when they hit the dusty floor.

"Have you checked the house you're staying in recently to make sure she hasn't come home?" the detective asked. A tall woman, she had brown shoulder-length hair and a lightly freckled face with a turned-up nose. Her name was Dianne Gomez, and she sat in an upholstered chair in Susan's living room. Cassandra and Susan sat on the couch.

"She's not there," Susan said. "We drove over there to check while we were waiting for you. And we left a note telling her to call us here, just in case she shows up."

"She won't call," Cassandra said. "Clark's got her. He found out where we are and came after us." Her voice sounded distant and tinny, as if it were coming over one of those string-and-tin-can phones kids made.

Like her life, the room and the people in it seemed to whirl around her, out of control. She could see it was stationary, of course; neither the couch nor the walls nor the detective was moving. And yet a part of her mind knew it was floating, spinning, caught up in the madness that had followed her here from Illinois, the madness that had just swallowed up her child.

Lisa, she thought. Lisa, Lisa, Lisa. The word was dragged away by the currents of madness, sucked into the maelstrom.

Susan said, "We've phoned Mrs. Schultz next door, Elizabeth's mother. And Mrs. Murphy, too. They all know to get in touch with us right away if Lisa shows up."

"Can you think of anywhere else she might be?" the police officer asked.

Both Cassandra and Susan shook their heads.

Gomez frowned. "The child has only been missing a few hours. Sometimes kids get it into their minds to do things. On impulse, they'll decide to explore a new neighborhood or investigate some construction project a few blocks away. So it's possible that—"

"No," Cassandra said. "Lisa never does things like

that. And she was really anxious to play with Kelly and Elizabeth today. They were going to use the Murphys' video equipment and put together a cooking show. She was real excited about it.''

The detective nodded. ''I understand your concern. I just wanted you to know that sometimes in these cases—even when the parents insist their child would never do anything like that—the kid shows up after a while, completely unaware of all the commotion his or her absense has caused.''

Cassandra tried as hard as she could to make herself believe that Lisa might be out exploring the neighborhood or something like that, but she was unable to do so. ''Clark's got her,'' she said. ''You don't know him. He's insane. And he threatened to kill her.''

''We've got a patrol unit checking the neighborhood right now,'' Gomez said. ''And we'll get in touch with the police department in Illinois. Maybe they can tell us whether this Clayton has left for New Mexico or whether he's still there. If he has left town, we'll try to get a picture of him.''

Is that all they're going to do? Cassandra wondered. Don't they understand that Lisa's life is at stake? ''Aren't—aren't you going to ask the neighbors if they've seen anything?''

''Of course we are. As soon as the patrol unit has covered the neighborhood, it will report back to me, and we'll begin going from door to door. We'll do everything we can to locate your daughter.''

''I'm sorry. I . . .'' Uncertain what she was going to say, Cassandra let her words trail off.

Fixing her eyes on Cassandra's, the police officer said, ''Listen, I've got a little girl of my own, eight years old. I know how I'd feel if she was missing.'' In her lap was a notebook in which she'd been jotting down some of the things Cassandra told her. She studied it a moment, then said, "Where is Lisa's father?"

"In Wisconsin. We're divorced."

"Was there a custody dispute?"

"No. I guess John figured I'd get custody anyway, so he didn't push it."

"How did he feel about your taking your daughter to another part of the country?"

"He was a little upset, but—but you're not thinking that . . ." Completing the sentence was unnecessary.

"It's very common," the detective said. "You'd be surprised how many child abductions turn out to be the work of whichever parent didn't get custody."

"John wouldn't do it," she said. "It's Clark. Clark has Lisa."

"It's still something we have to check out. Do you have his address?"

Cassandra gave it to her. Gomez asked a few more questions, which Cassandra answered mechanically. Then the doorbell rang, and a uniformed policeman entered, informing them that a search of the neighborhood had turned up no trace of the missing child.

"Okay," Gomez said. "Let's start the door-to-door."

After the officers left, Susan took Cassandra's hand. "I think you should stay here tonight," Susan said gently. "I don't think you should be alone."

Cassandra shook her head. "I've got to be there, just in case she does come home. And in case the—in case Clark tries to contact me."

"The number over there's unlisted. If anyone calls, they'll have to call here."

Cassandra didn't respond. What difference did it make where she spent the night? How could they sit here calmly discussing something so unimportant while Lisa was in the hands of a madman?

Lisa, where are you? Cassandra asked, trying to reach out with her mind and locate her daughter. Mommy's here, she thought. Mommy loves you.

Susan was holding her hand, looking at her sadly, and Cassandra was going to cry. But before the tears could start, she recalled Detective Gomez's words: "You'd be surprised how many child abductions turn out to be the work of whichever parent didn't get custody." Suddenly, she knew that was what had happened. John had taken Lisa. Grabbed her and taken her back to Wisconsin. Yes, Cassandra thought, that's it. That has to be it.

Quickly standing up, she said, "Is it all right if I use your phone? I have to call John." She was only vaguely aware of the high-pitched, almost-hysterical note in her voice.

"Of course it's all right," Susan said.

Cassandra headed for the kitchen; it was the closest room with a phone. Please let it be John, she thought. Please. And then she realized how absurd it would be under normal circumstances to be hoping desperately that your former husband had kidnapped your child. Cassandra pushed the thought away. It was meaningless.

Glancing at the kitchen clock as she dialed, Cassandra realized that it wasn't five o'clock yet, that John—if he was in Wisconsin at all—wouldn't be home from work. But it didn't matter. She would talk to Janice. If John had kidnapped Lisa, she would force Janice to admit it.

"Hello," a man said.

"John?" Cassandra was confused. He shouldn't be there. But then she realized that if John had flown to New Mexico to snatch Lisa, he wouldn't have gone to work today. And he'd had plenty of time to fly back to Milwaukee.

"Cassandra?"

"Yes, it's me. Why aren't you at work?"

"What?"

"Why aren't you at work? It's not five o'clock yet."

"What are you talking about? It's nearly six."

Six? Of course, the time zone. She'd forgotten about the time difference. "I . . ."

The words died unspoken. John didn't take Lisa. She was just grabbing at anything, no matter how unlikely.

"Is something wrong, Cassandra?"

"Yes," she said weakly, and then she told him what had happened. "I think it's him, John. I think it's Clark."

For a long moment, John was silent; then he said, "There's still time for her to turn up. We don't know for sure that she's been kidnapped yet."

"That's what the police said."

Suddenly, John exploded. "Damnit, Cassandra, if you hadn't taken her out there, none of this would have happened. Why didn't you send Lisa up to stay with me until you had this thing settled? She would have been safe with me. Or didn't you care about that? Whose welfare were you thinking of, Cassandra, hers or yours?"

Cassandra stared at the portion of the phone that was attached to the wall. A part of her was furious with him for saying what he just did, and yet another part of her agreed with him. It seemed to say, *It's your fault; it's your fault; it's your fault.*

No, she thought. No.

Your fault. Selfish, selfish, selfish. Had to keep the child with you.

"Cassandra," John said. "I'm sorry that I—"

She hung up.

As she walked slowly back into the living room, she began to cry. Susan helped her to the couch, and Cassandra put her head on her sister's shoulder. Then the tears came in earnest, her body shaking uncontrollably as she sobbed.

THE ATTRACTION

*   *   *

Lisa sat with her back against the wall, staring at her hands. She shivered. It was chilly in the cement room. The cold seemed to seep in through the walls and floor. Lisa guessed that because nobody ever came here, the place was unheated.

Although the shorts and T-shirt she had on had been perfect for a warm afternoon, they didn't do much to keep out the chilly dampness of her prison. I wish I had a coat, she thought. And then Lisa immediately cancelled the wish. She didn't want a coat, because she'd only need one if she was going to stay here, and what she really wished—wished with every bit of intensity she could put into it—was that the door would open and her mother would be there. And the police, who would have the bad man and the woman in handcuffs.

The bad man and the *bad* woman, she amended. If the woman was helping him do this, then she was bad, too.

Lisa wasn't wearing a watch. She wondered whether it was suppertime yet. If not, then her mom was probably watching TV or reading, unaware that anything was wrong. She'd merely assume that her daughter was at the Murphys', playing with Kelly and Elizabeth. Lisa shuddered. She didn't want to think about the possibility that no one knew she was missing, that no one was looking for her.

And she realized suddenly that in this windowless cement place she couldn't even tell whether it was day or night. If the bad man kept her here for a long time, before long she wouldn't know what day it was. She wouldn't know when it was her birthday—or Christmas.

But then in here it wouldn't matter.

From above her came a loud thunk that startled her. Looking up, she saw the cement ceiling, pipes, the electric lights. But the sound had reached her, broken the silence of this place, and if she could hear that thunk, then whoever made it might be able to hear her.

"Help!" she screamed.

Silence.

"Help me! I'm in here! I'm—I'm in a cement room downstairs!"

Silence.

And then she just screamed, that loud, piercing shriek that always made her mother cringe. She kept it up until she was too hoarse to continue. Then, with tears running down her cheeks, Lisa stared up at the ceiling, listening.

For a while, the only sound was her rapid breathing; then the room was filled with the noise of her sobs.

Later—Lisa was uncertain how much later—the bad woman brought her an Arby's and a Coke in a paper bag. The woman stared at her for a few moments, then left without staying a word. At first, Lisa wasn't going to eat the food, but eventually the smell of it made her change her mind. It tasted as good as it smelled. And Lisa hated herself for enjoying something given to her by the bad people.

21 SITTING IN THE KITCHEN OF THE SELlers house, Cassandra stared at her half-full cup of coffee. Susan sat across the table from her. Neither of them had slept last night.

Despite her sister's attempts to change her mind, Cassandra had spent the night in this house. Had she stayed at Susan's, she would have constantly worried that Clark would leave a message here—or that Lisa would somehow return. As it turned out, no attempt was made to contact her at this house or at Susan's. And Lisa was still missing.

Unwilling to let Cassandra be alone, Susan had stayed with her. Everyone wanted to help. Rob, who hadn't gone to work, was at his house just in case Clark tried to make contact there. The two boys were out on their bicycles, asking people in the neighborhood if they'd seen anything. The police had done that yesterday, discovering no witnesses to Lisa's abduction.

What had happened yesterday afternoon? Lisa would

never willingly go anywhere with a stranger; Cassandra was sure of that. So how had Clark done it? Had he driven by in a van, or something like that, and yanked the unsuspecting child inside?

And where was she now? Had he hurt her? Where had she spent the night? Had she had anything to eat? Questions whose answers she couldn't even guess at. And lurking in the shadows of her mind was a dark, menacing threat that was more important than all the questions.

"I'm going to kill the child."

No! Cassandra thought, forcing the image of Clark's pasted-together note from her mind. It can't happen. I won't let it happen.

Abruptly, she stood up purposefully, as if she were about to take some action that could rescue Lisa. But there was absolutely nothing she could do that would help her daughter, nothing at all. Susan was staring at her with red worried eyes.

Cassandra said, "I—I just couldn't stand sitting here anymore, doing nothing."

"It's in the hands of the police," Susan said. "I'm afraid that's all we can do, sit and wait."

"I feel so helpless, so—so useless. My daughter's in the hands of a lunatic, and all I can do is sit here and drink stale coffee."

Looking out the window above the sink, Cassandra saw that it was a sunny morning, but then it was always sunny here. The one time she'd seen it rain, a cloud had passed overhead, a patch of dark fluff in an otherwise clear sky, and it had rained big drops for maybe five minutes before the sun was out once more.

Was Lisa somewhere where she could see the sun? Or was she in some dark prisonlike place? Detective Gomez had been here earlier, but about all she could say was that they were working on it. The picture of Lisa that Cassandra had given her had been reproduced and distributed to all patrol shifts. Known child molesters were being rounded up and questioned.

Cassandra had insisted that no local pedophile had abducted Lisa; Clark Clayton from Illinois had done it. That, too, Gomez had said, was being checked out.

As Cassandra looked out the window, one of the postal service's white jeeps with the red-and-blue stripe went down the block, reminding her that one of her jobs while she stayed here was to bring in Marge Sellers' mail. She headed for the front porch.

In the mailbox were a number of letters, most of which appeared to be bills, and a gardening magazine. She started to add the mail to the growing pile on the dining-room table, and then she hesitated. Clark could use the mail to communicate with her. Suddenly, she was sure there would be a letter from him here. She began flipping through them. An electric bill, another from Wards, a letter from Marge Sellers' bank . . .

And suddenly there it was. A letter addressed to her, the address on the envelope formed by pasting letters cut from magazines. And she realized that she hadn't really believed that this would be here. It had been desperate wishing, nothing more.

"Susan," she cried, ripping open the envelope with shaking hands.

"What?" Susan said as she hurried into the room.

"It's—it's from him."

"Wait. Shouldn't you let the police open that?"

But it was too late, because Cassandra had already removed the letter from the envelope. Made of letters pasted to the page, the message was brief:

The child will die at 3 P.M. on Friday.

Friday was three days away.

"If it is this Clayton guy, do you think it could be a bluff?" Detective Gomez asked. She and Cassandra and Susan were in Marge Sellers' living room, the police officer in a chair, the sisters on the couch.

"There's no *if* about it," Cassandra said. "It's him. The note was made the same way. I know it's him."

The police officer nodded. "Would he hurt the child?"

Cassandra didn't know what to say. Clark was a madman. How did you predict the actions of a madman? She considered what she knew about Clark and tried to make her confused, terrified mind function. Finally, she said, "I think—" She shuddered, and when she spoke again, she said, "I think he'll really do it."

A tear rolled down her cheek, clung to her chin a moment, then dropped. Another followed it, and she wiped it away. Going to pieces wouldn't help. She had to maintain her composure.

"I've been in touch with the police in Illinois," Gomez said. "They can't tell us anything about Clayton's whereabouts, but they're wiring us a photo of him that they got from his former employer. I think he's the best lead we've got, so I'm going to give both his photo and the child's to the media. Maybe someone will have seen one of them."

"We've—we've only got three days," Cassandra said. Her voice had that distant, tinny sound again, as if the words were coming from one of those old phonographs with the big horn.

"We'll do everything we can to find her," the police officer said. Her tone was gentle, reassuring.

But Cassandra wasn't reassured. Three days. It wasn't enough time. Clark was smart, too smart to let them find Lisa in so short a time.

"What?" Cassandra said, suddenly realizing that the detective had been talking to her.

"I need to know how many people touched this." She held up the plastic bag in which she'd put the letter and envelope.

"I didn't touch it," Susan said. "Only Cassandra did."

"I'll have to fingerprint you," Gomez said, looking at Cassandra, "so I can eliminate your prints and concentrate on any others we find."

"There won't be any others," Cassandra said. "He never leaves prints on his notes."

The detective nodded. "We'll see. Oh, I almost forgot to tell you. The police in Illinois have established that your ex-husband was there all day yesterday. He's been eliminated as a suspect."

"I wish it was him," Cassandra said.

"Me, too," Susan said. "At least we know he'd never hurt Lisa."

Gomez stood up, picking up the plastic bag. "Your ex-husband phoned us this morning. He wanted to find out what the status of the investigation was."

Cassandra had wondered why he hadn't called her to check on what was happening. Now she knew.

"He says he's going to fly out here. I thought you'd better know so you can be prepared."

Leave me alone, John, Cassandra thought. Just leave me alone. Then she pushed the thought aside. What John did was unimportant.

"Find Lisa," she said, looking into the detective's eyes. "Please find her . . . before it's too late."

When Gomez left, Cassandra remained on the couch, using all her willpower to hold herself together. I have to keep my wits about me, she thought. I have to be strong. So I can help Lisa.

She was trembling.

*　　*　　*

Because it was the only thing she had to put between herself and the cold cement floor, Lisa had slept in the cardboard box in which she'd been carried here. While asleep, she had kicked the end out of it. Although she'd turned the carton so that the bent and torn end was against the wall, the damage was still apparent, and she was afraid the bad people would be angry when they saw it.

She was sitting with her back against the wall again. That was all there was to do here—sit and stare and think. And when she thought, it was always about how afraid and miserable she was. She wondered whether she would ever get out of here, whether she would ever see sunshine again, whether the bad people were going to hurt her.

At least she wasn't crying as much anymore. It didn't do any good to cry. It only made her feel worse.

Because there was no toilet in the cement room, Lisa had been relieving herself in a corner, which she thought of as "the stinky place." It was another thing that might make the bad people angry. When the bad woman had brought her the Arby's, Lisa had wanted to ask her where she should go to the bathroom, but she'd been afraid to speak.

What would they do when they saw the stinky corner, the broken box? The bad man had already threatened to kill her and her mom if she hurt the box. Closing her eyes, Lisa tried to make up a daydream of her having fun in some happy place. At first, she was unable to pull herself away from the cold, hard floor of the cement room, but then her mind abruptly filled with bright colors, and she was skipping along in a cartoonlike place, an *Alice in Wonderland* kind of place.

"Wait!" Lisa shouted to the purple teddy bear–like

creature that had just run across the path she was following. But the creature didn't stop, and Lisa ran after it, dashing into the pink-and-yellow forest.

That evening, when Wendy brought the girl another meal of fast food, she also brought her some blankets. Opening the door, she found the child sitting with her back against the wall. The girl seemed unaware of Wendy's presence. Wendy set the bag containing a hamburger and fries at the child's feet. The girl's eyes focused on it, but she didn't speak.

"I brought you some blankets," Wendy said, putting them down beside the paper bag.

The child said nothing.

Wendy felt sorry for her. Her dark hair a mass of tangles, the kid looked lost, confused, forlorn. She had done nothing to deserve what was being done to her. She was an innocent caught up in a game being played by others.

The child was ignoring the food and blankets. Wendy turned to go, and abruptly she had the urge to let the girl go, to hold the door open and tell her to run home to her mother. Although Wendy had been party to the kid's abduction, no harm had come to the girl; no ransom had been sought. And Wendy would be credited with letting her go. With a good lawyer . . .

But Wendy let the thought trail away uncompleted, for there was no chance she would do that. Clark had decided that the girl would be used to punish the mother. And Clark had to resolve this thing that was destroying him. He had to be free of it. I love him, Wendy thought. I can't betray him.

Could they pull it off, get away without being caught? Wendy decided not to try answering that. Her commitment to Clark was total. Wendy's mother had never interfered, even when her husband had come home and forced their daughter to have sex with him. Although she'd hated what Wendy's father did, she'd stood by her man; she hadn't turned against him. And Wendy would do the same; she would stand by Clark, no matter what. It was what she believed in.

The only thing that could make her turn against him was if he started hitting her, as her two husbands had done. Wendy would never let anyone beat her again. But she didn't think Clark would ever do that. Clark loved her too much to ever do anything like that.

"I broke the box," the girl said, suddenly breaking the silence.

"What?"

"The box. I broke it."

Wendy turned, spotting the large carton in which Clark had carried the child through the busy shopping center. One end was ripped and bowed. For a moment she was unable to understand why the child was telling her this, and then she remembered Clark's threat.

"We're through with it," Wendy said. "It doesn't matter." Suddenly, she found herself wanting to go to the child, hug her, console her. But she knew better than to do that. If she allowed herself to become attached to the girl, she might want to betray Clark.

The girl's eyes met Wendy's then, and Wendy saw just one thing there. Intense hatred. I'm sorry, Wendy thought. I'm sorry.

She locked the door as she left the room.

Feeling drained and numb, Cassandra sat in Marge Sellers' living room the next morning, staring at the carpet. Susan, who'd spent the night with her again, had gone home to get the morning paper, which was supposed to be carrying photos of both Lisa and Clark Clayton.

She had managed to get a few hours of fatigue-induced sleep last night. She had to sleep—she knew that—and yet she felt vaguely ashamed for having done so. How could she sleep while her daughter was in the hands of a maniac?

Detective Gomez was keeping her informed, but the police officer had nothing encouraging to report. As Cassandra had predicted, there had been no fingerprints on the note that had come in the mail—except for Cassandra's own, of course. All shifts had been issued the photos of Clark and Lisa, and officers were checking out motels in the area to see whether any desk clerks recognized the man or child. Police in Illinois were still unable to determine Clark's whereabouts, and they hadn't learned of any friends or relatives in New Mexico with whom Clark might be staying.

And John had arrived. Detective Gomez had given her the name of the motel at which he was staying, but Cassandra had no intention of contacting him. She had decided she didn't give a damn whether her former husband blamed her for what happened. His opinions were unimportant. *He* was unimportant.

The only thing that mattered was that there were only two days left. Two days before a madman killed her daughter. It was no bluff. She knew Clark had Lisa, and Clark would do what he'd threatened to do. And then she winced. How did she know he hadn't already—

Abruptly breaking the thought off, she forced it back into whatever dark place in her subconscious it had escaped from and slammed the door on it. I won't even consider that, she thought. I won't.

The doorbell chimes startled her. Going to the window, she pulled the curtain aside and peeked out, seeing

Susan with the paper under her arm. Cassandra opened the door.

"It's on the front page," Susan said as she stepped inside. She handed the paper to Cassandra.

Below its fold were side-by-side photos of Lisa and Clark. Cassandra had taken the picture of Lisa about six months ago. The girl was scrubbed and neat and wearing her best dress, a frilly yellow thing that she'd outgrown right after the picture was taken. The occasion had been the wedding of a woman who'd worked with Cassandra at the insurance company. The woman's name was Laura, and a month after the wedding she'd announced she was pregnant and quit her job.

And Cassandra wondered why she was thinking about these things. She shifted her attention to the photo of Clark.

Dressed in a business suit, he was looking at the camera with a pleasant, intelligent look on his face. This was a professional photograph, probably some official company picture. And the Clark who stared out at her from the newspaper was a younger Clark, probably in his late twenties.

Still studying the paper, Cassandra sat down on the couch. The accompanying story was brief, saying only that the authorities were asking for help in locating seven-year-old Lisa Jennings, who had apparently been abducted while on the way to visit some friends in Albuquerque's Northeast Heights, and that thirty-three-year-old Clark Clayton might be involved. Detective Gomez had promised that she wouldn't let any reporters know where to locate Cassandra, and apparently she had kept her word.

Cassandra's eyes returned to the two photos. She could feel her mood shift as she looked from one to the other. When she was looking at Lisa's photo, her eyes would grow moist as she recalled the yellow dress, Lisa's near miss as she attempted to catch the bridal bouquet, Lisa's face covered with wedding-cake crumbs . . .

And then, when she switched her attention to Clark's photo, her eyes immediately began to dry, and a searing lump seemed to develop in her stomach, its heat radiating outward, spreading throughout her body. It was rage, hatred. It was the overpowering desire to hurt Clark Clayton.

Suddenly unable to look at either photograph, Cassandra closed her eyes and rested her head on the back of the couch. Susan sat down beside her.

"They'll find her," Susan said. "Those pictures will help."

Cassandra nodded. She wanted to believe that. She desperately wanted to believe that. "I—"

She was interrupted by the phone. Instantly, she was on her feet, dashing into the kitchen. She had the receiver in her hand before the third ring had been completed.

"Mrs. Jennings, this is Detective Gomez. We've picked up someone who matches the description of Clark Clayton. We need you to come down and make a positive identification. A unit's on the way to pick you up right now."

22

THE UNIFORMED OFFICER DRIVING THE blue-and-white police car took her downtown, then turned onto a concrete down ramp that led beneath a building. Inside, he took her along a maze of corridors, finally opening a door and saying, "In here, ma'am," and Cassandra found herself alone in a room containing a wooden table and a few chairs. She sat down on one of the chairs.

The police had him. They had Clark. Now they could make him tell them where Lisa was. Unable to remain seated, Cassandra stood and began pacing the room. Now that he was in the hands of the police, he'd have to tell them. The sooner she made her identification, the sooner they would be able to make him reveal what he'd done with Lisa.

She was unwilling to even consider the possibility that it wasn't Clark. Detective Gomez had said she needed her to make a "positive identification." It had to be he.

Cassandra sat down again. After a few moments, she

was ready to resume pacing, but then the door opened, and Detective Gomez stepped into the room.

"Two officers on routine patrol spotted him at a shopping mall that hadn't opened yet," she said. "When they noticed that he looked like the photo of Clayton, they tried to stop him for an ID check, and he ran. They had to chase him through the mall and into the parking lot, but they finally got him. He wasn't carrying any identification."

"Has he said anything about Lisa?" Cassandra asked anxiously.

The detective shook her head. "He won't even tell us his name."

"Is—is it him?"

"That's why you're here, to answer that question."

Gomez, who had remained standing, moved to a curtain that covered one wall. Taking hold of the draw cord, she said, "He'll be behind one-way glass. You'll be able to see him, but he won't be able to see you. If it's him, I'll get some other officers in here to act as witnesses, and then I'll ask you to repeat your identification. You ready?"

Cassandra nodded, and the police officer drew the curtain aside, revealing another room, in which a man was seated at a small table. Rising so she could get a better view, Cassandra stared at the wiry frame, the thinning dark hair, the blue eyes. As she watched, he got up, glanced around the room, then moved casually to the glass, peering into it, moving his face within inches of it. Cassandra stepped back.

"To him it's a mirror," Gomez said. "He can't see you."

Then he stepped back a pace, grinned, and gave the finger to the two women watching him. Cassandra drew in her breath.

"He's just guessing," the detective said. "He suspects that he's being observed, but he really can't see us—honest."

Cassandra wasn't convinced, but it didn't matter. Only confirming the man's identity mattered. "It's not him," she said.

Gomez sighed. "Damn."

"It looks like him. It looks a lot like him. But I've never seen this guy before."

For a long moment, both women stared at the man who wasn't Clark Clayton. Two days, Cassandra thought. And she knew the police had been lucky to spot even this Clark look-alike. To find the real Clark in just two days—to find Lisa—was a nearly impossible task.

As if reading her thoughts, Gomez said, "Hang in there, okay? If we found this one, we can find the right one."

Cassandra nodded. She would hang in there. What else was there for her to do?

Abruptly, the door opened, and a man stepped into the room, a man Cassandra instantly recognized and definitely did not want to see. It was John.

"I asked you to wait out there, Mr. Browning," Gomez said, clearly irritated.

"Is it him?" John asked, glancing at the one-way glass, through which the unidentified man could be seen pacing.

"No," Gomez said. She drew the curtain.

And then they stared at each other. Finally, John broke the silence. "Cassandra, I'd like to have a word with you."

"I have nothing to say to you, John."

"Our daughter's been kidnapped. Don't you think this would give us something to talk about?"

Gomez said, "I've got to tend to our friend in the next room. You can stay in here if you want to."

The detective left, and Cassandra was alone with the man she'd loved once, the man who'd fathered her daughter, the man with whom she'd shared her life and her most intimate feelings.

John was the quintessential average man. Neither tall nor short, heavy nor slim, he had light brown hair and brown eyes, a face that was neither long nor round. There was absolutely nothing unique about him. And Cassandra wondered why she had never realized this before.

"All right, John," she said. "Talk." Where had all this hostility come from? Maybe it had always been there and it just took something like this to bring it out. Cassandra pushed the matter from her mind. Right now the complexities of her relationship with her ex-husband were insignificant.

"We have to put aside our differences, Cassandra. We have to work together to help our daughter."

"John, nothing we can do is going to make any difference. It's in the hands of the police."

He studied her silently, his sad expression indicating that he knew she was right.

"John—"

"When this is over," he said, interrupting her, "if we get Lisa back, I'm going to court and ask that custody be reconsidered."

"Thanks for picking such a wonderful time to tell me," Cassandra replied sarcastically.

His eyes grew hard. "I'm not concerned about your feelings, Cassandra. If Lisa hadn't been with you, none of this would have happened. It's as simple as that."

He glared at her a moment, driving home the point; then he turned and strode from the room. Why did he

seem so intent on using this to hurt her? She didn't
know. She only knew that he was hurting her, hurting
her with the truth. For had Lisa been with him and not
her, none of this would have happened.

Damn you, John, she thought as tears came to her
eyes. Damn you, damn you, damn you.

It was mid-morning when Clark awoke. Wendy lay
beside him, her slow, heavy breathing telling him that
she was still sound asleep. Last night, as on the night
following the kidnapping, they had made love repeatedly
and furiously. Sitting up, he watched her sleep for a
moment, then got out of bed.

After getting dressed, he put water and coffee in Wendy's electric percolator and plugged it in. Then he slipped
out of the apartment. He wanted to get a newspaper.

Clark considered using Wendy's car; then, deciding
that he needed the exercise, he strolled past the now-all-
yellow compact and turned right when he reached the
narrow two-lane street. This part of the city, he'd discovered, was called the Valley, because it stretched
north and south along the Rio Grande. The arrangement
of the streets and buildings seemed haphazard. Many of
the houses were old, probably made of adobe; a few had
roofs made of sheet metal.

It was a breezy day. A discarded candy wrapper
scooted across his path. Since they had taken the kid,
Clark had gone out every morning and evening to get the
newspapers. So far there hadn't been a word about the
missing girl. He was unable to see the television news,
because Wendy's old set had konked out. But that didn't
worry him too much, since the papers were much more
thorough than the TV stations. If the story had come
out, the papers would be sure to have it.

So why was there nothing about the abduction of the

girl? The papers wouldn't pass up a story like that, he was sure. The only answer was that the police had kept the story from getting out. He wondered why.

The drugstore where he'd been buying the papers was about three blocks from Wendy's place. Stepping inside, he turned to the racks by the cash register, finding them empty.

"No newspapers this morning?" he asked the heavy-set clerk.

"Sorry," the man said. "They've all been sold."

Outside the pharmacy, Clark hesitated. Should he walk the three blocks back to Wendy's and get the car or keep walking until he found another place to get a paper? He decided to keep walking. After two blocks, he came to a through street. Looking both ways, he saw no places likely to sell papers, so he arbitrarily turned right.

Although he didn't mind walking and knew the exercise was good for him, this twice-daily excursion to get a newspaper was going to become a pain before long, and he found himself wishing that Wendy had the papers delivered. Inwardly, he shrugged. No matter. In two days, the child would die, and shortly after that—after a few days during which the woman would be allowed to suffer the loss of her daughter—she, too, would die. And then he and Wendy would go away together, although exactly where they would go hadn't been decided.

As Clark walked along the four-lane street, he considered what would happen after the girl died. He had no plan yet for killing the woman, and he needed one. Nothing special was required. A bullet from a rifle with a telescopic sight would suffice, as would a blow on the head or a knife in the back or a bomb in her car.

A bomb. He considered the possibility. Although he'd never made one, it would be an easy enough project for a mechanical engineer. He was still playing with the idea when he saw a convenience store ahead. He'd walked about a dozen blocks.

Tyrone Jefferson had been a clerk at the convenience store for nearly a year. He didn't like the job. Some of the employees working other shifts had been robbed, and he figured it was only a matter of time before he found himself staring at the business end of some Saturday night special. The holdup guy could have the company's money; that was just fine with Tyrone. What worried him was that some of those dudes weren't happy just getting the limited take from the cash register. Some of them liked to hurt people.

But this was a line of thought he didn't like pursuing, and to give his mind something else to focus on, he turned on his portable radio, which he kept below the counter—a definite violation of company policy. But then, if they wanted to fire him from what he considered to be a high-risk job, one that paid the minimum wage . . . Tyrone shrugged.

If they fired him, maybe he could get one of those government loans and go to college. He was smart enough to go to college. And every time he drove by the campus, he marveled at the sheer quantity of pussy on the hoof. He'd heard stories that a lot of the white girls at the university liked to hump black. A twenty-two-year-old with a slim, muscular body and winning smile, Tyrone figured he might just be the black man to help them out.

He was mulling over this pleasant possibility when a white guy came in. Instantly, Tyrone sized him up, looking for some indication of whether this might be the guy with the Saturday night special who was going to show up eventually. He had a build like Tyrone's, except this guy was thinner, and if appearances were anything to go by, he seemed harmless enough. Despite his athletic build, he had a soft look about him, as if he earned his living in an office. Tyrone relaxed. The man got a newspaper from the rack and brought it to the counter.

"Anything else?" Tyrone asked.

"That's all," the man replied, studying the banner headline.

The man paid for the paper. When he picked it up, there was another one underneath. "Sorry," he said. "I guess I grabbed two of them. I'll put it back."

"Don't bother," Tyrone said. "I wanted to look at the paper, anyway."

"Good enough," the man said, smiling pleasantly as he left with the paper under his arm.

Relieved that this hadn't been his time to meet the dude with the Saturday night special, Tyrone watched the customer go. His thoughts drifted back to the university, and then it occurred to him that getting one of those government loans might not be so easy. Ever since Reagan got elected, the government had gotten pretty damned stingy with money for everything except bombs and missiles and such. But then that was another subject on which he didn't care to dwell.

Turning the newspaper so it was right side up, he absently scanned the top half of the front page, finding nothing of any great interest. Then he flipped the paper over, revealing the bottom half of the front page, and there, staring out at him, was a picture of the guy who'd just bought the paper. Beside it was a picture of a child. Tyrone read the caption.

Goddamn, he thought. Then he picked up the phone.

Officer Jay Aragon drove his cruiser slowly along a two-lane street lined with small flat-roofed houses. He was preoccupied, his thoughts focused on Darlene, the barmaid at a downtown watering hole where a lot of the Albuquerque cops hung out. In her early twenties, she was slender with large breasts and big brown eyes, and he'd been trying for six months to get her into bed.

It wasn't getting turned down that bothered him. He'd been turned down before. The problem was that she had made it with just about every other cop who hung out at the place, including a few who usually only got laid by women who felt sorry for them. And Aragon hardly fit that category. He was tall and muscular with thick dark hair, a handsome face, and a boyish grin. So why would she bed a dumpy booze hound with breath so bad he'd been nicknamed Halitosis Harrigan and say no to him? It bothered him.

"APD to one-Edward," the female dispatcher said, and the image of Darlene abruptly vanished.

Keying his microphone, Aragon said, "One-Edward. Go ahead."

"See the man at the convenience store at Grigson and Sanchez; reference, the subject possibly involved in the Jennings abduction."

"Is the subject there now?" Aragon asked.

"Negative, one-Edward. The man says the subject left about two minutes ago."

"One-Edward en route from Rio Lodoso and Cantrell," Aragon said, slipping the mike into its holder on the dash.

Turning right at the next intersection, he increased his speed. This was probably nothing. On the radio, he'd heard other units get calls to check out people who looked like the guy or the kid whose pictures were on the front page of this morning's paper, and nothing had come of any of them. Still, you never knew. He turned onto a four-lane thoroughfare. He was about three blocks from the convenience store.

On the radio, the dispatcher was assigning a unit to be his backup.

Clark Clayton walked leisurely along the narrow street, the paper still folded under his arm. He had planned to look through it while he walked, but he'd forgotten about the constant breeze, which was just strong enough to make handling a newspaper impossible. For a change of scenery, he was taking a different route, walking through a residential area rather than following the four-lane street on which the convenience store was located.

A block away, a police car sped by, going somewhere in a hurry. The sight of it made him uncomfortable. It was a new experience to be afraid of the police. Before, he'd always been an upstanding citizen, a person who automatically relied on the police for protection. But he was no longer an upstanding citizen. Now he was a criminal.

Anxious to look through the paper under his arm, he began walking faster.

"I'm sure it was the guy," the clerk at the convenience store said. "You know, it's like seeing the mayor or the governor on TV. When you finally see them in person, you recognize them right away. There's no doubt at all. Well, it was the same with this guy. It was him. I'm sure. He bought a copy of the paper with his picture on it, but the paper was turned so that side was down. I don't think he saw it."

"Did he have anyone with him?" Aragon asked.

"No."

"Did he have a car?"

"No."

"Which way'd he go?"

"That way," the clerk said, pointing.

Aragon hurried back to his car. He picked up the two-way radio microphone as he started the engine. "One-Edward to APD."

"Go ahead, one-Edward."

"Subject last seen heading south on Grigson on foot. I'm going to look for him."

"One-Adam," the dispatcher said. "What's your ETA?"

"Two minutes," a male voice answered. One-Adam was Aragon's backup.

"I didn't see him on Grigson," Aragon said into his microphone. "I'll check east of Grigson. You check west. If he's still on foot, we might get lucky."

"Ten-four," one-Adam replied.

Aragon began driving through the neighborhood, slowing and looking down the cross streets each time he came to an intersection. This was an older part of the city—small homes with small yards, the yards mostly bare of vegetation except for weeds. A big brown dog dashed out from a yard on his left and ran alongside the car, growling and showing its teeth. Aragon, who liked to use the open window for an armrest, pulled in his elbow. The dog, apparently satisfied that it had driven him from its territory, retreated.

As he entered another intersection, Aragon slowed, looking in both directions. To his left, he saw nothing but a cat walking across the street. To his right, in the next block, a man was walking. Aragon turned right.

As he closed the gap, he saw that the man had a newspaper tucked under his arm.

23

CLARK HEARD THE CAR APPROACHING. At first he paid little attention to it, but then he realized that something was wrong. The car should have passed him by now. Instead, it approached slowly, staying behind him. He turned to look, seeing a blue-and-white car with red-and-blue emergency lights on its roof.

Resisting the impulse to flee, he told himself that the officer might just be curious about him, that he was breaking no laws by walking through this neighborhood, and that running would only serve to prove his guilt. On the other hand, he had no identification, and if the cop took him in and if they discovered who he was . . .

He ran.

"He's running!" Aragon shouted into the microphone. "He just cut between two houses on the east side of the street."

"I'm almost there," said one-Adam, who'd headed for Aragon's location as soon as Aragon had radioed him that the subject had been spotted. "I'll head over a few blocks and see if I can head him off."

"Ten-four," Aragon said. "I'll be out of the unit. I'm going after him."

Dropping the microphone on the seat, he leaped out of the cruiser and ran toward the houses between which the fleeing subject had disappeared.

As he ran into a weed-choked backyard, Clark noticed a small child playing with a plastic bucket. The youngster watched him rush past, fascinated.

Ahead was a low wire fence, which Clark vaulted. There was an instant during which Clark waited to see whether he'd made it; then he decided that he had, that he was over the fence. At that same moment, his foot hit the top wire, caught, and Clark slid face first into the sandy earth. Scrambling to his feet, he glanced back the way he had come, spotting the uniformed cop coming after him. As he plunged through another yard, he recalled the last time he'd been chased by police and how he'd managed to bury the gun he'd been carrying in the hole in which a tree was to be planted. That time, in Illinois, he'd been caught. This time, he wasn't going to let that happen. He tried to run faster.

Breathing hard, pumping his legs as hard as he could, Clark rushed between two houses and into a narrow dirt street. Suddenly, a large black dog barreled out of the yard toward which he was running, forcing Clark to change directions. Immediately overtaking him, the dog barked and snapped at his heels.

"Blackie!" a woman called. "Get back here!"

The barking and snapping stopped. Clark kept running. And then he heard the barking again, farther behind him. Again, the woman yelled. Glancing behind him, he saw that the dog had done the same thing to the pursuing policeman and that the man had fallen.

I'm going to make it, Clark thought. I'm going to make it.

Patrol unit one-Adam was driven by Officer Elton Collins, who turned onto the narrow dirt road just in time to spot Aragon trip and fall when he was startled by a dog. Farther away was the fleeing subject, who'd just dashed into a vacant area.

Grabbing his microphone, Collins said, "One-Adam to APD."

"Go ahead, one-Adam."

"Subject has just run into a field at the end of Calle Acequia. We're getting pretty close to the city limits. You'd better notify the sheriff's office."

"Ten-four, one-Adam. Be advised that three of our units are on their way to assist you."

A few moments passed during which Collins was trying to find a road that would enable him to get ahead of the subject; then the dispatcher said, "One-Adam, the SO is en route."

"Ten-four." Collins had discovered some tracks that led across the field, and he stomped on the accelerator, his patrol car throwing up a cloud of dust as it roared into the open area.

Having no idea where he was going, Clark was just running, desperation keeping his legs working. Ahead was an embankment. Reaching the top, he rushed down the other side, stumbled, and found himself in the soft sand at the bottom of a dry ditch. Although he knew he should climb back up the bank and see where his pursuer was, he lacked the strength. He was breathing so hard that he was sure someone half a mile away could hear him. He tried to breathe more evenly, more quietly, but doing so was impossible.

The newspaper lay beside him, and he wondered why he hadn't dropped it. He supposed his brain had too much else to do to be bothered telling his fingers to release the newspaper. He was about to climb up the bank when the breeze caught the paper and flipped over a few pages. Clark found himself looking at his own picture, the company photo taken by the plumbing-supply manufacturer in Illinois. Beside it was a picture of the girl.

No wonder the police were chasing him. The clerk in the convenience store must have spotted him, or maybe the clerk in the pharmacy. What did it matter who had done it? Someone had, and he was in big trouble. Cautiously, he moved up the bank far enough to see over the top. There was no sign of the policeman who'd fallen, but a few hundred yards to his left, a patrol car was making its way across the field.

Staying in the dry ditch, Clark moved away from the car. The ditch went straight for a while, then began curving to the left, which would be back in the direction from which he'd just come. And Clark had no intention of going in that direction. Climbing up the bank and peering over the top again, he saw that the patrol car was farther away from him now. Looking in the direction he wanted to go, Clark saw another embankment about fifty feet away. The patrol car was stirring up a lot of dust, which might obscure the driver's vision. Clark decided to go for it.

Scrambling up the side of the ditch, Clark ran. He was in a plowed field now, the soft earth slipping beneath his feet, slowing him down. He had no time to worry about the patrol car. Either the cop spotted him, or he didn't. Clark concentrated on the embankment for which he was headed. Reaching it, out of breath, Clark dashed down the other side, not realizing his mistake until it was too late. He splashed into the muddy water that filled the ditch.

For a moment, he stood in the waist-deep water, trying to catch his breath. Then he realized that he had to keep going, that he had to get out of this filthy-looking water and run. His feet slipping in the mud, he climbed up the bank, peeked over the top, and nearly gasped. Directly in front of him was a white car with blue stripes on its side. On its door was a star and the words BERNALILLO COUNTY SHERIFF.

"Come on out of there," a voice to his left said. "Real slow."

Looking in that direction, Clark found himself staring at a young man in a khaki uniform. The gun the officer held in both hands was aimed at Clark. Clark tried to read the man's eyes. Will he shoot if I make a run for it? he wondered.

"Don't even think about it," the officer said. And Clark knew the policeman was serious.

"It's him!" Cassandra said excitedly. "It's definitely him!"

She was standing in the same room in downtown Albuquerque, looking at Clark through the same one-way glass. Inside her, hope began to bubble and churn. If they found Clark, they could find Lisa.

Detective Gomez stood beside her. The officer said, "We picked him up in the Valley. He bought a newspaper at a convenience store, and the clerk recognized him."

"Did he say anything about Lisa?"

Gomez shook her head. "He says his name's Fred Schwartz, that he's from Seattle, that he lives on the road and never carries identification because the Constitution says he doesn't have to. That's all he'll say."

Apprehension abruptly replaced the excited hopefulness Cassandra had been feeling. "You've got to make him tell you what he did with Lisa," she said. "You've got to."

"We'll keep working on him. You can count on that." The detective studied Cassandra a moment, then said, "Why don't you go home? I'll have an officer drive you. If anything comes up, you'll hear from us right away, I promise."

Cassandra shook her head. "I'll wait here."

"We'll keep working on him, but nothing may happen right away."

"I don't care. I'll wait."

After Gomez left, Cassandra continued to stand by the one-way glass and stare at Clark. Abruptly, she felt so weak she thought she was going to faint. Sitting down, she folded her arms on the wooden table and rested her head on them.

She could envision Clark smugly refusing to say anything other than the lie he'd already told about his identity. Conceivably, he could get tried, convicted, sent to prison, and never say a word about what had become of Lisa. Suddenly, Cassandra realized that he most likely would not be tried or convicted of anything. No one had seen him abduct Lisa. There were no fingerprints on the note. He could keep on telling his lies until they had to release him.

"Oh, no," she said to the empty room. "No, no, no." Her voice sounded weak, helpless, and it had the hollow ring of desperation.

Accompanied by Detectives Dale Carlin and Clarence Sherman, Gomez stepped into the interrogation room to which Clayton had been moved after Cassandra Jennings had identified him. Actually, it was the third room to which he'd been taken, and each time, he'd been allowed to sit and stew a while. Gomez was hoping to unnerve him a little bit.

Clayton, his clothes still wet from his plunge into the irrigation ditch, sat at a scarred gray metal table with an unidentifiable artificial surface. "What am I charged with?" he demanded as the officers entered the room.

"You resisted arrest, and you're a suspect in the kidnapping of Lisa Jennings."

Carlin and Sherman sat down at the same table. Both were husky men in their thirties, and Clayton eyed them warily.

"Your rights were explained to you when you were arrested," Gomez said. "Do you understand those rights? If not, I'll explain them to you again."

"I understand," he said.

"Good. Now where's Lisa Jennings?"

"Who?"

"Lisa Jennings, the little girl you snatched. Where is she?"

"Don't know anything about it."

Gomez, who'd remained standing, put her hands on the table and leaned forward, bringing her face close to his. "Look, as long as that little girl's okay, you can probably get out of this thing in one piece. But if anything happens to her, you're going to Santa Fe. Ever here of Santa Fe? It's so bad, they have riots there where a lot of people get killed. Books have been written about it. A guy like you, a white-collar type, you'll be nothing but fresh meat to those guys." She grinned.

Gomez could see a hint of fear in Clayton's eyes. Clearly, the thought of prison and what it would be like hadn't occurred to him.

"Hey," Carlin said. "I knew a guy like you went to Santa Fe. He came out with an asshole you could slip a watermelon into. They'd gang up on him, take turns, one guy screwing him in the ass while another did it in his mouth. He took it and didn't complain. He knew better than to complain."

"Shut up!" Clayton screamed, rising. Sherman forced him back down.

"We just thought you might like to know what you'd be getting into," Gomez said. "If anything happens to that little girl, you'll be a permanent resident of that place."

"Permanent meat," Carlin growled.

"I want a lawyer," Clayton said. "I'm entitled to a lawyer."

"Sure," Gomez said. "It's your right, and we would never try to deprive you of your rights. Can you afford an attorney?"

"No."

"Would you like a public defender, then?"

"Yes."

"Sherm, send for a PD."

"You bet," Detective Sherman said, rising. "Too bad those guys take so long getting here, you know? And it's too bad they're so overworked. They never seem to have more than a few minutes to spend with a client. It's always rush, rush, rush for those guys."

After Sherman had gone, Gomez said, "Look, Clayton—"

"Schwartz. The name's Schwartz."

Gomez shook her head sadly. "You've been positively identified as Clayton. And just to make sure there aren't any doubts, your fingerprints have been sent to Illinois. You're wasting your time by denying who you are."

He shrugged. "What's in a name?"

"Not much," Gomez said. "A piece of tender stuff like you serving hard time up in Santa Fe doesn't need a name. To those guys up there, your name's dinner." She smiled sweetly.

Clayton said nothing, but again a trace of fear appeared in his eyes. And there was something else in his eyes as well, something that worried the detective. It was a look that all experienced police officers knew well. It was the gleam in the eye of the man who walked into a crowded place and started shooting, the distant, unfocused stare of the mother who'd just blown away her husband and two kids, the excitement in the eyes of the arsonist who'd just sent a dozen people to a fiery death. It was madness. It was the most powerful driving force in a human being. And it was completely unpredictable.

"Where are you staying?" Gomez asked.

"Wherever I can find a place," he said.

"How about last night? Where did you stay?"

"Can't remember."

"You might as well cooperate with us," the detective said. "You're beaten, Clayton. You threatened to kill the kid the day after tomorrow, but you're going to be right here. How are you going to carry out your threat from a cell?"

A grin appeared on his face, and Gomez was afraid he'd say the girl was already dead, but he merely stared at her, smiling. Finally, he said, "I want a lawyer. I'm not saying anything else until I see a lawyer."

Wendy sat in her small living room, wondering what had happened to Clark. When she'd awakened, he was gone. At first, she'd assumed that he'd gone to get the morning paper, but an hour passed, then another, and still no Clark.

He loves me, she thought. He wouldn't just walk out on me. He wouldn't.

Which left only one possibility. He'd been picked up by the police. Wendy shuddered. For kidnapping a child, he would go to prison, and there would be nothing she could do to help him. I could see him on visiting days, she thought. I could wait for him.

No harm had come to the child yet. She could let the kid go and save Clark. As long as the girl was okay, Clark would serve a few years, but that was all. He'd get out, and they could be together. She realized that Clark might be forced to implicate her in the abduction, which meant that she would serve time, too. But she could handle that. It would be okay.

But there was no way she could let the girl go. Clark would hate her if she did that. The woman had to be severely punished. Until the matter of the woman was resolved once and for all, Clark would be unable to get on with the rest of his life.

Wendy got up, left the apartment, and walked to the street, hoping to find Clark walking leisurely toward her, hoping he'd grin and say that he'd gone for a stroll. She knew he was on foot because her car was still here. When she looked down the street, Wendy suddenly felt little prickles of excitement. A man *was* walking toward her, just as she'd pictured it. Unable to restrain herself, she rushed to hug him. Oh, Clark, she thought. Oh, Clark.

But she'd only gone about twenty feet when she realized that the approaching man was too short to be Clark, and too old. And he was Hispanic. Giving her a friendly wave, the man turned and walked into a driveway two houses away from where she stood.

Wendy walked slowly back toward her apartment, the prickles of excitement having been replaced by a numbing despair. She had made a promise to Clark, and that promise was a sacred pledge to the man she loved. The day after tomorrow, she would have to fulfill that pledge despite the consequences, even though doing so terrified her.

When she reached her apartment, she went into the kitchen and poured a cup of the now bitter coffee that Clark had made. It tasted awful, but her man had made it, and somehow it seemed important that she drink it. After the second swallow, she began to cry.

That night, after the blond woman had brought Lisa her daily meal of take-out food and a soft drink, Lisa sat alone in her prison, staring across the room, her eyes focusing on nothing.

Today's meal had been pizza. The empty carton sat beside her, as did the empty soft-drink cup. Lisa wondered whether pizza and hamburgers could ever again be her favorite foods.

The odor from the "stinky place" was starting to spread through the room now. And the used soft-drink cups and fast-food containers were starting to pile up in another corner, but at least they didn't stink.

She was so lonely that this time when her daily meal arrived, she had wanted to start a conversation with the blond woman, just to have someone to talk to. She'd wanted to ask for a game or some comic books—anything that would give her something to do besides stare at the cement room or make up things in her mind. But something inside had prevented her from speaking. She hated the bad people; she would not ask them for things. She would not do anything except what she was forced to do.

She kicked the pizza box and paper cup away from her. Those things had come from the bad people, and she didn't want them near her.

Lisa felt that terrible feeling coming on again, the feeling that she might never leave this cement prison, and she abruptly switched her thoughts to another place. It was pretty there, with lots of flowers and gold buildings that twinkled in the sunlight. But this time she was unable to hold the fantasy, because the flowers reminded her of the beautiful gardens at Aunt Susan's house and at the house she'd been at with her mom. And the sunlight reminded her of being outside, out of this place.

The terrible feeling was back, and Lisa began to shake. Closing her eyes, Lisa listened to the sounds of crying. But there was only sound, because no tears came. Lisa had no tears left.

24

GOMEZ AND SHERMAN SAT IN THE same interrogation room they'd used the day before, waiting for Clayton to be brought in. This time, he would be accompanied by his lawyer.

Earlier in the morning, Clayton had been arraigned in magistrate court, where bond had been set at fifty thousand dollars. Of course, he could get out if he could come up with ten percent of that, but because he had no cash and no property to put up as collateral, no bail bondsman would even talk to him. Although Gomez knew they had nothing they could take to the district attorney, the legal complexities were taken care of, and they could hang on to Clayton for a while. Long enough, Gomez hoped, to make him tell what he'd done with Lisa Jennings.

Gomez had been unable to come up with anything useful concerning Clayton's movements since he arrived in the city. Although a woman who operated a motel on Central Avenue thought Clayton had spent one night there, his name wasn't on any of the registration cards, which meant that the woman was mistaken or that he'd used an assumed name.

If he hadn't stayed in a motel, then someone had put him up. But who? Did he know someone here? Had he met someone? And these questions led to others. Had he used a car when he abducted the girl? And if he had, where had he gotten it? Police in Illinois had found Clayton's car at O'Hare. And he hadn't rented one in New Mexico.

"Do you think someone helped him?" Gomez asked.

Sherman shrugged. "We can't even prove that he did it."

"I know he did it."

"And I agree. But let's face it, Di, you and me, we can't go on the witness stand and say we know in our hearts he's guilty. If he just keeps his mouth shut and waits, we'll have to let him go."

"And then what happens to Lisa Jennings?"

Sherman rubbed his brow. "She could be dead already."

Gomez nodded, and she thought about her own daughter, Emilia. Dianne Gomez was glad she wasn't in Cassandra Jennings' place.

Jennings had been here until late last night. Gomez had finally convinced her to go home and get some rest. She'd returned about eight-thirty this morning.

The door opened, and a uniformed officer showed Clayton and his attorney into the room. The lawyer was Zoe Barrett, from the public defender's office. She was about thirty, slender, and had shoulder-length dark hair. Gomez thought she resembled Cassandra Jennings.

When they were seated at the table, Barrett said, "I'd like to make it clear that my client is talking to you voluntarily, freely cooperating in the hope that we can get this matter resolved. Also, he would like to state that his name is Clark Clayton and that he is a resident of the state of Illinois."

Gomez said, "May I ask why he lied about his identity when he was first picked up."

"He was confused and afraid, and he felt that if word of his arrest reached Illinois, it would be embarrassing for him."

Gomez started to ask why Clayton had fled from the officers who'd tried to pick him up, but she stopped herself, realizing that doing so would only elicit some vague excuse in smooth-sounding lawyer talk.

"Our main concern here," Gomez said, "is that the life of a child is involved."

"My client denies any involvement in the kidnapping of the Jennings girl."

"I understand that. Nevertheless, I'd like to point out that this matter isn't as serious as it could be—as long as no harm comes to the child. No ransom has been demanded, and it's possible that whoever took the girl was emotionally unstable at the time."

Barrett studied Gomez thoughtfully. Clearly, the attorney was seeing what Gomez was offering and liked the idea. But Clayton looked horrified.

"What are you suggesting?" he demanded.

Barrett tried to wave him to silence, but he ignored her. "Are you saying I'm insane?"

"I'm merely suggesting—"

"I'm not crazy!" he shouted. For a moment, he sat there glaring at her; then he said, "You said something about whether the child has been harmed. Well, the kid is alive and well."

"Mr. Clayton," the lawyer said angrily, "let's discuss this outside." She grabbed his arm.

He flung her hand away. "Well, you tell the woman that the girl will die tomorrow at three o'clock."

Realizing there was no way she could stop him, Barrett stared at Clayton, sadly shaking her head.

"You'll be in jail tomorrow afternoon at three o'clock," Gomez said. "You won't be able to hurt anyone."

Clayton smiled. "I won't be the one who does it. In fact, I'll have the perfect alibi. I'll be in jail."

"But you conspired with the person who did it," Gomez said. "Under the law, you're just as guilty as your partner."

Again, the attorney tried to grab Clayton's arm, and he yanked it away from her. "It doesn't matter. If I go to prison, it will be as a whole, intact human being—for the first time in my life. In a sense, there's not much those people up there can do to me that hasn't been done before—by the person who was supposed to love me."

"I wouldn't bet on that," Sherman said.

Clayton ignored him. "The other people in prison are there because they couldn't get their lives straightened out. I'll be there *because* I straightened out mine. I'll be ready for them." He looked smugly at Gomez.

This time, Clayton allowed his lawyer to lead him toward the door. When he reached it, he said, "I won't talk to you again until four o'clock tomorrow afternoon. Then I'll tell you where to find the body. Tell the woman. Tell her."

And then he was through the door. The uniformed officer who'd been waiting outside took his arm. Clayton didn't seem to notice.

Sherman let out a soft whistle. "Totally loony tunes. You believe him—about the accomplice?"

"I've gotta believe him," Gomez said.

"We could let him go," Sherman suggested. "Follow him, hope he leads us to the kid."

Gomez shook her head. "Can't take the chance that we might lose him—and without him we've got no chance of finding the kid. Besides, Clayton's smart enough to know that we'd try to follow him. If his accomplice is going to do the dirty work, he'd just go to a park somewhere, sit and wait."

"What are we going to do? I don't think there's a chance he'll tell us anything."

Gomez thought for a moment. "The only thing he had on him was a piece of paper in his shirt pocket. It had a lock of blond hair taped to it, and there was a message signed by someone named Wendy. It said, 'A part of me to have with you always,' or something like that. Wendy might be his accomplice."

"It could also be someone in Illinois."

Gomez frowned. "I hope she's not someone in Illinois, because I'm going to try a bluff."

She told Sherman what she had in mind.

Clark Clayton sat alone in his cell, thinking. He didn't regret what he'd done. It was important that the woman know that the child was still going to die on schedule. It was part of her punishment. She had to know when it would happen so she could wait helplessly while time ran out. It was important.

His attorney had been furious with him. But she didn't understand. There was no way she could. Nor was there any way a lawyer could get him off. When the body was found, his fingerprints would be discovered as well. Someone would recall having seen him carrying a big box through the mall. The evidence to convict him would be compiled.

It was the price of doing what he had to, and he would pay it.

He did have one regret—Wendy. If she got caught, she would go to prison, which Clark definitely did not want. And even if she did manage to get away, he would most likely never see her again. *I love her,* he thought. *I'll always love her. And I'm going to miss her terribly.*

Tears caused his vision to blur.

Wendy would keep her promise. She would go to the mall at the appointed time and turn the valve. He wondered whether she could do everything for him and kill the woman, too. He had not solicited a promise from her to do that. Though it would be better if the woman died too, if she lived, her punishment would haunt her for the rest of her life. It wasn't everything he'd wanted, but it would be enough.

"Hey, Clayton."

He'd been so engrossed in thought that he'd been unaware of the woman detective's presence. She stared through the bars at him, smiling, looking very pleased with herself. Unnerved, Clark waited for her to tell him what was on her mind.

"We know about Wendy," Gomez said. "We know all of it. We'll be waiting for her tomorrow afternoon. I just thought you might like to know."

Without waiting for him to respond, she turned and walked away.

Sherman was waiting for her in the passageway that led to the cells. "How'd it go?" he asked.

"He turned white when I laid it on him."

"What now?"

"Now we let him stew awhile."

THE ATTRACTION

* * *

Rocked by the detective's words, Clark paced back and forth in his small cell. It was over. Everything had fallen apart. He would go to jail while the woman went unpunished. She would have inflicted the final indignity on him, had the last laugh, come back from the grave to hurt him one more time.

Come back from the grave? Incapable of dealing with the paradox of wanting to punish and kill a woman who was already dead, he abruptly shifted his thoughts. He saw himself in a big prison. Men were holding him down, forcing him to do unspeakable things. . . .

"No!" a voice cried. "No!" And he realized it was a little boy's voice. And then the same voice, filled with terror, screamed:

"Mommmmmmmmmmeeeeeeeeee!!!"

And then she was there in the prison, watching as men forced him to do terrible things. "Disgusting," she said. "You're disgusting."

As he stared at the woman, horrified, he was unable to decide whether it was his mother or Cassandra Jennings. But the distinction was meaningless, he realized suddenly, for they were one and the same. The were *the woman*.

"Pleeeeeeeeease!" he shouted. "Please, Mommy, please." But she was gone. The men laughed. One of them muttered the same phrases over and over.

"Raw meat, raw meat, raw meat . . ."

The image vanished, and he was back in the jail cell again. Trembling, he stared at the cement floor, the crude beds, the filthy toilet. The prison and the men had been in his mind. They weren't real.

But his situation was real. He had failed, and he had dragged Wendy down with him. The police would be waiting when she arrived at the mall tomorrow, and Wendy would be arrested. It had all been for nothing. Wendy, my love, he thought. I'm sorry, so very, very sorry.

Sitting down on the bed, Clark rested his head in his hands.

It was at least a couple of hours later when another prisoner was put into the cell with him. He was a short man with thinning blond hair and blue eyes. Glancing disinterestedly at Clark, he lay down on the bed on the other side of the cell, folded his arms across his chest, and closed his eyes. For several minutes, he lay there silently; then, without looking at Clark, he said, "What's your name?"

"Clark."

"I'm Andy."

Uncertain how people were expected to act in a jail, Clark didn't know whether he should try to shake the man's hand or just do nothing. He did nothing.

A few silent minutes passed; then Andy said, "You play cards, Clark?"

"Sure. Sometimes."

"I'll see if I can get us a deck. Helps pass the time."

"What, uh, what are you in here for?"

Sitting up, Andy gave him a peculiar look. "This must be your first time. That right?"

"The first time in jail, yes."

"Not everybody likes to be asked questions. You've got to be careful who you ask them to and what you ask."

"I'm sorry."

Andy dismissed the matter with a wave of his hand. "I don't mind telling you. I'm charged with burglary. You?"

"Kidnapping and resisting arrest."

Andy grunted. Clark noted that Andy didn't ask whether he'd actually kidnapped anyone. Apparently, that was a no-no in some unwritten code. It was okay to say you were charged with something, but you admitted to nothing, and no one asked you to. But then he was just guessing. He'd stepped into a world with which he was totally unfamiliar.

Time passed, and the men talked. Clark learned that Andy's last name was Tallon, that he had a wife and two kids, that he was originally from a small farming community in Ontario. A trustee showed up with two dinners on metal trays—beans, corn bread, and an unidentifiable vegetable. Shortly after that, a guard showed up with some things that had been delivered to the jail by Andy's wife.

Andy looked through them. There were socks, blue jeans, and blue-tinted underwear that looked as though it had been washed with the jeans. "Ah," Andy said, holding up a deck of cards, "I can always count on Judy."

Clark wondered whether that meant Andy's wife was accustomed to his being in jail. But he didn't ask, for doing so would most likely violate some unwritten taboo of jailhouse behavior.

The men played rummy for a while; then Andy took out a pack of cigarettes and divided them up. "Poker chips," he said.

"I didn't know you smoked," Clark said.

"I don't." Andy grinned. "Judy always sends me a pack or two of smokes. You can make a lot of friends in here when you've got smokes to give away. And in here you need all the friends you can get. These are just on loan, by the way. When the game's over, I get them back."

Which wouldn't have been a problem in any case, because Andy won them all back playing poker. After he carefully slipped the cigarettes back into the pack, Andy lay back on his bunk and said, "Well, at least it'll only be for one night."

A sudden loneliness came over Clark. Andy's presence made it possible for Clark to think about something other than his failure to punish the woman and what would happen to Wendy tomorrow. Sitting on his bed, Clark wished there was some way he could get out of the cell and warn Wendy.

"Are you getting out tomorrow?" Clark asked.

"Yeah." Andy lay on the bed with his arm covering his eyes. "As a rule, you can figure on spending a night here, because it almost always takes a day before they get you over to magistrate court so bond can be set. Tomorrow I'll be out on bail."

"I wish I was getting out tomorrow," Clark said. "I'd give almost anything."

Uncovering his eyes, Andy looked at him but didn't speak.

Clark said, "There's someone I need to warn. A friend. She's—she's walking into a trap."

"That's too bad," Andy said. He poked through the things his wife had sent him and produced a paperback book. "Here," he said, tossing it to Clark. "Read this. It'll get your mind off things."

Clark stared at it. It was a spy novel.

"Come on," Andy said. "Read it. There's no point worrying about things you can't do anything about."

Although Clark tried to concentrate on the book, he was unable to do so. When Andy drifted off to sleep, Clark put it down without bothering to mark his place.

Clark slept fitfully that night. Several times he was

awakened by nightmares. In one, the woman had been bending over him, laughing, and then she'd taken a long stick with a red-hot coil on its end, a thing like the heating element on an electric stove, and pressed it into his flesh. Later, he'd dreamed that he was on trial in some dark place illuminated by torches and that Wendy had been pointing at him, shouting, "Betrayer! Betrayer! Betrayer!"

In the morning, a guard brought them a breakfast of funny-tasting scrambled eggs and coffee. Then Andy brought out the cards. Clark tried to concentrate on the games, but he couldn't. Because neither he nor Andy had a watch, Clark had to wait for a guard to pass to discover what time it was. The morning passed, and the afternoon came. Clark found he was unable to play cards anymore because he was too worried about Wendy. Andy shrugged and read one of the paperback books his wife had sent him.

A guard came to the cell and said, "Tallon, get your stuff gathered up. You'll be going over to magistrate court in about ten minutes."

"What time is it?" Clark asked anxiously.

"About one-thirty," the guard said.

An hour and a half, Clark thought. He considered trying to overpower the guard when he came to get Andy, but then he dropped the idea. His chances of getting out of the building were extremely slim.

"Well," Andy said as he put his belongings into a pile on the bed, "I don't think I'll be coming back here, so I guess this is it." He stepped over to Clark and offered his hand.

Standing, Clark shook it.

"You've been a decent cell mate," Andy said. "Some of the guys you get locked in with are real animals." He smiled.

The two men stood there in silence for a moment; then Andy said, "Anything you'd like me to do for you? Any messages you'd like me to deliver, or anything like that?"

Suddenly, Clark saw a way to save Wendy. "Yes," he said excitedly. "Can you get a message to Wendy?"

"I can try. Where do I find her?"

Clark considered that. By the time Andy was out of court, it might be too late to go to Wendy's house. He'd have to go to the mall. He told Andy the name of the mall. "She'll be there at three o'clock. The cops will be waiting for her. Tell her what happened. Tell her not to go inside—and just to forget about the kid."

He realized then that if Wendy did that, the kid might die, anyway, because no one would find her in that room. He might win, after all. He grabbed the other man by the shoulders. "Please, Andy, will you do it for me? Will you?"

Andy frowned. "What about the cops?"

"If you see her before she goes in, you'll be in time. They'll be waiting inside. Please, Andy. Please save Wendy."

Andy nodded. "Okay. As long as I don't see any cops. What does she look like? How will I recognize her?"

"She's—" Suddenly, Clark wasn't sure about this. How did he know that Andy was who he said he was? It all seemed so convenient—Andy showing up, being friendly, then getting released just in time to save Wendy if Clark would only tell him where she was and what she looked like. He backed away from Andy.

"This is a trick," he whispered. "You're a cop."

It had all been a setup. The police didn't know about Wendy. They'd gotten her name from the paper with some of her hair taped to it. He'd had it in his shirt pocket when he'd been arrested. No one would have been waiting for Wendy at the mall if he hadn't just told this cop where to look for her. And he had to make sure this cop didn't tell anyone. He hurled himself at the man.

THE POLICEMAN WAS READY FOR HIM. Clark was grabbed and he suddenly found the momentum of his lunge carrying him into the bars of the cell. Slamming into them, he heard himself cry out. Dizzy, he clung to the bars as he turned to face the cop.

"Guard!" the policeman yelled, his eyes remaining on Clark.

From the corirdor came the sound of approaching footsteps, and then the cell door was opening. All was lost. The child would be rescued. Wendy—poor Wendy— would be arrested.

No! he thought. Can't let it happen. Can't.

The cop was stepping through the open cell door. In a moment, it would close, sealing him within, powerless to prevent the child's rescue and Wendy's capture. Pushing himself off the bars, he plunged through the opening, hitting the cop, who was shoved into the jailer, both men slamming into the wall. The guard sank to the floor, apparently unconscious.

"Prisoner escaping!" yelled the police officer, who was trying to get to his feet.

Clark kicked him in the head. The man grunted and tried to roll away from him. "Help!" he shouted, but the word came out strangely garbled.

Clark was about to kick him again when he heard more footsteps approaching. The heavy metal door at the end of the passageway was flung open, revealing a uniformed officer. The cop's eyes widened as he realized that Clark was rushing at him, and then the two men collided. For a moment, Clark was tangled in the other man's limbs, but suddenly he was free, running down a passageway, opening a door to another corirdor, plunging toward freedom, the chance to save Wendy.

From somewhere came shouts. Ahead of him suddenly was a policeman aiming a handgun at him, holding it with both hands.

"Freeze!" the cop yelled.

But Clark had no intention of stopping. He needed the vengeance that was the only way to undo the things the woman had done to him, and he had to save Wendy. Neither the officer nor his gun mattered, for to give up now would mean the end of everything Clark cared about. He ran at the cop, grabbing for the gun.

For a moment, the two men struggled, and then there was a bang. Overloaded with pain and confusion, Clark's mind reeled. What had happened? And then he realized that the officer's gun had gone off. But he was unhurt. He was running, almost floating down a corridor. The policeman was gone now, for this was a safe place and not a jail. Although darkness seemed to be closing in around him, there was a light ahead. Wendy was there, motioning for him to hurry. The police hadn't caught her.

He sensed a presence in the shadows, a shape he

couldn't quite make out. It was the woman; he knew her without seeing her. And she no longer mattered. I reject you, he thought. You wouldn't love me, so I renounce you. You are no longer my mother.

Ahead was his love, the only love that mattered. But the strange blackness swirled around her just as he reached for Wendy's hand, engulfing her, hiding her. He stretched, groped, and then he saw her hand poking into the darkness through a tiny lighted hole. He had it then; he had Wendy's hand.

He opened his eyes at that moment, seeing policemen staring down at him. Their lips moved, but he was unable to hear any words. The faces began to blur, and then the blackness came again, cocooned him, claimed him.

Sitting in the small, sparse interrogation room, Cassandra tried to concentrate on the magazine that lay before her on the table. The article dealt with the dos and don'ts of buying a new car, and Cassandra had read the first paragraph about four times. Giving up, she pushed the publication away from her.

Although Detective Gomez kept trying to get her to wait at home, Cassandra had to be here, near what was happening. Susan was at the house Cassandra was sitting just in case anyone tried to contact her there. So far she hadn't encountered John again, which was fine with her. She was under too much emotional stress as it was.

Unable to stop herself, she looked at her watch, discovering that two minutes had passed since she last looked at it. It was 2:15. If Clark's threat was true, his accomplice would murder Lisa in forty-five minutes.

She thought about the countdown for launches conducted by NASA, about how the clock was stopped when something went wrong. Minus forty-five minutes and holding. Cassandra wished she could find some way of doing that with her watch, some way of making the damn thing stop its inexorable movement toward three o'clock.

She dismissed the notion; it was silly. The she slammed her fist down on the table. Instead of trying to trick Clark, why couldn't they make him tell what he'd done with Lisa? At that moment, Cassandra knew she could make him tell. With her daughter's life at stake, she could be unmerciful with implements that administered pain. She didn't give a damn about Clark Clayton's constitutional rights. Clark Clayton was a psychopath who was going to kill an innocent child, and in a situation like this a murdering lunatic had no rights.

Forty-three minutes.

Don't look, she told herself. Don't look. Her eyes filled with tears, but she held them back. Crying wouldn't help Lisa.

Abruptly, the door opened, and Detective Gomez rushed in. "We know where the girl is," she said hurriedly. "She's at a shopping mall, somewhere in the mall. We don't know exactly where."

"Make him tell you," Cassandra said, rising. "Make him tell you."

Gomez shook her head. "We can't. He's dead. He tried to escape. He was shot by an officer. We're on our way to the mall now. We know for sure now that the accomplice is named Wendy, but we don't know her last name or what she looks like. That's all I've got time to explain right now. I've got to get to the mall."

"I'm going with you," Cassandra said.

"Please, I'd rather you . . ." Letting her words trail off, Gomez nodded. "Okay, let's go."

Its rooftop strobe lights flashing and its siren screaming, the police car sped through downtown Albuquerque, then got on a freeway. Cassandra sat in back beside a blond detective with a bruised face. Gomez was driving. Beside her was another detective, a stocky man she called Sherm who kept talking over the radio, getting things organized for a massive search of the mall. Cassandra looked at her watch. Thirty-two minutes.

Gomez left the freeway, and a moment later they were in a traffic jam. Although the other drivers tried to get out of the way, there was simply nowhere for them to go. The police car was moving about ten miles an hour despite its lights and siren. Please, Cassandra thought. Please get out of our way.

But the traffic jam was only getting worse. And then Cassandra saw the reason for it. Because of construction, the six-lane street was reduced to two lanes, one in each direction, orange barrels marking the open lanes.

"Shit," Gomez said. "I was here two days ago, and none of this was here."

"No other way would have been any better," Sherman said. "They got these orange barrels on half the streets in this city."

Finally, they were through it, and a moment later Cassandra could see the mall ahead. Shutting off the light and siren, Gomez drove into the parking lot, then wheeled into a parking space for the handicapped.

"Stay here," she said to Cassandra.

"No, I want to—"

"Stay here," Gomez said more firmly. "Please. We know how to handle these things. You'd just be underfoot."

Before Cassandra could respond, Gomez and the two men hurried toward the shopping center. Resisting the impulse to run after them, Cassandra watched until they disappeared into the mall. She looked at her watch. Twenty-one minutes.

Fidgeting, Cassandra sat in the car, waiting. She was unable to see any sign of the large search party the detectives had been organizing, which could mean either that the officers had gathered in another part of the complex or that they were searching surreptitiously, to prevent Wendy from becoming aware of what they were doing.

Wendy. Who was she? What kind of person would agree to help Clark kidnap a child? No matter how hard she tried, Cassandra was unable to picture Wendy—and unable to understand her. Gomez had told Cassandra about the lock of hair taped to the note. It indicated love. But what kind of love? Cassandra was sure that she would instantly drop anyone who suggested kidnapping and murder no matter how much she loved them. But not Wendy. And again Cassandra wondered what kind of love would make a person do such a thing.

Seventeen minutes.

Shoppers came and went, but Cassandra saw no sign of the police officers. Where were they? What were they doing? Cassandra began to have doubts. Could Clark have realized that the police were trying to trick him? Could he have lied? A shopping mall was crawling with people. Where could you hide a child in such a place? It didn't make sense.

Desperate to find out what was going on, Cassandra reached for the door handle. But before she could open the door, she saw someone familiar. A woman with curly blond hair. And something made Cassandra hesitate. Where had she seen the woman before?

The woman was walking toward the same entrance the detectives had used. As she approached the building, she glanced around her. She seemed worried, tense. And suddenly Cassandra knew where she had seen the woman before. She had been parked near Susan's house

in a compact sedan with a fender that didn't match the
color of the rest of the car. But the blond woman hadn't
just been parked there, Cassandra realized; she'd been
watching. She was Wendy.

Hurriedly scanning the huge parking area, Cassandra
searched for a police officer. But there were no cops to
see. And the blond woman had just entered the mall.
Quickly climbing out of the car, Cassandra rushed after
her.

As she stepped into the complex, Cassandra saw the
usual throng of shoppers but no police officers. And no
blond woman. Oh, no, Cassandra thought, I can't lose
her. I can't.

Moving through the shoppers, Cassandra desperately
studied the heads in front of her, hunting for one that
had curly blond hair. And then she spotted the one she
was looking for. Quickly closing the gap, Cassandra
followed the blond woman. Wendy was moving slowly,
casually. Abruptly, she angled toward one of the benches
that had been placed in the center of the walkway. As
she approached, a man rose and smiled. Together, they
turned and walked toward the entrance to a large department store. Cassandra watched them, icy, numbing horror spreading through her body. The woman wasn't
Wendy.

She had blond curly hair like Wendy's, and she was
dressed in jeans and a blue shirt like Wendy, but
Cassandra had never seen her before. Frantically, she
began looking for the real Wendy, who was on her way
to murder Lisa.

Cassandra turned in a circle, her eyes scanning the
faces, looking for blond hair, a blue shirt. She was
jostled suddenly as a man bumped into her. "Sorry," he
said mechanically, without sincerity. Cassandra ignored

him. She had to find the woman who was here to kill Lisa.

She was surrounded by places Wendy could have gone. There were stores large and small, movie theaters, restaurants. Which one of them could have a place to conceal a captive child? The signs giving the names of shoes shops and clothing stores and fast-food places swirled around her, a blur of letters and colors. Cassandra had to assume that none of these places was Wendy's destination, for if she had stepped into one of them, Cassandra would never find her.

She ran deeper into the mall. If Wendy had gone straight ahead, she might still be overtaken before she reached her destination.

Glancing at her watch, Cassandra tried to focus on its face and run at the same time, but she was unable to do so. Even so, she knew it was almost three o'clock and that she had only minutes left in which to save her daughter.

Propelled by desperation, she ran, dodging the people who appeared in front of her, frantically scanning the faces around her. And then, ahead of her, a blond head turned right and disappeared into another section of the mall. Nearly colliding with a woman carrying a large package, Cassandra rushed to the spot where she'd seen the blond woman, arriving just in time to see her disappear again, into a passageway. Cassandra ran after her.

She dashed into the passageway, finding it empty. No! she thought. No! But then she saw the door that was automatically closing. A sign affixed to it said EMPLOYEES ONLY. Cassandra grabbed the door just before it would have latched, locking her out.

Pushing the door open, she saw a set of stairs that descended into whatever lay beneath the mall. Cassandra hesitated. Was the woman she'd seen Wendy? A glimpse of some curly blond hair was all she'd had. She glanced at her watch. It was three. This was the only chance she would have. She started down the steps.

Reaching the bottom, Cassandra found herself in a wide passageway with some lockers against one wall. To her left was a heavy-looking door. To her right, the passageway abruptly ended where a wall had been constructed across it. For a moment, Cassandra thought the blond woman must have gone through the heavy door. Then she saw her in the shadows at the end of the passageway. And it was unquestionably Wendy. Having removed a metal plate from the floor, Wendy was reaching into the opening, turning something.

Cassandra started toward her.

Sitting on the floor in her cement prison, Lisa heard a sound, a sort of throaty hiss. Getting up, she walked across the room to where the pipes protruded from the floor. The noise was coming from the pipe that had had its cover removed. Putting her hand over the opening, she could feel the air blowing through it.

Except that it wasn't air, because air didn't smell like that. And then she remembered what did. Lisa backed away from the pipe.

Suddenly aware of Cassandra's presence, Wendy looked up, disbelief appearing on her face.

"You . . ." she said as she slowly stood. "How . . . ?"

"Where's my daughter?" Cassandra demanded.

Stunned, the other woman just stared at her.

"Where is she?" Cassandra screamed. "Tell me!"

Wendy shook her head. "I can't do that," she said softly. "I promised. I love him."

"Tell me, damn you! Tell me what you've done with Lisa!"

The two women stared at each other, neither sure what to do. Then Cassandra grabbed Wendy, determined to do whatever she had to, to make her reveal what she had done to Lisa. Shoving the woman against the wall, she struck her in the face.

"Where's Lisa?" she demanded, only vaguely aware of the hysteria in her voice.

Cassandra drew back her hand to strike Wendy again, but her opponent lunged forward, grabbing her around the waist, and both women were on the floor, each struggling to control the other's hands. Wendy managed to free one of hers and gouged at Cassandra's eyes. When Cassandra tried to protect her eyes, Wendy managed to yank her other hand from Cassandra's grasp. She began choking Cassandra.

Suddenly unable to breathe, Cassandra put all her efforts into prying the woman's hands from her throat, but Wendy held on with tremendous strength. Looking into Wendy's face, Cassandra saw a fierce determination and a hint of the craziness that had gleamed in Clark's eyes. The madness had been transferred.

Struggling for breath that wouldn't come, Cassandra was weakening. Clark still lived in this woman. He was killing her, and when she was dead, he would slay Lisa as well. But she couldn't let that happen. She couldn't.

Summoning all her remaining strength, Cassandra heaved herself upward, encircling Wendy with her arms, and rolled her over. Forced to release her hold on Cassandra's throat, Wendy clawed at her. Gasping for breath, Cassandra tried to strike her, but it was a blow with no power behind it, and Wendy deflected it easily, throwing Cassandra off of her and scrambling to her feet.

Cassandra tried to stand, too, but she was too dazed, too busy just sucking air into her lungs. Wendy/Clark kicked at her, her foot glancing off Cassandra's shoulder. Backing off a step, the blond woman brought her foot forward again, but this time Cassandra grabbed it, held on, and twisted, sending her opponent sprawling.

Getting to her feet as quickly as she could, Cassandra saw that Wendy was still on the floor. Weak and lightheaded, Cassandra was unable to take advantage of her momentary upper hand. She leaned against the wall, her back hitting something hard.

Wendy was getting to her feet now. Having risen to her hands and knees, she stared at Cassandra, and her blond hair and feminine features seemed to disappear. Instead of Wendy, it was Clark who gazed at Cassandra now, his eyes burning with hate and madness. Although Cassandra knew she should attack before her adversary could stand, if she took a single step, she would probably collapse.

Wendy was on her feet now. Realizing that victory was hers, she moved toward Cassandra confidently. The object Cassandra had hit was pushing painfully into her back. Suddenly, Cassandra realized what it was. She was leaning against a fire extinguisher. Moving to the side, she lifted it off its bracket, turned, and swung it at Wendy. It smacked her squarely in the side of the head, and Wendy collapsed as if someone had dropped a truck on her.

She lay face down on the cement floor. Putting down the fire extinguisher, Cassandra moved to her on shaky legs and rolled her over. "Where's Lisa?" she asked with as much strength as she could put into her voice.

But Wendy wasn't going to answer her, because Wendy was unconscious.

Cassandra simply stared at her, uncertain what to do. Then she looked around her. The only thing in this dead end passageway besides the lockers was the heavy-looking door. Ignoring the weakness in her legs, Cassandra rushed to the door and pulled on the knob, finding it locked. Hurrying back to Wendy, she patted the woman's pockets, instantly finding the lump that had to be keys. She pulled out a ring with about ten keys on it. As she started back to the locked door, she glanced at the lockers, then pushed the notion from her mind. She didn't even want to consider that possibility, for if Lisa was in one of the lockers, she wasn't alive.

Reaching the door, Cassandra tried a key. It wouldn't fit, so she tried another, then another, then another. Then she dropped them and had to start again.

Finally, Cassandra found a key that turned the lock. Pushing the door open, she was nearly overwhelmed by the odor of gas. The lights were on, revealing a room that seemed empty except for a large cardboard box. Taking a cautious step into the room, Cassandra saw her daughter. Lisa lay behind the carton, motionless. Cassandra rushed to her.

The girl was on her side, her eyes closed. Be all right, Cassandra thought. Please be all right.

Cassandra was reaching down to pick up her daughter when something hit her, knocking her to the floor. Suddenly, Wendy was on top of her, trying to pry her fingers apart.

"Give them to me!" she screamed.

And then Cassandra realized that she had kept Wendy's keys, that she was clutching them in her right hand, and that Wendy wanted to lock both her and Lisa in this gas-filled room. With her free arm, she hit Wendy in the head, and the woman cried out. Cassandra had found the spot where the fire extinguisher had struck Wendy. She hit her again, and Wendy rolled off her.

Getting to her feet, Cassandra braced herself for an attack, but none came. Wendy lay on the floor, moaning. Forgetting her, Cassandra picked up her daughter and rushed out of the room. As she stepped into the passageway, the door at the top of the stairs burst open, and Gomez was there, along with some other detectives. They hurried down the stairs.

Taking one look at the limp child in Cassandra's arms, Gomez instantly took Lisa away from her, and laying the girl on the floor, began giving mouth-to-mouth resuscitation.

"Get rescue and an ambulance," Gomez snapped, looking up as she filled her own lungs with air. She immediately placed her mouth over the child's again.

One of the detectives spoke into a walkie-talkie. "Seven-forty-nine, APD."

"Go ahead, seven-forty-nine."

"We need a ten-forty-three and a ten-fifty-five. Advise them to go to the west entrance. Someone will show them where to go."

"Ten-four."

Watching as Gomez breathed for Lisa, Cassandra tried to empty her mind, to keep herself from thinking the unthinkable. And somewhere inside, some very basic part of herself was pleading desperately for Lisa to be all right. The detective with the walkie-talkie was speaking into it again, telling the other officers that the child had been located.

Suddenly, Cassandra realized that Lisa's chest was rising and falling without Gomez's help. The detective looked at her triumphantly.

"Lisa," Cassandra said, dropping to her knees and clutching the child to her.

"Not too tightly," Gomez warned. "Let her breathe."

Still holding the child, Cassandra relaxed her grip. "Oh, Lisa," she said softly, her eyes filling with tears. "Oh, my little girl, my lovely little girl."

"Mommy? . . ." the child said weakly.

"Yes, honey, yes. It's me. And everything's all right."

Tears ran from the girl's eyes, and both mother and daughter cried.

"How did you find her?" Gomez asked.

After taking a moment to let her tears subside, Cassandra found her voice. "I—I spotted Wendy. I knew it was her because I saw her parked across the street from my sister's house. She must have been watching it."

Gomez frowned. "Where is she?"

"In there," Cassandra said, indicating the room in which she'd found Lisa.

One of the detectives turned the knob. "It's locked," he said.

Suddenly, Cassandra realized that she no longer had the keys. She must have dropped them as she picked up Lisa. "The gas is still on in there," she said. Pointing to the metal cover Wendy had removed from the floor, she added, "I think the valve is over there."

One of the detectives hurried over to the spot.

Looking at another detective, Gomez said, "Get the manager. We need a key to that door." To a different officer, she said, "Take Mrs. Jennings and her daughter upstairs."

Carrying Lisa, Cassandra followed the officer up the steps. It's over, she thought. It's finally, undeniably over.

Ten minutes later, Cassandra was sitting in some sort of waiting room in the administrative section of the mall. Lisa sat beside her on the couch, an oxygen mask covering her nose and mouth. The ambulance that would take Lisa to be checked out at the hospital hadn't arrived yet.

The mask made communication difficult, so Lisa hadn't spoken much since the firemen put it on her. She would have a lot to tell, and Cassandra hoped she would do so. If the child could talk about it, she'd be able to work it out of her system and get back to living a normal life.

Normal? Could their lives ever be normal again? Yes, Cassandra decided. Now things could indeed be normal again. She smiled at Lisa, who returned the smile with her eyes.

After seeing to Lisa, the rescue firemen had left them to see what they could do for Wendy. So far no one had told her anything about Wendy's condition. Cassandra was sure she would never be able to understand why Wendy had done what she did. The only thing she'd been able to conclude was that madness, like so many maladies, was contagious.

The door opened, and Gomez stepped into the room. She studied Lisa a moment, then shifted her gaze to Cassandra. "The rescue firemen were unable to revive Wendy," she said softly.

Cassandra nodded.

"The ambulance will be here in a moment. Later on, if you're up to it, I'm afraid we're going to have to get your statement." She smiled apologetically.

"It'll be okay," Cassandra said.

Gomez patted her hand. "It's over," she said gently.

Yes, Cassandra thought. It's over. Lisa hugged her.

Epilogue

"YOU ARE ABOUT TO ENTER ONE OF of the most dangerous professions there is," the mayor said, his voice amplified by the loudspeakers. "But it's also one of the most rewarding, and certainly one of the most important to this community. . . ."

Standing with the other graduates, Cassandra only half listened to the mayor of Albuquerque, who stood at the podium flanked by two police captains and a deputy chief. It was a beautiful sunny day. The ceremony was being conducted outside, and Cassandra wished she could take off her shoes and run through the grass instead of standing on it with her body held straight and motionless.

The things that Clark and Wendy had done were in the past now. Many months had passed since the day Cassandra had fought with Wendy and carried Lisa from the gas-filled room. Although it was a day Cassandra would never forget, she didn't talk about it much anymore. And neither did Lisa. They'd discussed it a lot right after it had happened, but when the time had come for pushing it to the backs of their minds and getting on with their lives, they had done so. There were no permanent scars for either of them.

John, Cassandra had learned, had been at the police station when she and the detectives had left for the mall. The reason he hadn't demanded to come along was that Gomez hadn't been able to find him to tell him what was happening. It turned out that he'd been in the rest room.

Before he left for Wisconsin, Cassandra had told him that she'd just fought to save Lisa's life and that she'd fight just as hard to keep her. Although John had left without saying what he planned to do, a few days later he'd phoned to say that he wasn't going to try to get custody.

Cassandra and Lisa were living in an apartment now. Lisa was in school and seemed to like it better than the school she'd attended in Illinois. She'd quickly made friends with the other kids in the complex.

Now that she had a good job, Cassandra was thinking of saving her money for the down payment on a house. But that was just a dream, something to wish for.

She'd been seeing a lot of a man named Will Leighton, a friend of Susan's husband, Rob. Although she liked him a lot, she didn't know where the relationship was going. For one thing, she'd decided that she liked the freedom of being single and beholden to no one, and she suspected that Will, who was also divorced, missed the companionship of wife and family.

The mayor said, "As you take your place among the other fine men and women who have become officers of the law . . ."

The phrase officers of the law repeated itself in Cassandra's mind. If there was one thing she had never dreamed of becoming, it was a cop. Dianne Gomez had suggested it to her, saying that the force needed female officers. Although Cassandra had dismissed the idea at first, it grew on her. And eventually she found herself taking examinations and going to interviews. And, to her surprise, she got the job.

When the mayor finished, a captain read the oath, which the graduates of the police academy repeated. He declared them duly sworn officers, and Cassandra, along with the other newest members of the Albuquerque Police Department, cheered.

When they were dismissed, Cassandra hurried over to the spot where Susan, Lisa, and Dianne Gomez waited along with the other spectators.

"Congratulations," Gomez said.

Susan hugged her. And so did Lisa.